SUSAN A. JENNINGS

Prelude to Sophie's War

Sophie's War - Book One

SaRaKa InPrint

Images:

Author photo and cover design SAJ

Images: Shutteestock/Olga Lutina ID:196736366 (Woman) Shutterstock/Kletr ID: 52431325 (Aeroplanes) Shutterstock/ Tkemot ID:127854155 (London)

Second edition

ISBN: 978-1-989553-14-5

Editing by Meghan Negrijn

This book was professionally typeset on Reedsy.
Find out more at reedsy.com

To my wonderful writing groups,
Historical Writing Ladies
and
The Ottawa Story Spinners,
whose support make my books possible.

The old men were still running the country. The politicians who had caused millions of deaths were now celebrating, as if they had done something wonderful.

KEN FOLLET

Contents

Prologue

Prelude to Sophie's War is a spinoff from *The Blue Pendant, Book 1 of The Sackville Hotel Trilogy* and it is the continuation of Sophie Romano's story, the head maid at The Sackville Hotel. Sophie is also the main character in *Ruins in Silk*, the prequel to both the trilogy and the *Sophie's War Series* and, because of the continuing and expanded story, please note … **Spoiler alerts.**

Sophie's story begins in the early 1900s in Italy, as a young girl growing up on her family's silk farm. Seeing a need to expand the business, her father and uncle purchase a silk mill in Derby, England where they produce fine silk for lucrative British aristocrats. Alberto, Sophie's father, moves his family to Derby to manage the silk mill, leaving his brother to look after the silk farm in Italy.

After her mother's death, Sophie, an only child, becomes close to her father. Alberto raises his daughter to think for herself and grooms her to run the business, an unusual situation for the Edwardian era. A double tragedy of brutal murders in Italy and a devastating and all destroying fire in Derby ruins the family and Sophie loses everything, including her father. Forced to take a maid's position at the prestigious Sackville Hotel, she works her way up to head maid and ultimately to a role in the Great War.

1

1914 - Bexhill on Sea

The Sackville Hotel

The heartbreak in his face told her all she needed to know. She felt his pain deep inside and the sense of finality as the announcement ripped at his heart. Carlos had done the same to her, shattering her heart into tiny pieces at a time when she needed him the most. The scars never healed completely, but a corner of Sophie's heart had opened to love again. Could she hope that, given time, Bill's heart would too?

She liked Bill. His kindness and understanding had comforted her and, since her father's death, the loss of privilege and everything she held dear, understanding was a rarity. Her feelings, although she would never admit it to Bill, had grown beyond liking. It also occurred to her that loving Bill might fill the void and give her purpose in life. Under-chef to the hotel's executive chef, Bill was quietly ambitious for his own kitchen. Sophie had worked hard, moving quickly from maid-of-all-work to head-maid. Although grateful for the work, it was not fulfilling. Tragedy had curbed her ambition but knowing Bill had kindled a spark for wanting more. His reaction to Anna's engagement to another man had not escaped her, confirming her suspicions that Bill's affection for Anna was perhaps a secret love.

No stranger to love's cruelties, Sophie was determined to mend Bill's heart. He had taught her to play chess and the game had bonded them in friendship, it was only a matter of time before he would fall in love with her.

Saturday afternoon, their day off, Sophie and Bill walked along the promenade, he slipped his hand into hers as they arrived at the Pavilion for tea. Finding a table by the window, Sophie ordered tea and scones and they contentedly watched the waves pound on the beach. The sky had filled with grey storm clouds, prompting Sophie to think about the war, battleships seen in the English Channel, khaki uniforms everywhere. Something told her the euphoria and eagerness to fight for England was edged with grief and suffering not yet experienced. Inexplicably, she sensed she would be part of relieving that suffering. A shiver of excitement tingled down her spine.

"Sophie!" Bill's voice brought her back to tea as the waiter rattled cups and saucers. Bill's aqua eyes gave her a puzzled look. "Are you alright?"

"I'm fine. The grey, stormy clouds made me think of the war and when it will end. Christmas they predict." She squeezed his hand. "I'm just miles away. It must be the sea air."

"Too many are dying," he replied pensively, "Word has it that it is much worse than the propaganda leads us to believe."

A chill swept over her as she nodded in agreement and quickly pushed it away with a smile and cheerfully changed the subject. "Time to get back. The London train arrives at four, full of guests escaping the city before it gets too cold." Staring out to sea, Sophie added, "It looks as though they will have a cold, stormy first night."

On the walk back to the hotel, Bill asked, "What do you think will become of us as the war escalates?"

"I wish I knew, but I doubt it will be over by Christmas."

"I agree," Bill replied. "Have you thought about what you might do to contribute to the war?"

"I've thought about it." She frowned. "But rolling bandages doesn't appeal to me. I'd like to do something meaningful." Sophie quietened, thinking.

Bill stopped walking with a shocked expression on his face. "You're not considering working in the munitions factory, are you? I hear the kitchen maids babbling on about it."

"Never. I value my life." She punched him playfully in the arm. "However, I had this strange premonition that I will help ease the suffering." Sophie giggled. "I know that sounds silly and, if truth be told, I am needed at The Sackville. Many distressed guests are escaping London. Have you thought about how you can contribute?"

"I really want to finish my apprenticeship with Chef Louis. The man is tough to work for but he is the most renowned chef in Britain." Bill put his arm around Sophie. "To answer your question, no, not now anyway. Maybe later." They walked the rest of the way in a comfortable silence. It pleased her that Bill seemed his old self. The news of Anna's engagement was never mentioned but the greyness of her premonition lingered with a sense of foreboding. Of what, she did not know.

3

Sophie hadn't seen Bill since the arrival of the Saturday train; more guests had come than usual and, with the shortage of staff, everyone was busy. She deliberately went to the staff dining hall early before the rest of the staff arrived hoping to see Bill, who, among other things, was in charge of the staff meals. The room was quite empty and so was the table. No food had been prepared. She could hear Chef Louis yelling in the kitchen, assuming he was yelling at Bill. To her surprise, the hotel housekeeper exited the kitchen and appeared to be the cause of Chef's yelling.

"My apologies, Miss Romano. That man just... just... upsets me. I informed him that Mr. Blaine is not well and is confined to his bed. I can't have the staff catching colds and fevers."

"Mr. Blaine is ill? Have you called the doctor?" Sophie took a breath to hide her panic as the housekeeper's head went to one side, her expression quizzical.

"He has a minor fever. Nothing to worry about, Miss Romano." She sighed. "My sitting room. I must speak with you about the housekeeping." She held two pieces of note paper. "Resignations. A kitchen maid and one of senior housemaids have been seduced by the high wages of the munitions factories."

"I had heard maids talking about the factories. The conditions are terrible. I thought it was nothing more than talk." Sophie tried to stay focused, but Bill's sudden illness worried her.

"The wages are double what we can offer and the euphoria of patriotism is almost epidemic. Men going to war, women working in factories or even doing men's jobs. Mrs. Banks sighed yet again. "We have to make some changes. Do you think we can promote Amy?"

4

"Yes. She's young, but sensible, hard-working and willing. I can keep an eye on her. We are going into the slow season. It might be a problem for Christmas but we can hire local help."

"I'm concerned for the smooth running of the hotel as the glamour of being a fighting soldier has seen the men enlist in droves and the maids are finding better hours and better pay in factories."

A knock on the door announced the arrival of tea. As Mrs. Banks poured, Sophie tried to make sense of all the events in her head. Anna's engagement, resigning staff, and not the least of which was Bill's state of health. He had been ordered to bed with a mysterious ailment, an aliment he showed no signs of yesterday.

Sophie and Mrs. Banks finalized the changes to housekeeping staff duties and finished their tea.

"May I have permission to visit Mr. Blaine?" Sophie held her breath, hoping it would stop the pink in her cheeks.

"I'm afraid not. No one is allowed in his room until I'm sure he is not contagious." Mrs. Banks looked up from her ledger. "Is there something going on between you two? You know the hotel's policy on romance."

"No, we are friends and play chess together. I thought he might like to play." Sophie willed herself not to blush.

"Mr. Blaine needs to rest, perhaps tomorrow. That will be all, Miss Romano. Please speak with Amy and prepare her for extra duties." Sophie nodded her compliance.

The following day, Sophie tapped on Bill's bedroom door, feeling naughty as women were not allowed in the men's quarters. Although she had permission from Mrs. Banks, she still felt guilty. When no answer came, she knocked louder

5

and called through the door. "Bill, it's me, Sophie. Mrs. Banks has sent me up with your meal. Can I come in?" Suddenly she felt flushed, wondering if perhaps he wasn't decent.

"Come in," Bill called, a hint of surprise in his voice and a broad smile welcomed her. "This is a surprise. Mrs. Banks must have decided that I'm not about to infect the hotel with the plague."

Sophie placed the tray on his lap and plumped his pillows. "There, does that feel comfortable?

"Thank you, Nurse Romano," Bill teased. "You would make a good nurse."

Sophie giggled. "Maybe! Mrs. Banks said your temperature was back to normal but you are to stay in bed for one more day, which sent Chef Louis off into another, quite unnecessary, rant. There are only ten rooms occupied and only a trickle of dinner reservations tonight."

"Chef's ranting never stops. Even I am weary of his constant bullying. I couldn't take it anymore. I needed this break."

"Bill Blaine, are you telling me you faked a fever to get away from Chef?" Sophie's eyes were bright with mischief.

"No. I was upset," His eyes dropped to the tray on his lap, and Sophie didn't have to guess why he was upset. He quickly took a breath and continued, "and I was somewhat overheated. Mrs. Banks interpreted it as illness and I didn't object. I do feel guilty but who am I to argue with the housekeeper." Bill laughed and touched Sophie's hand. "I needed time to gather my thoughts. It is good to see you."

Sophie moved to the chair by the bed and rested her hands in her lap, aware of an awkward silence.

Eager to break that silence she asked, "Shall I bring the chess set up tonight, that is if Mrs. Banks gives us permission?"

"I would like a game of chess with my beautiful chess player. Sweet Sophie, always so kind." His words fluttered her heart and his aqua blue eyes stared with such tenderness.

She stood up quickly, almost knocking the chair over. "I had better get back. Mrs. Banks will be on the war path." She giggled, aware she was blushing. "Enjoy your meal. I'll see you later."

The grandfather clock struck eleven times, as though announcing Sophie's arrival into the empty staff dining hall. Her evening duties had not allowed for a chess game. Tired and cold, she stoked the fire and rubbed her hands together for warmth. She was cold from exhaustion rather than temperature; training new staff, filling in for others and worrying about everything took all her energy.

It wasn't like Sophie but she felt moody, tired and not as content as usual. She sat in the rocking chair by the fire, rocking and thinking about Bill's comment that she'd make a good nurse. Was nursing so different from being a maid? It seemed far-fetched but she did like caring for people. She was always telling the maids to work hard and to strive for better things. Maybe it was time to take her own advice. Did she want a change? Was nursing something she could do? "But," she said aloud. "On the other hand, I'm happy here. I like my job most of the time and there's Bill. He will stay until he's a chef himself."

"Hello. I wondered if you would still be up." Bill's voice made her jump and clasp her hand to her mouth, hoping he hadn't heard her comment.

"Bill, what are you doing out of bed?"

"Mrs. Banks brought me my dinner and declared me well enough to get up. I'm back to work in the morning. I have slept so much in the last two days I couldn't sleep and wondered if there was any cocoa. Why are you up so late?"

"An exhausting day and I needed some time to think. If you're making cocoa, I'll join you. I'm sorry about chess tonight, I've only just finished but we could play now if you like." Sounding more energetic than she felt, she hoped she had enough energy to play. Being with Bill was what she really wanted.

Sophie's tiredness showed in her moves. Her brain too tired to follow, she finally conceded defeat.

"It is time you went to bed," he chuckled. "I have never won so easily. May I walk you home? I am a gentleman after all." They both laughed.

"All the way up the servants' stairs," she teased.

He nodded. "Can I take you to the cinema on Saturday?"

"I'd like that." Sophie felt his arms around her in a goodnight hug. She waited for a kiss but the hug would do.

2

Everything Changes

During the next few weeks, Sophie enjoyed Bill's attention. They played chess in the evenings, walked on the beach and held hands in the back row of the cinema on Saturdays. She was falling in love and she believed Bill was too.

Sophie made a valiant attempt to deny the contradictions the war caused both in her everyday life and her love for Bill. Deep down she knew the truth. A veil of positive euphoria covered her, the hotel, staff and guests alike. The fear of the unknown and fear of change. She didn't believe the propaganda that Britain was winning the war. Her intuition was telling her the government was holding back on the number of casualties and battles lost.

The similarity of a long ago memory of being happy, in love with Carlos, and the prospect of a wonderful life ahead gripped her in panic, because she'd had no warning of that impending disaster. That same feeling filled her today and it scared her. This time there was a warning but an unheeded warning. The old memory of disaster haunted her. What could she have done differently in the past? Could she have saved her father? If she'd been warned would she have made different choices. Could she atone for the past by warning them in the present? Warn them of what? She gave herself a shake, a reprimand. Her mind was playing tricks, or was it? She sensed her attempts to hold onto her life and, if she was honest, to Bill, were beginning to unravel. She felt as though she was losing her grasp.

And then it happened.

Taking a break in the staff dining hall, Sophie's tea cup rattled as she placed it in the saucer. Seeing Bill in the doorway, she smiled until she saw his serious expression. Her eyes scanned him to his feet and she saw his brown suitcase.

"Bill! Are you going somewhere?" Sophie stuttered, her heart pounding and unbidden tears flowing down her cheeks.

Bill nodded. "I was going to leave you a note, but you deserve to hear it from me. I'm sorry, Sophie. I tried, I really did. I do love you as a friend and I wanted it to be more but ..."

"Your heart belongs to someone else," Sophie whispered. "Where are you going?"

"Another hotel. Not as big as the Sackville. I've been hired as executive chef with my own kitchen." He gave a forced laugh. "Something I've always wanted. Now I can yell at the under-chef." He laughed again. "I'd never do that. It's partly because of Chef's bullying that I'm leaving."

"Is it far away?" Sophie's eyes brightened. "Is it close enough that I can visit? Could we go to the cinema?"

Bill shook his head. "No one knows where I'm going. I leave on the afternoon omnibus to Eastbourne. I wrote a letter of

10

resignation to Mr. Pickles." He laughed again, harder this time. "I'm afraid all hell will let lose when Chef Louis realizes I've gone. I'd love to see that."

Sophie's tears started again as she desperately tried to think of something, anything, that would stop him from leaving.

Bill's gentle, aqua eyes filled with moisture and regret as he stared at Sophie. "I am so sorry, but it is for the best." He took a step towards her and handed her his chess set. "I want you to have this and find someone more deserving than me to play." He gave a wry smile. "And beat them. You are the best opponent I have ever had." He took her in his arms, kissed her cheek and said, "Goodbye, my sweet Sophie."

Before Sophie could catch her breath, he was gone. She hugged the chess board to her chest and cried.

She thought of Bill every day and wondered where he was, which hotel, but no one had heard of a new chef at any of the hotels in the area. He had hidden his whereabouts well. Most of the joy had gone from Sophie's life. After Bill's departure, she hardly spoke to Anna. She did her work, looked after the maids, made sure the guest rooms were clean and comfortable. She frequently took out the chess board and set it up as if to play but put it away again. Even that was too painful and she hid the chess set at the bottom of her chest of drawers. If she was honest, she not only missed Bill but she missed Anna's friendship. Passing in the hall with cursory good mornings or hellos hurt as much as the cause of the parting.

The war was not over by Christmas as predicted and, as Sophie had thought, the fighting and casualties had escalated. Past Christmases at the Sackville had been exciting and fun but

Sophie's melancholy mood, lack of trained staff and dampened spirits were not conducive to merriment. Celebrations went ahead, management wanting the appearance of normality for the comfort of the guests.

The Saturday before Christmas, she took the omnibus to Eastbourne to buy presents; a pendant for Amy and a fancy tin of tea for Mrs. Banks. She had no one else to buy for. Picking up a dainty shell shaped brooch, she thought of Anna and, on impulse, bought it.

When she returned to Bexhill, she wondered along the promenade until the wind chilled her to the bone, forcing her to run for the warmth of the staff dining hall to make a hot cup of tea, which she took upstairs to her room. Engrossed in wrapping her little presents and tying red ribbon around the white tissue paper, she didn't, at first, hear the knock on the door and then a voice whispered, "Sophie, are you in there?" It was Anna.

Sophie opened the door. "I brought you something to wish you a Merry Christmas." She hesitated. "A peace offering?" Anna stood, holding a parcel tied with blue ribbon as Sophie stared at her, amazed at the coincidence.

"Anna, come in. I am so pleased to see you. Thank you," she said, accepting the parcel.

"I bought you something too." Sophie handed her the little box tied with red ribbon. "I saw it today when I was shopping and thought of you."

Anna took the box. "Thank you. Fancy both of us missing each other at the same time."

They each opened their present: the brooch for Anna and a Rudyard Kipling book for Sophie. In unison they said 'thank you' and hugged each other. Sophie looked at Anna and said,

"A lovely Christmas present."

Christmas companionship healed Sophie and Anna's friendship somewhat, but it had left some deep, long lasting bruising. Despite the reconciliation, Sophie found herself torn by loyalty and bitterness towards her friend, for ruining her chance of happiness and hurting Bill. She might have been more forgiving except she'd received a letter from Bill.

Dear Sophie,

I expect you heard the news from Anna, that I am sailing the high seas. Anna found me in Eastbourne today, the day I set sail on a merchant ship for some far off land. Anna just left The Grand Hotel where I am, or was, working. I decided to write to you so you hear my plans from me. I will be gone by the time you receive this. I intend to find a postbox near the docks just before we set sail.

My sweet chess player, Sophie. I miss you and if we had met under different circumstances, we may have had a chance.

I reached my goal of being an executive chef and I was treated very well at The Grand in Eastbourne. Had it been peace time, I would have stayed. The staff were great and I no longer had to put up with Chef Louis yelling. I learned to treat my staff well. In spite of my success, there was a void in my life and I wanted to serve my fellow countrymen. I hoped to join the cavalry, where my past horsemanship would be put to good use but alas, they turned me down. My next option was a galley cook as a merchant seaman, so here I am travelling the world.

This is truly farewell. I don't know if I'll survive the German U-boats or what is in store for me but I won't be coming back. I may settle in America after the war. Who knows what will happen?

You deserve a good life. Maybe think about nursing? You have a natural aptitude for caring. Or work your way to housekeeper? Mrs. Banks is bound to retire eventually. Whatever you do, be sure it is what you want.

Yours Affectionately,

Bill

P.S. Please do not tell Anna about this letter. It is our secret.

'Our secret' felt nice, particularly as Anna had omitted to tell her she'd found Bill in Eastbourne and paid him a visit. She sensed she should be sad and she was, but something in the letter touched her deeply and she knew she had a tiny corner of Bill's heart and he would always have a place in her heart.

The summer of 1915, after Anna's wedding, turned out to be busy and challenging. The war had claimed almost all of the permanent staff and Sophie struggled to keep up with the high standards expected at the Sackville. The very young maids giggled more than worked and the guests were quite often unreasonably demanding. The typical Sackville guests were prestigious, aristocratic lords and ladies, their habits predictable and easy for the hotel staff to manage but in wartime the type of guests had changed. The aristocrats retreated from their London residences to their country estates, forgoing the fashionable seaside holiday. It was the nouveau rich, often in trade with no inherited country estate, who sent their families to the seaside to escape the London Zeppelin attacks.

Bexhill-on-Sea was situated on the shores of the English Channel, where ships of war frequented the waters, as did the German U-boats. Enemy aeroplanes flew over the coast most nights. Although no bombs had dropped on Bexhill yet, it didn't seem to Sophie such a safe haven.

Even in wartime August, Saturday was the busiest day at reception as guests departed in the morning and new guests arrived in the late afternoon. Sophie and Anna hardly had time for a short walk but made time for tea at the Pavilion. Anna sipped her tea, bright and confident. Sophie wished she felt the same. Although busy, she was bored, the work mundane, the maids impossible and the guests demanding and it didn't help that her relationship with her friend was strained at best.

"What's wrong, Sophie? You don't seem yourself."

"I don't enjoy my work anymore. Everyone is trying to help the war effort and I feel as though cleaning up after rich people is a worthless occupation."

"You are not worthless," Anna said, forcefully

Sophie smiled to herself, remembering Bill's letter suggesting the housekeeper position. "Perhaps. But cleaning water closets and making beds is not what I dreamed of doing for the rest of my life. My father taught me to run a business, albeit I was only sixteen and he had no idea of the tragedy that would befall us. But mopping floors is a far cry from managing a silk mill."

"I can see your dilemma," Anna said as a loud train whistle

made them both jump.

"The train! We'd better hurry." Sophie lifted her skirts and started running, Anna close behind, giggling as they ran through the servants' door of the hotel.

Side by side climbing the stairs two at a time, Anna waved as she pushed the baize door into the reception area, just as the first taxi pulled into the portico. Sophie continued up the stairs to the guest suites.

3

Leaving the Sackville

Checking the towels in Suite 304, Sophie heard the excited chatter of children, the first to enter the suite. She rolled her eyes, hoping the nanny would appear. No nanny, but a tall, important looking man with heavy side whiskers and a happy smile followed the children.

Sophie curtsied. "Welcome to the Sackville, sir. I'm the head maid, Miss Romano, and I was checking your suite. If you require anything, please ring down to reception." She pointed to the telephone as she prepared to leave.

"Thank you. It all looks splendid. What do you think, children?" He bent down and picked up a little girl of about five and tousled the hair of a boy standing next to him, about eight or nine. A fine looking lady, presumably his wife, walked in, followed by a nurse pushing a bath chair occupied by a rather cross looking, elderly lady. Sophie glanced at the party, wondering if the two bedroom suite was large enough for everyone.

"Pardon me, sir. Would you like me to convert the study into sleeping quarters? This suite has only two bedrooms."

Sophie offered, as the porter arrived with copious amounts of baggage.

"No. That is kind of you. I will need the study until I return to London." Seeing Sophie's eyes scan the party, he rubbed his whiskers and smiled. "Oh dear, I see the confusion. Too many people." He gave a hearty laugh. "My mother and her nurse have the suite next door to us."

"My mistake, sir. You must be tired after you long journey. May I order you tea?" She took a side glance. "And perhaps some brandy for you, sir?"

"Thank you. My wife and mother would indeed appreciate some refreshment. I'll join the ladies for tea. It is a little early for brandy."

Sophie smiled at the children. "And would you like some lemonade and maybe I'll see if I can find some chocolate cake?" Sophie glanced at the father for approval as the children nodded enthusiastically.

Closing the suite door, she slipped through the baize door to the servants' stairs, suddenly aware she had company.

"Miss Romano," the nurse called. "May I enquire about a special diet for Madam?"

"Of course. Come with me. I'll order the tea first and then we can chat, if you don't mind the staff dining hall? Would you like some tea, or do you have to get back to your invalid?"

"No, she'll be fine with the family for a while. Sir Lionel is very attentive."

"They seem like a nice family. Have you been in their employ for long?

"About six weeks, since Mrs. Osbourne's accident. Sir Lionel is a gentleman and treats me well but his wife acts the lady of the manor, with no manor, if you know what I mean."

Sophie nodded. "Trades? Maids see it all."

"The old lady loves to order me around and is difficult most of the time." She grinned. "Like most old ladies. But I've been nursing long enough to know she's all bark. Please forgive me. I didn't introduce myself. Eva Smart. This looks like a nice place to work."

"It is, most of the time, but not as exciting as nursing. Have you always been a private nurse?"

"No. The Osbourne appointment is my first private nursing position. I worked at St Thomas's for many years, where I met Mrs. Osbourne after her legs were badly injured in a Zeppelin bomb attack. Sir Lionel offered me a good wage to be her nurse and companion. It is a different kind of work but I felt guilty leaving the hospital and accepting what is perceived to be an easy job. I'm not as young as I used to be and need to look after my own health."

"I'm sure it is not nearly as easy as it looks." Sophie smiled, taking a deep breath and plucking up the courage to ask Eva about training to be a nurse. "I have been considering leaving here and becoming a nurse. I want to nurse soldiers in France, or maybe Belgium. Is it difficult?"

Eva smiled and tapped her hand. "I admire your enthusiasm and if you have a passion for nursing it is wonderful and rewarding work. It's not for everyone. The work is hard and definitely not glamorous. Whether or not you would nurse soldiers overseas will depend on how long the war goes on." She gave a long sigh. "I hope it doesn't go on for three years, which is the length of time required for nurses' training. The pay is terrible."

"Three years isn't long and I have some money saved, but

I'd have to find somewhere to live," Sophie said.

"Most London hospitals have a nurses' residence. If you want to nurse near battlefields, maybe consider Voluntary Aide Detachment. The training is only three months but you need your own income, a family to support you."

Sophie shook her head. "I have no family or income to support me."

"I see. If nursing soldiers is important to you, look no further. There are plenty of injured and ill soldiers right here, sent home from the front to recover. A very rewarding part of nursing." Eva hesitated. "Civilians get hurt too in this war. The burns from bomb injuries are as horrific as a battlefield and shockingly, in London, it is mostly women and children. Do you think you can face such suffering?"

"I do." A jolt of memory hit her hard. The image of her father's burning flesh flashed in her mind. For a brief second, she questioned herself.

Eva must have seen Sophie's face blanch because she quickly added, "There is no shame in turning away from gruesome scenes. Nursing isn't for everyone and it is a myth that we get used to it. When it no longer shocks or repulses, it becomes a problem and threatens compassion, an attribute essential for a good nurse. Forgive me, I speak too freely. I am a little jaded after too many years on the floor. I loved being a hospital nurse and have lost count of how many patients I've treated but knowing I can be part of easing someone's suffering more than makes up for the challenging times. If you are compassionate, then I think you'll make a grand nurse."

"I understand what you're saying about compassion. I'm not squeamish and I don't faint at the sight of blood." She forced a laugh, quickly brushing away her father's image. "You should see some of the messes I've cleaned up here. I really want to become a good nurse. I'm tired of not having a purpose. It is compassion, kindness and being able to help that is at the root of my desire to be a nurse. I can really make a difference."

"In my opinion, with that attitude, you will find the work rewarding. May I suggest you apply at the Bartley Hospital in London? It is a smaller hospital than Guys or St. Thomas. My friend, Clara Kay, trains the probationers. You would get along well with her and they have a very nice nurses' residence."

"Thank you. How helpful you have been." Sophie took a breath. Eva sounded so certain, even suggesting a hospital. It all felt rather sudden. Was this possible? She felt a fluttering of excitement.

"I'm glad to help."

"Eva, you mentioned a special diet for your patient?"

"Mrs. Osbourne has a nervous constitution and is distraught after the journey from London." Eva grinned at Sophie, rolling her eyes in a conciliatory fashion. "She would like a modest dinner tonight, of lightly poached sole with puree of vegetables and egg custard for sweet, served in her suite at seven o'clock sharp. She always takes breakfast in her room, a poached egg, toast, seasonal fruit and she likes coffee in the morning served at nine o'clock on the dot. She may dine with the family for luncheon and dinner. I will let you know."

"I will inform chef of your request. Eva, will you eat with the patient or shall I send something more appetizing for you?"

"I will eat after Mrs. Osborne has retired. I'll order from the menu and have it sent up, if that is permissible. I must return to my charge."

"Of course. I do hope we have chance to talk again. Perhaps a walk on the beach, if you have a day off?"

"When Sir Lionel is with the family on Saturday and Sunday, I get some free time."

"That's perfect. My afternoon off is Saturday," Sophie said with enthusiasm.

Sophie escorted Eva back to the guest area and, having finished for the day, she wearily climbed the servants' stairs to her room. The attic bedrooms were hot in the summer. She undressed to her chemise and flung the window open, allowing the brisk sea breeze to cool her face. Heavy thunder clouds moved away as the sun and blue sky peaked through. It felt like a sign for a new future, just as the chance meeting with Eva had been. A nursing career seemed imminent.

Sophie sat at the desk in front of the dormer window and opened her treasure box. Taking out her fountain pen, she immediately sensed her father's affection. The pen had been a gift from him on her sixteenth birthday. "Papa, am I doing the right thing?" A gust of wind caught the corner of a sheet of writing paper and placed it in front of her. "Is that you, Papa?" She felt his presence, his love and his approval. The pen felt like his hand as she wrote to Matron at Bartley Hospital, London.

Every day Sophie surreptitiously checked the post. She had told no one. The only person privy to the secret was Eva. Not having received any kind of reply, her hopes of training as a nurse dwindled. The Osbourne family were returning to London and she would miss Eva. Although a brief acquaintance, it had been pleasant to talk to someone about London and nursing.

Eva knocked on the staff dining room door. "Sophie, I'm glad I caught you."

"I thought you had departed for the train station. Come in. Can I offer you tea?"

"No, thank you. The luggage has gone ahead by train. Sir Lionel drove down in his Rolls Royce last night and we return by automobile. I wanted to say goodbye and wish you luck with your nursing career."

"That is kind of you but I have not had any correspondence. Perhaps my letter went astray or I'm not suitable." Sophie couldn't keep the disappointment out of her voice.

Eva frowned. "I do not agree about your suitability but I do agree it is strange that you have not had any reply. I will contact Clara, Sister Kay. She will know the status of the training program. Be patient a little while longer. I will write to you as soon as I hear anything." Eva handed her a piece of paper. "My address in London. If you hear anything, write. Take care, my dear. It was a pleasure getting to know you."

September was drawing to a close and no letters from either the Bartley or Eva arrived. Sophie had given up. Tired of being morose and melancholy, she attempted to make peace with the situation and looked in a different direction. Perhaps a housekeeper's position was an option. She endeavoured to pluck up enough enthusiasm to send enquiries to select hotels in Eastbourne but her pen would not write. She wondered if her father was telling her to be patient. He always said she was in too much haste. Thoughts of her father made her smile.

Anna knocked on her door and poked her head around. "Smiling at last." Anna's cheery voice filled the room.

"I was just thinking about my father. He gave me this pen."

"Sophie, is something wrong? You seem so melancholy."

"No, I'm fine. It seems strange with so few guests, winter is coming and this war drags on." Sophie yawned feigning tiredness. "I'm really tired so let's talk tomorrow."

Anna looked disappointed but said, "Good night" and closed Sophie's bedroom door.

Sliding under the covers, Sophie closed her eyes, only to be woken with a repetitive rapping noise. She stomped to the door and swung it open, ready to yell at Anna for waking her.

"Mrs. Banks?"

"I was on my way to bed and thought I'd drop these off for you. They arrived in the afternoon post." She handed two letters to Sophie, her eyes steady on the crest and name in the corner of the envelope, Bartley Hospital. "Is everything all right, Miss Romano?"

"Oh yes, thank you, Mrs. Banks." She chose not to give any explanation, since she didn't know if they contained good news or bad. Sophie eased the door to encourage Mrs. Banks to leave.

"If you're sure, I'll say good night."

"Good night!" Sophie closed the door and listened for Anna but she must have been sleeping because no sound came from her room.

Her heart thumped in her chest as she clutched the letters, deciding which to open first. She ran the letter opener along what she assumed was Eva's.

Dear Sophie,

I hope you are keeping well. Please forgive my tardiness. Life has been hectic since our return to London. The bombs fall around us and we spend our nights in the cellar. Mrs. Osbourne's health has deteriorated as a result and the children are terrified. Sir Lionel has acquired a country house and will be moving the family to the safety of the Cotswolds in the next few days.

I wrote to Clara Kay at the Bartley and received a reply today. It appears that your letter was misdirected and Matron did not receive it. After my enquiry, it has been found and is in the correct hands, along with my recommendation. Expect to receive a letter in the next day or two from either Sister Kay or Matron Hartford, requesting information of your work experience and a letter of reference from Mrs. Banks.

I wish you every success. You will make a fine nurse. Affectionately,
Eva Smart

Sophie jumped around the room, doing a jig and wanting to shout to the world. But at eleven o'clock at night, she thought better of it and carefully slit the envelope of the second letter. As Eva had indicated, the letter requested information and a letter of reference. It was a pleasant one, apologizing for the delay. It was encouraging to hear that there were several spaces available for probationary nurses. It was signed by Clara Kay, Senior Sister at the Bartley Hospital.

Picking up her fountain pen, she replied to Eva immediately.

Dear Eva,
I hope you are well, despite the chaos. I can't imagine sleeping in a cellar and I hope your health has not

suffered. It will be pleasant to escape to the countryside. I hear the Cotswolds are beautiful and there is nothing like clean country air to heal the body and mind. I hope Mrs. Osbourne recovers quickly.

I am well and so happy to receive your letter. The letter arrived from the Bartley the same day.

My sincere and profuse thanks for writing to Sister Kay. I surmise that without your intervention, my letter would not have been seen. Thank you again.

As you predicted, Sister Kay has requested a letter of reference and employment experience. Her letter sounded promising and I am excited. I will speak with Mrs. Banks tomorrow and reply post haste. Of course, I will keep you informed of my progress.

With much appreciation,
Affectionately,
Sophie Romano

Mrs. Banks was already in the staff dining hall when Sophie came down for breakfast. "Mrs. Banks, may I speak with you?"

"Of course. Bring your breakfast and join me in my sitting room." Mrs. Banks turned. "Does this have something to do with the letter?"

"It does," Sophie whispered, almost losing her courage.

The sitting room was warm, a fire burned in the grate and Mrs. Banks sat by it, gesturing for Sophie to sit opposite.

"The letter you brought to me last night was from the Bartley Hospital in London. I have made enquiries about nurses' training. The letter requested a letter of reference. I was hoping you would oblige." Sophie stopped talking. Feeling an awkward silence, she added, "I know the timing is bad and I could stay as long as you need me…" Sophie wondered what she was saying and was relieved when Mrs. Banks raised her hand to stop her.

"Miss Romano, you would make an excellent nurse and I am delighted to write a letter of reference. I hate to see you go but I am pleased for you. You deserve more than maids' work. You will be missed."

"I appreciate your understanding, although I haven't been accepted yet." Sophie took a step towards the door and turned. "Mrs. Banks, if I am accepted, I shall be sorry to leave. I have liked working here and I will always remember your kindness when I arrived. I was a very young, frightened girl, not knowing one end of a broom to another. Thank you."

"My pleasure. Over the years I have grown fond of you. I'll leave the reference in the staff dining hall this evening. Please keep me apprised of developments."

"I will, and thank you."

The Bartley Hospital accepted Sophie Romano as a nurse probationer and she was to report to River House, Residence for Nurses, in one week's time. Taking the stairs two at time, she went to her room and wrote two letters, one to Eva to pass on the good news and a letter of resignation that she delivered to Mrs. Banks' sitting room.

Literally skipping into the staff dining hall, she bumped into Anna. "I have some wonderful news!" Suddenly Sophie realized Anna didn't know about her application to the Bartley and quickly pulled herself together, figuring out how to tell her.

"What is it? I haven't seen you so excited for months. Has Bill come back?"

"Bill? No." Sophie frowned and looked puzzled. "Why would you think of Bill?" It surprised her that the mention of Bill's name from Anna's lips brought back the pain. "It's something quite different."

"Different? How?"

"Anna, I made enquiries about training to be a nurse." Sophie paused, waiting for Anna's reaction. None came so she continued. "I've been accepted at the Bartley Hospital in London as a probationary nurse."

"A nurse! You didn't tell me." Anna looked hurt and her bottom lip was close to pouting, irritating Sophie. To be fair, they were friends and Sophie had kept her dream from Anna.

"I'm sorry." Sophie tried to look remorseful but she really wasn't. "Today I received a letter to report to the nurse's residence in a week."

"So soon! I can't believe you didn't tell me."

"I'm telling you now. I thought you'd be happy for me. I've always been happy for you, your marriage and your plans with Alex."

"You're right. I'm sorry and I am happy for you. This is an incredible opportunity for you."

Half an hour before the taxi was due to arrive, Anna pushed Sophie into the staff dining hall, where the staff had gathered. Mrs. Banks made a little speech and presented Sophie with a nurse's timepiece to wear on her uniform and remember the Sackville. She glanced at Anna, knowing that it would have been her idea. Close to tears, Sophie declined offers of company to the train station, preferring to go alone. Anna was offended but Sophie felt unreasonable resentment towards her. Reminding her of Bill had stirred up some old feelings.

She walked out of the servants' entrance to the automobile. The driver opened the door. Sophie wound down the window and waved as the automobile drove away. She resisted turning and looking back, preferring to look forward to her future.

4

London - August 1915

The train puffed and snaked into Bexhill-on-Sea station. Sophie tingled with excitement, clutching her ticket to a new life. She didn't even hear the porter.

"Excuse me, miss. Are you for the London train?"

Sophie's mind could only think of the journey ahead.

"Miss! Can I load ya trunk?"

She stared at her luggage: a large trunk, a suitcase and her reticule at her feet. "Oh yes, thank you." She picked up her reticule and taking out some coins, thanked the porter. She waited for the passengers to exit the train before moving towards the 'Ladies Only' compartment.

The porter placed her suitcase in the overhead rack. "I'll put ya trunk in the luggage compartment, miss."

Sophie nodded her thanks and sat by the window, her stomach doing flip-flops. Barely able to keep from laughing out loud, she felt so happy, looking forward to a new life. She pulled the leather strap to drop down the window, peering at the guard as he yelled 'all aboard', waved his green flag towards the engine and blew his whistle.

Sophie closed the window as the train slowly moved along the platform, passing strangers waving to relatives, mostly women waving off husbands and sons leaving for war. Bexhill was a small town so the houses quickly passed by followed by a long stretch of coastline. She watched the waves break on the beach silently from her carriage. She would miss the sea, the fresh salty air, the crunch of beach shingles under her feet, Saturday strolls and tea with her friends. Her lips curled in a cynical smile at this last thought. Although she would miss the latter, she would not miss hearing Anna's constant chatter about the happy couple. She really didn't care about their plans. At last, she could be honest. She would never forgive Anna for breaking Bill's heart, for being the cause of placing him in great danger as he escaped to the high seas. She seemed to have a proclivity for falling in love with men unable to share their hearts.

Sophie lay her head back, pleased she was a lone passenger. She watched the green countryside replace the sea and sand dunes and allowed herself to dream of her future, which would absolutely not include romance.

The changing motion of the train prompted Sophie to open her eyes. The rolling green countryside of southern England had turned grey. Dark smoke swirled from chimney pots and clothes flapped on washing-lines, shaking off the lingering black soot. The greyness of London matched a small sense of darkness that wouldn't let the happiness inside escape. Surprisingly, it gave her comfort. It gave her permission to wallow in self-pity and grieve for a love lost. She stared, not

31

seeing the streets or houses, only aware of the train slowing down. Suddenly her hand flew to her mouth to stop her crying out. A gaping hole full of rubble appeared in the middle of a row of terraced houses, once a family home. She had read the newspapers and remembered Eva's letter about the spring attack of Zeppelin airships dropping bombs on London, but seeing it made it real and shocking. Indulging in her morose thoughts seemed trivial and selfish compared to the destruction of bombs. Had someone died in that bombed out home?

She sat up as the train slowed and clattered into a siding. Sophie peered through the window as it jolted to a stop and waited. The silence was intense at first, until she heard a distant rumble and then the clackety-clack of another train, a troop train passing in the opposite direction. Sophie felt a chill as the faces of young men in uniform blurred into one. Young men going to war and some would not return. Would she nurse others back to health?

Confident in her decision to come to London, she abandoned her selfish thoughts as the train eased out of the siding and back onto the main tracks to slowly move towards London's Victoria Station. She reached up to the luggage rack and grabbed her suitcase. Standing by the window, she steadied herself by holding the door frame as the train crawled to a halt. Taking a deep breath, she smiled. She was determined to shed her old life and embrace the new.

A single ray of sunshine pushed through the grey clouds shining directly on Sophie. She leaned her head back and saw a ghostly barrage balloon floating in and out of the clouds. She'd read about these balloons, installed after the bombing, especially designed to protect London from bomb laden Zeppelins. A shiver rolled down her spine. Bomb attacks were real. Despite the ordinariness of people going about their business, she sensed the barrage balloons simply gave Londoners a false sense of security—more bombs would come! She forced the thought out of her mind and hailed a taxi.

The cab pulled up to a drab red brick building with a polished brass plaque by the door that read: River House - Residence for Nurses; home for the next three years. Sophie paid the cabbie, giving him a sizeable tip she could ill afford, before asking him to carry her trunk to the front door and wait. As she lifted the brass knocker, the highly polished head of a smirking lion, she wondered if it was guarding the premises or warning the guests.

"Good afternoon!" A trim lady, with grey hair wound in neat curls, said with a soothing smile. "You must be Miss Romano, the new probationer." She extended her hand, took Sophie's in a warm, firm grip and announced, "Mrs. Wilderby. Housekeeper. Please come in." Sophie smiled. She hated the term probationer. It sounded temporary and she wanted nursing to be permanent but it was the term used for new recruits.

Mrs. Wilderby turned to the cabbie, engaging him with a warm smile. "Would you be so kind as to carry the trunk upstairs to leave it outside Room 2?"

"Thank you," Sophie said, feeling apologetic and pleased she had given him a generous tip. He muttered under his breath, swung the heavy trunk on his shoulder and grunted as he climbed the stairs.

"Welcome to River House. I take care of everything domestic in the house and, on occasions, I will nurse you if you are ill.

33

I'm a good listener if you need to talk. The rules are for safety and well-being. I expect you to abide by them, at all times." Sophie nodded "First, let's have a cup of tea and then I'll show you around. The other probationers are out, except Miss King, your roommate, who arrived about an hour ago. Probationer's orientation starts tomorrow at the hospital so you have the remainder of the day to yourself. It's quiet at the moment because the nurses don't finish their shift until six. Most of the nurses are like yourself, probationers, but we do have some fully qualified nurses staying with us."

Sophie enjoyed the tea and followed Mrs. Wilderby from the common room, to the dining room, laundry and kitchen. The house was squeaky-clean, an expression she used on the young maids at the hotel. But even the smell of disinfectant and furniture polish could not mask the overall odour of mustiness and age. The large dining table was scratched by years of meals, the sofa had holes in the upholstery and the coloured pattern had long gone from the threadbare carpet. When they returned to the entrance hall, Mrs. Wilderby pointed to a framed list with the heading 'Rules of River House.'

"Why River House?" Sophie asked.

"River was the name of the original family who owned the house. I found it strange at first as the Thames River is some distance from here." Mrs. Wilderby smiled, making Sophie feel safe and warm. "Now for the rules." Sophie listened and read the notice. They were mostly about curfews, meal times, and protocol for entertaining visitors, no gentleman friends allowed and the household duties expected of the residents. Other than the early curfew, Sophie found nothing restrictive.

"That is early," Sophie commented, "although, I expect I'll be studying in the evenings."

"It is the first time away from home for some probationers. We have to be careful. I understand you worked in a hotel."

"I was sixteen when I started at the Sackville. That was six years ago. I am used to rules. Mrs. Banks the housekeeper was quite strict but fair and kind. My day started at 5 a.m. and during the busy season I often worked until ten or eleven at night; too late to go out."

"You are well prepared for a nurse's schedule. I don't think I've ever said this before, but the probationers schedule is not as long. Unless you are on night duty, your shift ends at six." She raised an eyebrow. "But remember you are no longer supervising. You will be taking orders, not giving them." Mrs. Wilderby looked puzzled. "I'm curious, why did you leave such a good position?"

"I wanted to serve my country…" Sophie paused, thinking of Bill and the Sackville. She struggled to hold back tears, wondering if she had done the right thing, leaving Bexhill.

"My apologies, Miss Romano. I didn't intend to intrude. Losing someone in this wretched war is hard to bear."

"Yes." Sophie brushed her moist face. Not wanting to explain she allowed the assumption to remain.

"Now follow me. I'll show you to your room and introduce you to Miss King."

"Enter!" A young lady's voice called as Mrs. Wilderby knocked on the door of Room 2. Sophie noticed a brass frame containing a handwritten label that read Miss Sophie Romano and underneath Miss Beatrix King.

Mrs. Wilderby stood by the open door, ushering Sophie to step inside but making no attempt to enter. "Miss King, I'd like to introduce you to Miss Romano. I'll leave you girls to unpack." She closed the door.

35

Sophie smiled and reached out to shake hands. "Call me Sophie. Miss Romano is much too formal."

"My parents call me Beatrix. Still too formal. Call me Trixie." She giggled and her lips curled into a smile, but Sophie saw sadness as she stared at Trixie's pale porcelain complexion and equally pale blond hair, almost invisible as it curled around her face

"Welcome to our abode. Not exactly a palace—bare necessities at best. You'd think they would give us decent bedding and some comfortable chairs. And only one wardrobe, barely enough room for my clothes." Trixie giggled and spread her arms spinning around the room.

"I don't have many clothes. Take all the space you need. This room is larger than my room at the hotel." *And*, Sophie thought *pretty much what I'm used to. A wardrobe is a luxury after storing clothes in the sloping roof. The only difference for me is that I'm back to sharing.* Sophie had coveted her own room and remembered how upset she was when she'd had to share with Anna, the receptionist. Eventually they both had their own rooms.

"You lived in a hotel with your parents?"

"No, I was the head-maid at the Sackville Hotel in Bexhill." Sophie heard the pride in her voice and a doubt flashed across her mind again. Was she doing the right thing?

"You don't talk like a maid." Trixie poised her head to the side. "Did you defy your parents? How exciting!" She clapped her hands and giggled again.

"Both my parents are dead. I didn't have a choice." Sophie's words snapped as she glared at Trixie. Her flippant attitude and incessant giggles were annoying, but she felt compelled to give her some kind of explanation. "My father owned a silk

mill in Derby and a silk farm in Lucca, Italy where I was born."
She paused wondering why she was telling this stranger her
life story. "My mother died when we moved to England and
my father died in a fire. I lost everything and I had to work
as a maid to survive." Sophie pursed her lips, took a breath.
"Now, which bed is mine?"

Trixie sat heavily on one bed, her bright face suddenly
sorrowful. Stating the obvious, she pointed to the other bed
and said, "That one. I'm so sorry I didn't mean to be flippant.
My mother tells me all the time that I talk too much and I
don't think before I speak. How awful. I can't imagine losing
my parents." She frowned and bit her bottom lip. "What a
terrible thing to happen."

"It was a long time ago but thank you. There's no need to
apologize. How were you to know?" Sophie felt uncomfortable for snapping at Trixie. Under that giggly persona she was
a sensitive woman. Trixie's apology and concern was genuine.
Sophie dared to think she had found a friend.

"Why did you choose nursing?" Sophie asked, as she
unpacked her trunk.

"Escape!"

"Escape? From what?"

"Marriage to boring suitors! My parents even paraded me
as a debutante, following in mother's footsteps, except she was
the daughter of an earl." Trixie rolled her eyes. "And refused
the suitors and married beneath her. My father had no title
until he was knighted for services to the government."

"You were escaping a charmed life?"

"Not as charmed as you might think. Mummy is okay. Not
thrilled about her daughter being a nurse of course but Daddy
was angry." Trixie paused and tears gathered on her lower

eyelids. Sophie wondered if the sadness, or was it fear, related to her father.

"I'm sorry. Now, I'm the one making assumptions."

"My father is not always a nice man," Trixie said.

"I guess we both have our reasons for being here. I'm looking forward to helping people and serving my country. I need a purpose in life." The words were a statement and Sophie said them with pride and conviction.

"Me too!" Trixie nodded. "You and I will get along well." She giggled. "Look at us as opposite as can be. You have lovely dark olive skin and black hair and you're skinny thin. I'm blond, pale skinned and chubby. Mother says these are child bearing hips." Trixie wiggled her hips and giggled again. "Daddy says I'm plump. What a terrible word, it sounds like one of Cook's puddings."

Sophie smiled but didn't answer. This friendship thing was coming on too strong. She admitted there was something endearing about Trixie and they might become friends, but she needed to get used to Trixie's enthusiasm. Thinking of Anna, she reminded herself friendships change.

Noises came from the hallway; female voices and doors opening and closing. "The other girls are back." Trixie looked at the clock on her bedside table. "Dinner time. We'd better freshen up. At least we don't have to dress for dinner."

Sophie and Trixie entered the dining room and stared at the number of chairs squeezed around the table. Two girls in full nurse's uniform, not probationers, sat on one side. A tall thin girl stood up. "Hello, my name is Hillary West and this is Mavis Riding."

"Pleased to meet you. Sophie Romano and my roommate, Trixie King." Sophie glanced at Mavis who stared while twisting a strand of gorgeous golden-brown hair. She took her time but reached out and gave Sophie a limp handshake, ignoring Trixie.

Trixie giggled and waved her arms. "My goodness there are a lot of chairs." Her eyes narrowed, glaring at Mavis, noting her rudeness.

"Where should we sit?"

"Wherever you like, except the head of the table where I sit." Mrs. Wilderby's voice boomed from the doorway. "No one owns these chairs. Sit and make yourselves scarce."

Sophie sat by Hillary and Trixie sat opposite. Mrs. Wilderby placed a steaming casserole on the table, followed by two large dishes of mashed potatoes. She waited until everyone was seated, bowed her head and said grace.

5

Harsh Beginnings

The alarm rattled on the nightstand beside Trixie. Sophie stretched and waited for the noise to stop. She had woken long before the alarm but Trixie had not stirred.

"Turn the darn thing off, Trixie!"

The noise continued. Sophie jumped out of bed and slammed down the button. Trixie didn't move. She shook her shoulders. "Wake up. Its five past five."

Finally, the covers moved and Trixie sat up on her elbows. "You're chipper this morning. Are you always like this?"

"I'm used to getting up at 5 a.m. And I don't want to be late for our first morning. I'm heading to the bathroom before it gets busy."

Dressed in their new uniforms, Sophie and Trixie skipped downstairs for breakfast, surprised to find only Hillary at the dining room table.

"Good morning! I see you are early birds like me," Hillary said. "I like to start my day with a good breakfast and Cook makes the best. Most of the girls come rushing in at the last minute and grab a piece of bread."

"Sophie's the early bird. I'm not," Trixie said, standing at the end of the table. "I think I'll be joining the last-minute girls for an extra half-hour in bed."

Mrs. Wilderby placed a plate of eggs and bacon in front of Hillary. "Good morning, Miss Romano, Miss King! What would you like for breakfast?"

Sophie looked at Hillary's plate, "I'd like eggs and bacon please and coffee." She glanced at the tea pot on the table. "I see you have tea. Tea will do nicely."

"Not for me." Trixie said, "I'd like some fruit, fresh if you have it and toasted bread. I don't like marmalade. What kind of preserve do you have?" Trixie glanced towards Hillary and Sophie, puzzled by their shocked faces. "And I really do prefer coffee."

Mrs. Wilderby grunted and glared at Trixie with her blue-grey eyes, anger reddening her cheeks. "Miss King, this is not the manor house and I am not your servant. I do not have time to stand over a grill and toast bread. Cook makes fresh bread every morning, bread and marmalade with tea or nothing."

"Oh dear! No, I don't expect you to toast my bread. I am quite comfortable toasting my own in the electric…" Trixie's words trailed off as she glanced at the sideboard which had no toaster. Her porcelain face coloured pink. She pulled her chair up to the table, her eyes fixed on the white tablecloth. "Bread and marmalade with tea would be very nice. Thank you."

Mrs. Wilderby clasped her hands on her waist, pursed her lips and stood straight with a steely cold stare. "I'm pleased you understand, Miss King. I see you have a lot to learn."

Sophie stole a glance towards Hillary and saw her lips lift at the corners. She quickly looked away, aware she might trigger a burst of giggles. Hillary, well-mannered but not a society girl, enjoyed a hearty breakfast, encouraged by a mother rather than servants. Sophie felt a different kinship to Hillary. Although amused by Trixie, she pitied her because Trixie had no idea she was being demanding. Poor girl would struggle with the discipline. Sophie wondered if Mrs. Wilderby's show of anger was for Trixie or privileged ladies in general.

The first day at the hospital began with a lecture from an officious woman on cleanliness and infection. Sister Singleton was as stiff and starched as her uniform. The lecture contained nothing about nursing patients, anatomy or disease but a great deal about the correct method of scrubbing a floor, washing linen and the importance of cleanliness. Sophie recognized the teachings from studying Florence Nightingale.

Sister continued with graphic descriptions of disposing of bedpan waste with far more detail than necessary. She had the distinct impression Sister enjoyed seeing the squished disgusted faces and reflex gagging of young ladies accustomed to chintz drawing rooms. Sophie had never dealt with bedpans, but she had cleaned up disgusting messes, particularly from drunk guests at the hotel. She glanced at Trixie's green face, patted her hand and leaned towards her to whisper. "Think of spring lilacs."

A voice boomed through the room, "Miss Romano, will you please share your comments?"

Sophie stood up, colour burning her face. "I'm sorry, Sister. Miss King found the discussion difficult and I merely suggested she think of spring lilacs."

"Do you think your knowledge is better than mine?"

"No, Sister!" Sophie paused, wondering if it was wise to continue, but seeing her colleagues' pale faces, she took the risk. "I worked as a maid in a hotel and occasionally I had to deal with an unpleasant mess in the bathrooms. I taught myself to think of my favourite fragrance. I thought it might…" Sophie felt the back of her knees push into the chair at Sister's stare.

"Enough, Miss Romano!" Sister twisted her face, her eyes witch-like. "The fragrance of diseases, dying men and death cannot be expunged with lilacs!" Her voice dropped to a whisper. "I know. I've seen what happens in battle." Sophie saw deep emotion in Sister's eyes. "I'll speak to you later."

Sophie sat down, aware she had unwittingly made an enemy. Sister finished lecturing and led the girls on a tour of the hospital. It was a big disappointment for Sophie to learn that they would not be attending lectures or be in contact with patients for three months. The tour was to clarify their cleaning duties in the wards without disturbing the patients or getting in the way of nurses and doctors.

The Women's Ward had several empty beds but the Men's Ward overflowed, mostly with war wounded who were too ill to go home. Sophie felt the despair as they entered the Men's Ward. She smiled at a young man as his fearful eyes flashed from side to side. His face was grey, contrasting against the white bandage around his head. He leaned heavily on a crutch, trying to get out of bed. She glanced down and realized he was missing a leg. She had an urge to weep. He couldn't have been more than seventeen. She wanted to comfort him and tell him everything would be okay, but it wouldn't be okay ever again for this young soldier. Sister called for the group to hurry. Sophie smiled and he tried to return it. At that moment, Sophie knew why she wanted to be a nurse.

"Miss Romano, fraternizing with patients is a sin."

His smile widened at Sister's remark. Sophie nodded and joined the group. Once again, she had crossed Sister Singleton.

The tour finished deep down in the bowels of the building. A wall of moist heat and the smell of wet linen hit them and the disgusted looks returned. Sister stopped briefly at the laundry room and nodded to two probationers as they hauled loads of steaming wet linen from enormous washtubs. Sophie felt the sweat trickle down her back as the group moved towards a black hole in the wall, the odour of lye stinging her nostrils. Sister walked into the blackness and switched on a single light bulb hanging from the ceiling. The light revealed a windowless cupboard full of brooms, buckets, mops and cleaning materials. Each probationer was instructed to take a bucket, mop, scrubbing-brush and directed to a particular ward or section of the hospital.

As Sophie went to pick up a bucket, Sister stopped her. "Not you, Miss Romano." Sister's chin eased upwards as she smirked. "I have a special task for you. Follow me, Miss Romano. The rest of you, get to work."

Trixie leaned in to Sophie. "Lucky you."

Afraid Sister might hear, Sophie didn't answer. *I doubt it. I'm being punished for speaking out.*

"Enjoy the fragrance of lilacs," Sister said as they reached the top of the stairs. An evil smirk pinched her face as she pointed to a door. Sophie opened the door and almost delivered her breakfast to the floor. Bedpans were stacked on shelves waiting to be cleaned. Swallowing the bile, she did indeed think of lilacs and struggled to repress her retching stomach. With stubborn determination, she began cleaning the offending bedpans. When the door opened again, Sophie spun around, expecting to see Sister.

A friendly voice said, "Oh dear! What did you do to upset Sister Sin?"

Sophie frowned, puzzled by the name. "Hillary, it is nice to see a friendly face. It was Sister Singl... Oh, that's her nickname. Sister Sin, that's clever."

"Well, actually it's not just her name, although it makes it simple. So, what did you do?"

"I suggested to Trixie that she think of spring lilacs, to overcome her disgust at Sister's description of bodily waste." Sophie rolled her eyes. "Sister overheard me and here I am. Oh, and I should mention that I am sinful for smiling at a patient."

"Sister's sins!" Hillary burst out laughing and Sophie joined in, appreciating the release of tension. "Sister is religious and punctuates her sentences with the words sin or sinful. Rumour has it that she left a convent to nurse in the Boer War."

"It seems I have a lot to learn."

"She's a miserable woman and not liked by either nurses or staff. I'm afraid that once in her bad books, she does not forgive."

"My first day and I've upset Sister twice."

"You have three months with her and then you move to Sister Kay."

"I wondered when I would meet Sister Kay. A guest at the hotel put me in touch with her," Sophie said, sounding nasal as she tried not to smell.

"You'll like her. She's nice and really cares about probationers. I'll see you tonight. Perhaps we can chat then." Hillary paused. "Sorry," she said and placed a bedpan on the shelf."

The smell lessened as the pile of clean bedpans exceeded the dirty ones and by the time Sister came by, they were all clean. She nodded her approval and sent Sophie to scrub the entrance floor. The rhythmic motion of scrubbing took her back to the early days at the Sackville Hotel. She recalled the determined young woman who had lost everything and her pledge to make something of herself. Mrs. Banks at the Sackville Hotel was encouraging, which could not be said for Sister Sin. But now that she was older and wiser, people like Sister could not deter Sophie's ambition to nurse and help young men like the soldier she met today. I can handle three months, she reassured herself.

Expecting to see a black hole when she returned with her bucket, it surprised Sophie to see a light shining from the broom closet. The light gave her an odd sense of relief. She called, "Hello!" but there was no answer. She glanced at her watch. It was 6:15 and she was late. Everyone had already finished. Her arm raised to switch off the light but she hesitated, afraid of the darkness. She couldn't explain it but the black hole felt sinister.

Out of nowhere, Sister's sharp voice bellowed. "Electric lights cost money. Switch it off."

Clasping her hand to her chest, Sophie swallowed. "Sister you startled me." Where had she come from? Sophie wondered. Did she always creep around?

Sister pushed past and plunged Sophie into darkness.

"Good night, Sister." Sophie ran up the stairs and bumped into Hillary at the nurses' entrance.

"Sophie! Is everything all right?"

"Hillary, yes. I'm being silly. Can I walk with you to River

House?"

"I'd like that. What happened?"

"Yet another encounter with Sister. I had left the light on in the broom closet." Sophie hesitated. "I know it sounds silly, but I had the strangest feeling that something bad had happened in that closet."

"I'm not aware of anything but since my probation days I have no reason to go down there. It is creepy. I hated working in the laundry room."

"I'm tired and my mind is playing tricks. It's years since I scrubbed floors."

"I heard you say you were a maid. Didn't you scrub floors then?"

"When I was a junior maid. But by the time I left the Sackville, I was head-maid, instructing and supervising all the maids. The Sackville is a large hotel catering to society families. It was a lot of responsibility, but I enjoyed it."

"Why did you leave?"

"A broken heart and a desire to serve in the war, although the war will probably be over before I finish training. What about you?"

"My father's a clergyman and, with three daughters and no sons, he worried about our futures. So he educated us to take care of ourselves. I loved the lessons and grew close to my father but my sisters hated learning. Marriage was the only option for them. Dot is happy with two children but Mary is miserable. She married an older man. I didn't like him but he had money which impressed my sister and father."

"You didn't want to get married?"

"I never really thought about it. My father said I was too tall and not handsome enough to find a beau. I wanted to learn and travel."

"What a terrible thing to say!" Sophie thought about her own father and how he had always been proud of her.

"Papa was being practical. He acknowledged my love of learning, which meant far more to me than being pretty. Mama thought I should be a governess. On parish calls, she constantly dropped hints to society ladies about how clever I was. I shuddered at the thought of teaching spoiled upper class children and I hated how society ladies looked down on my mother."

"My father taught me how to run a business until the fire destroyed everything. It's unusual that both our fathers respected and supported us as intelligent women."

"Sophie Romano, you are a mystery! First you tell me you were a maid, now you are a nurse and your father wanted you to run a business?"

"It is a long story. A fire destroyed both my father and the silk business. I was destitute and worked as a maid to survive."

"I'm sorry."

"No need. It was a long time ago. I was never sure I wanted to run the business, but I wanted to please my father. I am sure I want to be a nurse."

"Medical science was a hobby for Papa. He never actually said, but I think he wanted to be a doctor. He was delighted when I told him I wanted to be a nurse." Hillary paused. "Nursing is only a stepping stone for me. My goal is to become a doctor."

"Wow! That is ambitious, but things are changing. Some medical schools accept women now," Sophie said, opening the front door and climbing the stairs. They parted ways at the landing.

Sobbing greeted Sophie as she opened the bedroom door. Trixie sat on her bed, her face in her hands.

"Trixie, whatever is the matter?"

"I'm a failure. My father was right." Trixie blew her nose and wiped her face. "He said my hands were too soft to manage the training." Tears filled her eyes again. "I can't even scrub a floor. I was in the Women's Ward. Sister Sin grabbed my arm, pushing at the scrubbing brush." Trixie rolled her sleeve to show a big bruise above her wrist. "Then Mavis tripped over the bucket and water spilled on Sister. I have never seen anyone so angry, not even my father... it was..." Trixie dissolved into sobs.

Sophie sat down and gently wrapped her arm around Trixie's shoulders. "Sh... Shush... Sister is an angry person and takes it out on people she sees as weak. I'm sure she does this to all the probationers. She had me cleaning bedpans. Now that's disgusting." Sophie screwed up her nose. "Come on, wash your face and let's go and have dinner."

There were only three places vacant at the table. Trixie sat next to Mavis. "I'm sorry about the bucket. I hope you didn't get wet."

Sophie watched Mavis as she gleaned pleasure from Trixie's distress. "Oh, I didn't get wet but Sister did. You should be more careful."

Sophie glared at Mavis. "You must have been distracted to have tripped over a bucket. One might think you did it deliberately."

Mavis opened her mouth to reply but said nothing as Mrs. Wilderby placed a cast-iron pot on the table.

The next morning, as they walked to the hospital, Trixie asked Sophie, "Why were you mean to Mavis last night at dinner?"

"Because I'm sure she deliberately kicked the bucket to get you into trouble."

"I don't need protecting. You aren't my mother."

Sophie stopped walking and held Trixie's arm. "Listen to me. Mavis manipulates people. You are kind and trusting but that makes you gullible. I don't want you to get hurt."

Trixie flipped her arm. "Let go of me! I had a nice long chat with Mavis after dinner last night and she's not like that. It was an accident. Mavis comes from a society family like mine. We have a lot in common." She hesitated. "But you wouldn't understand. My mother warned me I'd be mixing with all sorts at nursing school."

Eager to lash out at Trixie's hurtful remark, Sophie reluctantly held her tongue. She never wallowed in her misfortune but often missed the privileged lifestyle, even though it was many years ago. She remembered evenings in the drawing room with her father and society guests. Without saying a word, Sophie quickened her step, arriving at the hospital alone. She avoided Trixie all day. Something about Mavis bothered her. She doubted the girl came from a society family. She suspected Mavis was a fraud.

6

Relationships

The friendship between Sophie and Trixie didn't recover. They were civil to each other as roommates but nothing more. Sophie, having been betrayed by her friend Anna in the past, although for different reasons, she had no intention of patching up the friendship with Trixie. She watched with concern as Mavis drew Trixie closer, sensing the friendship would end in disaster. On Mavis's advice, Trixie's father had paid for her probation, a system that allowed probationers with privileged families and delicate hands to avoid the floor scrubbing. Sophie did not have such means but her hotel experience, competence and hard work meant she moved to assist nurses on the wards ahead of her colleagues.

Sharing the same interests, Hillary and Sophie's friendship strengthened; even though, for the past month, they had seen little of each other, since Hillary was working the night shift. Sophie missed their conversations about medicine and the practicalities of life. She compensated by spending her days off studying in the library, not only for Christmas exams, but because the human body fascinated her. Her interests went beyond nursing the sick and wounded.

The librarian, familiar with Sophie's studies, handed her a medical journal about the effects of war on soldiers. The article featured soldiers with minor physical wounds who seemed to have an invisible condition that prevented them from getting well. It described how the wounded brain showed no external evidence of injury. Doctors on the Western Front suggested the cause was horrific memories of the battlefield but they couldn't explain why these memories lingered on for months, even years or why it affected some soldiers and not others. Medical officers acknowledged the problem, but most commanding officers considered these men to be philanderers, cowards or worse, deserters attempting to get home. It often resulted in an unfair court martial.

Sophie felt compassion for these men. She understood their trauma. She never spoke of it but her own memory of her father being burnt to death was the same kind of horrific memory as war atrocities. As much as she tried to forget; often, and without warning, flames would suddenly leap into her head and nothing could stop the image of his burning body. She had always put it down to the shock so it fit that the army called this nervous condition shell-shock. However, there was still a lack of understanding as soldiers were expected to get over it and go back into battle. Not having seen a battlefield, even Sophie wondered why these men wouldn't heal. The rest of the article had nothing significant to add. She returned the journal to the librarian and packed up her books. Glancing at the clock, she sighed. "I'll be late again." Knowing Sophie studied at the library, Mrs. Wilderby merely huffed when Sophie was late for dinner.

Wrapping her scarf tighter around her neck against the

damp cold of winter, Sophie walked towards River House, pondering her future. A mist hovered in the air, caught in the beam of the searchlights scanning the skies for Zeppelins. She glanced upwards. *I may not have a future if we get bombed.* Attacks from the air had been increasing; but so far had spared Bartley Hospital. She suspected a different kind of war was emerging; one right there in London. How would that affect their futures? She admired Hillary's desire to be a doctor and wondered if she should consider medical school too. She certainly studied far beyond nursing, but she could never raise the money for university. On reflection, Sophie decided she preferred nursing and caring for people. The article about brain injuries had opened her mind to something more than nursing the physically sick. She wanted to help heal the mind too.

Sophie, deep in thought, and completely unaware of her surrounding, suddenly felt the hackles on her neck jump to attention, altering her to danger. She heard running footsteps too close for comfort and seconds later heavy breath brushed her back. Was she being attacked? Bracing herself, she took a deep breath and swung around, ready for a fight. She was shocked to see Trixie, hysterical with blood on her face and one eye swollen shut as her arms grabbed onto Sophie's.

"Trixie, what happened?" Sophie pulled her close and felt her body trembling. She peered over her shoulder but saw no one following. "Did someone attack you?"

Trixie tried to talk but the only word Sophie heard was Sister. The other words blurred together in between sobs. Only feet away from River House, Sophie held Trixie tight and walked her to the door.

"Shush, it's okay. Let's get you home."

Mrs. Wilderby, checking for late comers from the front parlour saw them struggling up the steps and opened the front door.

"Good gracious! What happened, Nurse King?"

"I can't understand what she's saying. She just ran to me in the street. I think someone has attacked her," she replied,

Sophie helped Trixie to her room and Mrs. Wilderby followed with a bowl of warm water and a bottle of iodine.

"Ouch!" Trixie yelped.

Mrs. Wilderby continued to clean the cut above her eye. "For all that blood, the cut is quite small; but you will have a black eye. Now tell me what happened?"

Trixie glanced towards Sophie who sat beside her and held her hand.

"Trixie, we need to know who did this to you," Sophie said kindly. "Take your time and tell us what happened."

Trixie leaned on Sophie's shoulder. "You were right. Mavis is not a nice person. Little things keep happening. She gives me wrong information and I get into trouble on the ward. I just didn't want to see it until today." Trixie took a deep breath and cleared her throat, her face taut as she held back tears. "I saw her whispering to Sister and they giggled and laughed. Sister put her arm around Mavis and kissed her... on the mouth..." she paused, glanced at Sophie and stared at Mrs. Wilderby, waiting for comments. Sophie thought it better that Mrs. Wilderby took the lead and stayed silent.

Trixie continued, "I don't understand. Mavis had never mentioned Sister was a relative so why were they kissing?" Trixie's shoulders trembled and her face wrinkled. "It felt creepy. I called to Mavis to tell her I was leaving and we needed to get back for dinner." She didn't answer, but they both spun around and stared at me. Sister's face turned scarlet, the way she gets when she's angry. I said I was sorry that I didn't know they were relatives. They both laughed and Sister wagged her finger at me. She poked me in the chest, saying, 'Nurse King, you saw nothing and never speak of it. You are a sinful girl.' Her tone was frightening and I asked Mavis if we could please leave. Sister smiled at Mavis and said, 'Nurse King's sinful ways must be punished.' Mavis laughed and grabbed my arm and together they pulled me down the stairs to the broom cupboard."

Trixie burst into tears. "Sister... pushed me against the shelves. I tried to get away and she slapped my face and punched me and then..." Trixie was almost in hysterics. "Then... she pulled my uniform up and put her hand... up my skirt and Mavis... didn't try to stop her... I screamed and she let go. Trying to cover my mouth, I escaped. I ran up the stairs. Mavis followed me. Sister Kay was at the top of the stairs and I just kept running. Sister Kay must have stopped Mavis because she didn't follow me. Once on the street, I saw Sophie and ran to her."

Mrs. Wilderby didn't comment but turned to Sophie. "Run Trixie a bath and I'll ask Cook to heat some soup for you both. I'll bring a tray up rather than you going to the dining room. I'll tell the others you aren't well."

Trixie soaked in the tub and was much calmer as she wrapped herself in her dressing gown. Her sad puppy look was made even sadder by her pale skin. "I'm sorry I treated you so badly."

"It's all right. I have met girls like Mavis before. Working in a hotel exposes you to a lot of different people. I worried for you because I knew Mavis would hurt you, but you were not to know. Sister's behaviour is inexcusable. I suspect she lost her temper because you caught her."

"Caught! Doing what and why were they kissing like that?" Trixie's puppy look turned to wide eyed bewilderment. Shaking her head from side to side, she added, "I don't understand."

Before Sophie could reply, there was a knock on the door. The kitchen maid arrived with a supper tray, explaining that Mrs. Wilderby was delayed on the telephone.

The chicken soup was hot and flavourful and Sophie smiled at the plate of buttered toast on the tray. Mrs. Wilderby had a good heart. Trixie sipped on the soup but Sophie ate heartily; having not eaten since lunch, she was hungry.

"This is so nice," Trixie said, holding up the toast. "I love buttered toast. Why did you say, Sister was caught?'"

"You know about homosexuals, don't you? It's against the law but some men can't help it. They are usually bachelors who like men instead of women."

Trixie nodded giggling. "Daddy says they are sick and to avoid contact."

"Women can be like that too; lesbians who prefer other women to men. It's easier for women to cover up their affections because people don't pay attention to women kissing or hugging, unless the kissing is on the mouth and hugging becomes caressing."

Trixie's hand flew to her mouth, her eyes so wide they might have popped from their sockets. "Oh no! Is that what Mavis and Sister were doing? Do they... you know... sleep together?"

Sophie nodded. "I think so. We had suspicious female couples in the hotel but it's hard to say whether they were just travelling companions or more. It's a weird kind of relationship. Some women dress in a masculine fashion, taking on the male role. They are mostly nice people that love each other. Unfortunately, there are a few, like Sister, who are twisted and sick and take advantage of young women."

"Is that why she tried to pull my uniform off?" Sophie watched Trixie's expression change and tears rolled down her cheeks.

Sophie sat beside her, patting her hand, "You are all right, nothing happened."

The bedroom door opened and Mrs. Wilderby came in with two dishes of Cook's apple pie. "I thought you would enjoy a treat. I have news." She stopped, seeing horror in Trixie's face. "Trixie, what is it?"

Sophie answered for her. "I explained Mavis and Sister's behaviour. Trixie had no idea what she was seeing."

"I'm sorry you had such an awful experience, but the news will cheer you up." Mrs. Wilderby sat on Sophie's bed. "Sister Kay called me to say that Nurse Riding would not be in for supper and she inquired about you, Nurse King. She was worried and reported the incident. Matron immediately called Sister Singleton and Nurse Riding to her office. Sister's behaviour has come under scrutiny before, but there was always an explanation until now."

"How did Matron know what happened in the cupboard?" Trixie asked, her face askew with one eye closed and puffy and the other wide with disbelief.

"About an hour later, Matron returned my call. Mavis accused Sister of... things." Mrs. Wilderby blushed and looked flustered, glancing at Sophie and obviously not prepared to describe things. "She said Sister threatened her if she didn't comply or told anyone. Mavis is going home. Her father will pick her up in the morning. They have relieved Sister of her duties."

Trixie's rattling alarm woke Sophie the next morning. Exhausted from yesterday's events, she didn't feel like getting out of bed. As usual, Trixie slept through the noise. Once up and with the alarm stopped, Sophie dressed, leaving Trixie to sleep, her face buried in the pillow.

Sophie joined Hillary at the breakfast table. "Good morning!" Hillary frowned. "You look as though you had a bad night? What's wrong?"

"It was an eventful night." Sophie replied as Mrs. Wilderby place the teapot on the table. "We'll talk later."

"Eggs and bacon for two?" she asked. "How is Nurse King this morning?"

"She's still sleeping, so I didn't wake her."

"She should stay in bed today." Mrs. Wilderby glanced at Sophie, moving her head slightly to one side with a raised eyebrow. "Until she is feeling better. That was a nasty fall she had last night."

Sophie nodded and poured two cups of tea, realizing Sister's crime would be covered up. How would they explain Mavis's departure? She glanced at Hillary's puzzled face. "Walk with me to the hospital and I'll tell the story," she whispered.

Feeling better after a good breakfast, Sophie welcomed the fresh air, waiting for Hillary on the front step. A green van stopped outside River House with Riding Plumbing & Electric written on the side. A tall wiry man got out of the van and jumped up the steps. "Where's our Mavis?" he yelled.

"You must talk to Mrs. Wilderby. I'll fetch her for you."

Sophie opened the door to find Mrs. Wilderby and Mavis holding a suitcase, already at the door.

The man grabbed the suitcase and pulled Mavis with it. "Get in the van, Mavis."

Mavis was sobbing and Sophie saw this spiteful young woman turn into a troubled little girl. "Pa, I'm sorry!" Mavis's eyes never left her feet as she jumped in the van, slamming the door. Her cupped hands hid her face and her shoulders shook with unheard sobs.

His cap in hand, he looked at Mrs. Wilderby. "Are you in charge here?"

"I'm the housekeeper. Matron is the person to speak to and she's at the hospital. Mr. Riding, this is an unfortunate incident and I'm sure we can sort it out. Matron thought Mavis would be more comfortable at home."

"I want some answers and if I don't get 'em there'll be trouble." He shook his fist and bounded down the steps to the van. Once in the driver's seat, he yelled at Mavis and once again shook his fist, this time right in front of Mavis's face.

Mrs. Wilderby's forehead creased with worry. "I'm not sure home is the best place for Nurse Riding."

Sophie nodded in agreement. "Poor Mavis. That little scene explains a lot about her background. She is a victim in more ways than one."

"You are older and wiser than your years, Nurse Romano. Let's keep this between ourselves, shall we? Except for Matron, she will need to know."

"Of course."

Mrs. Wilderby turned as Hillary stepped through the front door. "And you too, Nurse West."

Hillary looked startled and repeated Sophie's 'Of course'

with a quizzical expression.

Mrs. Wilderby went back into the house and the girls began their walk to work.

"What is going on?" Hillary said, "Did I miss something this morning, as well as last night?"

"Mrs. Wilderby thinks you saw Mavis leaving. I'm sworn to secrecy but as she thinks you saw, I can tell you what happened. Mavis's father picked her up in a trades van. Riding Plumbing and Electric."

"You were right. Mavis is no privileged lady. Why would she put on such an act?"

"Mavis is a victim." Sophie continued to explain the morning's events and Trixie's trauma of the night before.

Hillary nodded. "Mavis and I are the same year. We trained together and sometimes..." Hillary hesitated. "Her speech was just odd. There were rumours about Sister Sin but I didn't know about Mavis except that she was Sister's favourite. I feel sorry for her. I wonder if she will come back?"

"I don't know. We'd better hurry or we'll be late."

7

Old Flame

Sympathetic eyes followed Sophie as she arrived for duty that morning. Sister Kay told her to report to Matron, which usually meant trouble.

Matron looked up from her papers. "Nurse Romano, please take a seat. I want to talk about last night. How is Nurse King?"

"She was sleeping when I came down to breakfast. Mrs. Wilderby took her some tea and said she was tired and had a headache from the bump on her head."

Matron nodded with approval. "Mrs. Wilderby will take good care of her." She hesitated, biting her bottom lip. "Sister feels remorseful for having lost her temper with Nurse King. Overwrought and overtired, Sister has returned to the convent for rest and prayer." Silence followed. Matron stared at Sophie who stared back. She realized the hospital would take no disciplinary action against Sister. Sister would eventually return and hurt another young nurse.

"Nurse Riding has gone home to what looks like a less than ideal situation." Sophie's words were stiff. "And yet you know that Sister coerced her. Don't you care about your nurses?"

Sophie caught her breath. Had she gone too far? Although she didn't like Mavis, she sensed Sister had taken advantage of her vulnerability and traumatized Trixie.

"What I know, or how I feel personally, about a situation is immaterial. The hospital's reputation is at stake." Matron sighed, the corners of her mouth tried to lift but no smile came. "And, I do care, very much, about my nurses. Mrs. Wilderby called me about her concerns for Nurse Riding. I will consider re-instating her." Matron paused. "That was an impertinent question, deserving of reprimand."

"Yes, Matron, I'm sorry." Sophie dropped her gaze to her feet.

"I like you Nurse Romano, and I don't say that often. You have all the qualities of an exceptional nurse. Your previous hotel experience has given you a maturity I rarely see in the young women who pass through my care. Heed my advice and let the situation go. Concentrate on your career."

"Yes, Matron. Thank you. I will take your advice." Sophie understood Matron's situation. A kind person doing her job. Matron had a good heart.

"Have you decided what to do when you finish training?"

"Serve my country and work in a field hospital." Sophie paused. "I have been studying shell-shock. Careful nursing with an understanding of this nervous condition would help soldiers recover faster."

"I commend you for your extracurricular studies. Doctors at the front have been talking about shell-shock for some time but the military still doesn't take it seriously." Matron lifted her watch. "Please excuse me. I have to welcome Mr. Wainwright, a new orthopaedic surgeon from Italy." Matron laughed. "I'm curious to meet this Italian doctor with an English name."

Wainwright. Sophie took a sharp breath. Could it be? Matron came from behind her desk and walked Sophie to the door. "Can I rely on your discretion about the other matter?"

"Yes, Matron, I must return to duty."

She stopped in the nurses' lounge, thankful to be alone. Her heart was pounding and she felt clammy and bilious. Could it be him? When had Carlos become a doctor? No, it must be a coincidence. But how many Italians had an English name like Wainwright?

An exceptionally busy morning on the Men's Ward took Sophie's mind off whether Mr. Wainwright was in fact Carlos. Sister Kay, the ward sister, greeted her with a concerned look. "Is everything all right with Matron?"

"Yes a pep talk about…" Sophie hesitated, knowing Sister would understand, "about last night."

Sister nodded with a commiserating smile. "We have two new patients, young men from Passchendaele. Neither have a trace of beard stubble and both with leg injuries." Sister sighed. "Settle these boys first and then finish the bed-baths." She pointed to an orderly pushing a bath chair.

Private Skinner's long gangly arms and legs hung like a puppet without strings, except for one leg that stretched out in front of the bath chair. The orderly maneuvered Private Skinner alongside the bed. Sophie moved the blanket that covered his trouser-less legs, a splint went from the top of his thigh to his ankle, the white bandages red with blood. The other leg had several sutured cuts and an ankle the size of a football.

Sophie took his hand. "Private Skinner, I'm afraid this will hurt but we'll be as careful as we can." She pulled the bed sheets back and called a second orderly to help lift him onto the bed.

The poor boy gripped Sophie's hand until it turned white. He creased his face into a tight ball, his breath suspended to hold back a scream as they lifted him onto the bed. She eased pillows under his broken leg and placed a cool cloth on his head. Her fingers gently wiped the tears of pain from his cheeks and she glanced at his chart, surprised that his last morphine shot was over twelve hours ago. Placing the chart at the end of the bed, she almost hooked it on his swollen foot. His long legs spilled over the foot of the mattress.

"Private Skinner, are you in pain?" She felt silly asking as the answer was obvious.

He moved his head hesitating before speaking. "It's real bad when I move. Sorry…" Involuntary tears trickled onto his cheeks. "I try not to show it." He sniffed, attempting a smile. "My sisters would call me a crybaby."

"Your sisters would be wrong. You are very brave. The doctor will be in to see you soon. He'll make you more comfortable."

He grabbed Sophie's arm. "Nurse, will they cut my leg off…?" Fear and misery released more tears and his bottom lip trembled.

"I'm not a doctor but I am sure they will mend your leg." Sophie glanced at the misshapen leg, swollen and bloody. She wondered if she was misleading the young soldier, but she had to give him hope.

"Skinner, are you flirting?" A cheerful voice shouted from the next bed.

"Johnny! I thought they'd split us up."

"Not a chance. You and me are mates."

Sophie approached the next bed and took the chart from the orderly. "Private Bigsby, how's the knee?" she asked, reading the chart. The knee wasn't his only problem. Someone had noted shell-shock with an exclamation mark.

"Ah, it's just a knee, and I have another one." Raising his good knee, he chuckled. "They said I might need an operation." His voice dropped, the cheeriness gone. "The bloody Huns. Did you see what they did to Mike…" His voice trailed off and Sophie got a glimpse of his fear.

"Private Bigsby, I want you to lie back and relax. The doctor will do his rounds soon." Sophie puffed up his pillows and gently eased his shoulders back until he relaxed. "Take it easy."

"Good morning, Sister!"

Sophie froze at the sound of the voice, one she had not heard for seven years. But there was no mistaking Carlos' warm gentle voice. She fussed with Private Bigsby's blankets, not daring to turn around.

"Sister Kay," Matron said, "I would like to introduce you to Mr. Wainwright, our new orthopaedic surgeon. Have Private Skinner and Private Bigsby arrived on the ward?"

"Yes, Matron. Nurse Romano is settling them now."

"Mr. Wainwright is here to assess them for surgery. I'll leave you to take over." Matron's footsteps marched out of the ward.

Sophie gasped as Carlos said. "Nurse Romano… from Derby?"

"As far as I know she came from Bexhill, in Sussex?" Sister said, the intonation a question rather than an answer.

Carlos cleared his throat. "I worked with an Italian family by that name years ago. A coincidence, no doubt."

Sophie concentrated on her patient, keeping her back to the group. As she heard them approach, she had no choice but to turn around. Her knees almost buckled under her. Carlos was as handsome as she remembered; his eyes even bluer and his smile melted in her heart.

"Nurse Romano, it has been a long time."

"Seven years, and now you are a surgeon," Sophie said, remembering how he had abandoned her when she needed him. Anger bubbled through the tenderness. She needed to change the subject. "Private Skinner is in a great deal of pain. His chart indicates his last morphine was ten o'clock last night."

Carlos lifted the chart and scribbled something as he leaned in to Private Skinner. "I will give you an injection to ease the pain." He turned to Sister Kay. "And Sister, every four hours, please." He replaced the chart and Sister beckoned to Nurse West to prepare the syringe.

"Once the pain has eased, I'll examine the leg."

Private Skinner tried to smile but moisture gathered along his eyelids. "I don't want to lose my leg... Sir!"

Carlos sat beside the bed. "It will take a long time to heal and some hard work on your part, but you will keep your leg and you will walk again." He patted the soldier's arm.

Hillary wheeled a cart to the side of the bed. Carlos filled the glass syringe and quickly plunged the needle into Private Skinner. "Nurse Romano will take good care of you." His smile lingered, not on the patient but on Sophie and his tenderness stirred feelings she didn't want to remember.

Sister Kay cleared her throat. "Nurse Romano, return to the morning routine. Mr. Watson's bed needs changing. Nurse West will take over here."

Sophie's eyes dropped to the floor, her face on fire and her hands clammy. She could feel the quizzical glances piercing her back. Knowing her flushed face had been noticed, she hurried towards Mr. Watson's bed.

"Oh my. What happened to you? Your face is as bright as a beacon flashing across an angry Irish sea."

The colourful words and Irish accent coming from a stranger annoyed Sophie. "I don't think we've met," she said, holding Mr. Watson on his side.

"No, we haven't. I was sent down from the Children's Ward as you are short staffed here. Emily Finnegan. I'd shake hands but mine are full," she said while pushing a rolled sheet under Mr. Watson.

"You sure have handsome doctors on this ward. And, he has eyes for you. Do you know him?" Emily asked.

"Who?"

"The new doctor. I saw the way he looked at you."

"We met many years ago in Italy. It's none of your business and I don't want to talk about it." Finding Emily's questions intrusive, she changed the subject. "You must find the Men's Ward different from the children's ward?"

"I've nursed children for years. It used to be that they came with illnesses we could cure or at least make them feel better. But now, they have terrible injuries from the bombs. Some have lost parents and parents come looking for lost children. It's heartbreaking."

"Oh, that is sad." Sophie imagined sleeping children being wakened by a bomb falling on their bed. "It's more terrifying than the battlefield." She nodded towards Private Skinner's bed. "These soldiers are barely adults."

Sophie felt empathy for Emily and wanted to redeem herself. "I'm sorry I spoke in haste. I've had a... strange morning."

Emily patted her shoulder. "We all have those days and I do have a habit of asking questions. It's the Irish in me. Da teased me and said I kissed the Blarney Stone one time too many. I grew up only a stone's throw from Blarney Castle, County Cork." She laughed a contagious chuckle. "He was worse than me but a great storyteller. That's where I learned. The Blarney Stone might have helped. I tell his stories to the children. It takes their mind off the loss and pain." Emily's voice trailed off.

Tucking the sheets around Mr. Watson, Sophie glanced up, hearing the jovial chuckle turn sad. "I enjoy stories. Reading takes my mind off things but I'm no good at reciting," she said.

"I'm not much of a reader," Emily replied, as she eased Mr. Watson back on his clean pillows. "There we are, Mr. Watson, as clean as a whistle. The tea trolley will be around shortly."

"We'd better get on. There are still three more patients to settle." Sophie couldn't help smiling at Emily's use of words. Her accent and Irish pronunciation were quite charming.

The day had gone by fast. Emily was fun to work with and Sophie almost forgot about Carlos until Hillary mentioned him on the walk home to River house.

"So…" Hillary paused. "Tell me about the handsome Italian surgeon?"

"There's nothing to tell."

"I don't believe you. It's obvious you know him."

Sophie sighed. "I was staying on the silk farm with my aunt and uncle one summer. My father hired Carlos to keep an eye on the farm and learn the silk business. I was sixteen and it was just a teenage crush."

"It looked like more than that." Hillary waited for a comment.

"I was just surprised to see him. That's all!"

"Sophie Romano, you are a dark horse. Italian lovers on a silk farm! I thought you worked in a hotel."

"I did, but not by choice. After the murder of my father, uncle and aunt, we lost everything. I still own the villa in Italy. It isn't worth much and I haven't been back to Italy for years so it's probably in ruins now."

"What happened to your mother?"

"Oh, she died of a fever when I was twelve. My dad and I were very close." Sophie felt tears spring to her eyes. "I haven't thought about my family in a long time. I keep it in the past. It's safer that way."

"I had no idea, but it explains your tenacity and dedication. Your father would be proud of you," Hillary said, as she opened the door to River House. Hearing Trixie talking to Mrs. Wilderby in the kitchen, Sophie crept upstairs to her room and lay on the bed, sensing tears hovering behind her eyes. Seeing Carlos had stirred memories she thought she had put away, memories of abandonment. First her mother, then her father and at her greatest time of need, Carlos. Then there was Bill. He knew she loved him, but rejected by Anna, he ran off. She had been abandoned again. It was probably for the best as she realized she still loved Carlos. "No!" she said aloud. "I must love no one."

"Talking to yourself?" Trixie said, as she closed the bedroom door. "You look exhausted."

Sophie sat up on her elbows. "It was an eventful day. A new nurse, Emily, from Children's Ward helped out today. She's Irish and hilarious." Sophie avoided talking about the new doctor. She didn't want to explain. "How are you? You look much better."

"I feel fine but Matron won't let me go back to the ward until this heals." Trixie pointed to the cut and a bruise over her eye. Sophie thought about Matron covering up Sister Sin's crime although the incident had angered her. Had Sister gone too far this time or would she be back? But then nurses, and especially sisters, were in short supply as so many were in field hospitals nursing injured soldiers. She would probably be back.

8

Love and Friendship

Fully recovered, Trixie returned to the hospital and Emily returned to the Children's Ward. Sophie had enjoyed Emily's sense of humour and funny stories. They helped her push her emotions back inside her where they belonged. And she had avoided Carlos for a week.

Private Skinner took a turn for the worse after his operation and was in an intensive care ward. Private Bigsby's knee operation was a success and they discharged him to a convalescent home. She thought about what the two soldiers had endured on the battlefield. Her desire to nurse in a field hospital and comfort more young soldiers grew stronger by the day and, she admitted, it would take her away from Carlos. *Are my desires motivated by the right reasons? Honestly, I'm not sure.*

On a whim, she visited Private Skinner. "Knock, knock," she said as she approached his bed, shocked to see his grey pasty face and his limp arm attempting to greet her. "I wondered how you were doing. The operation went well, I hear." His lips moved into a smile but if she hadn't been staring at him, she would have missed it. "What's this about you not feeling well?"

"I'm tired and can't sleep. I'm afraid to close my eyes because of the nightmares." Sophie pulled the chair close to the bed and took his hand. She felt him relax. "Close your eyes and think of something beautiful. Do you have a sweetheart?" He nodded. "Think of her eyes, her hair blowing in the wind." A trace of a smile crossed his face and the furrows on his forehead smoothed out for a few minutes. But suddenly his face squeezed into a ball and his eyes shot open with horror. "Private Skinner, you are here in the hospital and you are safe." He took a deep breath.

Sophie let him rest for a minute. "Tell me about your sweetheart. What's her name and has she been to see you?"

"Molly. I don't want her, or my mum, to see me like this."

"You look fine. Most of your cuts and abrasions have healed and your leg is in plaster. You look good to me."

"Don't feel good. They think I'm a hero and I'm not. Johnny was the hero. He saved my life."

Sophie looked at his chart. She could see no reason for the continued intensive care but she was sure he was suffering from shell-shock. He needed company and someone to talk to. "Private Skinner, I have to go now but may I visit you tomorrow?"

"I'd like that. Can I ask you to call me Mike?"

"As long as we're out of earshot." She looked towards the duty nurses' desk. "It has to be Private Skinner when Sister is around. Now try to sleep and think of Molly."

"Excellent advice, Nurse Romano." Carlos tapped her on the shoulder and his touch sent her into a tailspin. "Private Skinner is going back to the Men's Ward tomorrow morning. His leg is healing well and he needs encouragement to walk

72

with crutches. In fact, he needs someone like you to nurse him back to health."

"Thank you. I must leave or I'll be late for dinner." Sophie hurried out of the ward, angry with herself for reacting. What was it with that man? Taking a deep calming breath, she started down the corridor and then heard his footsteps.

"Sophie! Wait!"

She spun around, almost knocking him over.

"Can we talk?"

"I have to get back for dinner. What is there to talk about?"

"I'm sorry for what happened all those years ago. I regretted writing that letter. Sophie, I am so sorry."

Sophie couldn't believe her ears. She had waited a long time to hear him say he was sorry but now she felt numb. "I didn't believe the letter at first. I needed you so badly but your mother convinced me you meant what you said."

"My mother?" Carlos frowned as the paging system drowned his voice. "What does she have to do with this?".

"MR. WAINWRIGHT PLEASE REPORT TO WARD 9 IMMEDIATELY!"

"Sorry I have to go. We'll talk later," he called over his shoulder. "Can I take you to dinner?"

"Yes!" Sophie replied as he disappeared into the next corridor.

The chatter from the dining room greeted Sophie as she hung her winter coat on the hall stand, too late to go to her room.

"Lost in studies again, Nurse Romano?" Mrs. Wilderby asked, carrying a large platter into the dining room.

"Sorry…" Sophie hesitated and said nothing more. Studying

was Sophie's usual excuse on her day off, so she let the assumption lie. She could hardly tell her she was flirting with the new surgeon. She had an urge to giggle which did not escape Trixie. Her head bent slightly to one side, a question in her stare. Sophie sat next to her. "I'll tell you later," she whispered. Hillary frowned at the two of them with one eyebrow raised. Sophie smiled and mouthed, 'Later.'

After dinner, not that Sophie could eat much, she felt giddy climbing the stairs. I'm behaving like a schoolgirl. Trixie and Hillary were on her heels as they rushed into the bedroom and closed the door.

"What is going on with you?" Hillary asked in her matter-of-fact tone.

Trixie jumped up and down, not sure what she was excited about. "I can't stand the suspense. If I didn't know better, I'd say you were in love."

"Oh, my goodness!" Hillary gasped. "It's Dr. Wainwright. I knew it. I saw him looking at you this morning and you were blushing. Not something I normally see in you."

"It's Mr. Wainwright. Remember, doctors are addressed as Mr. when they become surgeons. And Trixie, stop jumping or you'll open that cut on your head."

Hillary held on to Sophie's shoulders, looking her in the eye. "You are changing the subject. What happened with Mr. Wainwright?"

"Well, I went to see Private Skinner and he appeared at the bedside. We had a brief conversation in the corridor and he asked me to dinner." Sophie shrugged. "There was a misunderstanding all those years ago." Her mind flashed back to dinner at the house in Derby. He'd been quiet that night, not even reacting when her father had hinted that marriage might be a good thing. Then she remembered the intensity of his last kiss. "I'll always love you." Not just I love you but he'd added always followed by no matter what happens. She hadn't noticed at the time. He was leaving for Italy to sort out an account in Bologna and check on Uncle Roberto at the farm in Lucca. He said they would talk when he returned. On reflection, she thought he knew things had changed.

"What misunderstanding?" Trixie asked.

Sophie remembered as though it was yesterday. He had mentioned his father was in Bologna and they were to meet. At the time, she thought nothing of it, a coincidence. But now it was obvious there was no coincidence. His father had planned to be there. He talked Carlos into taking over his Bologna office and Carlos had no intention of returning to Derby.

Frustrated, Trixie yelled again. "What misunderstanding?! Hillary, do you know what she's talking about?"

"Carlos worked for her father and they had a fling when she was sixteen. Before he was a doctor. Right?" Hillary directed her question to Sophie.

Sophie only heard the word 'fling' and came back from her memories. "It wasn't a fling. That was what his mother called it. I might as well tell you, but please don't tell anyone. Carlos promised to marry me and then he wrote me a letter and said I was too young and ended it. I thought he'd abandoned me but his mother interfered. However, the end result was the same; I never saw or heard from him again."

"This is so romantic. Now you've found each other again, you can get married." Trixie twirled around the room, almost knocking over the lamp.

"Trixie, stop twirling. You're making me dizzy, and, no, we

are not getting married. I'm not even sure I'll accept his dinner invitation." Sophie stared off into space. A dinner invitation was hardly a marriage proposal.

"Not everyone wants to get married," Hillary stated.

"Well, I do. But not to the mindless creatures my mother chooses for me. I'll find my own husband." Trixie shrugged. "It's been a long time and he's very handsome. Do you think Carlos is married?"

Sophie felt a sharp pain in her heart. The room fell silent and even Trixie stopped chattering. Sophie had never considered he might have married, but it made sense. His mother would find him a suitable debutante.

Hillary broke the silence and smiled. "If he's been studying to be a doctor and then a surgeon, he hasn't had time for romance."

"You're right. When would he have had time?" Sophie said.

"Speaking of medical studies, I have some news. I met with Matron today and she is going to help me apply to medical school. They are accepting a limited number of female candidates."

"Hillary, that is wonderful news! Why didn't you say earlier, instead of talking about my silly not-to-be romance?"

"It's a slim chance I'll be accepted but Matron said enrolment is low because of the war. She thinks this would be a good time to apply. My father has offered to pay the tuition. I had no idea that he had saved so much money. He saved it for me and my sisters so we would have something when he died." Hillary's mouth twisted into a strange smile. "Mary and Dot won't be happy when they find out he spent it on medical school for me. Papa said they don't need the money as they have husbands to take care of them. Dot is happy and her husband provides for her and the children. Mary hates her husband. He's old but very wealthy and Mary loves his big house and society friends." Hillary's eyes were moist. "Papa always said I was too intelligent for society."

"I have trouble understanding the anatomy they teach us nurses. How are you going to understand all those..." Trixie paused, wafting her arms in a big circle. "All those... everything!" Both Hillary and Sophie burst out laughing.

"Trixie, you are funny. All those everything is a lot to learn but I find learning easy and I want to be a doctor."

Sophie hugged Hillary. "I am pleased for you and I know you'll get in to medical school."

Sister Kay was waiting for her when she arrived at the ward the next morning. Sophie wondered what had happened as this was unusual. "Is something wrong, Sister?"

"Not wrong... but a warning or, perhaps a reminder. The hospital frowns on romantic involvement between doctors and nurses. I know it's none of my business but I saw how you looked at Mr. Wainwright."

Sophie took a deep breath and willed herself not to blush. "Sorry, Sister. Mr. Wainwright worked for my father many years ago and it surprised me to see him."

"I see. Heed my words, anyway, Nurse Romano. Now, change the beds. Nurse Finnegan's on her way down from children's. She'll be working with you and Nurse West today."

"Yes, Sister." Sophie hurried onto the ward.

"Nurse!" Sophie turned to see Private Skinner. "They brought me down this morning."

"Welcome back. You are looking much better. How's the leg

doing?"

"Not bad; the doc says I have to use the crutches and walk about."

"Good, I have to change your bed. Let's start by getting you up and into that chair." Sophie pulled the covers back and eased his legs to the side of the bed. She placed the crutches; one on each side of him. "Put the crutches under your arms, your weight on your good leg and lift yourself up. You can't fall. I've got you and the bed is behind you."

Private Skinner heaved his body up. A wide grin spread across his face. "I did it. I'm standing."

"You certainly are. Now move your crutches slightly forward and lean on them, gently swing your good leg forward. Now do it again." Once he reached the chair, Sophie helped him to settle. Private Skinner stayed in the chair while Sophie helped Emily deal with the bedridden patients. It was always a rush in the mornings, getting the patients ready for the doctor's morning rounds.

"Private Skinner, are you ready to get back into bed?"

"I'd like to see if I can walk. Can you help me?" He pushed his crutches into his armpits and heaved out of the chair. Giving a long sigh accompanied with an enormous grin, he took several steps towards Sophie.

"Well done, Private Skinner," Carlos' voice boomed from the nurses' station.

"Thank you, Sir. Nurse Romano showed me how to use the crutches. She's the best. I was in a funk and she talked to me, real gentle-like. Thank you, Nurse."

Carlos was standing next to Sophie and she could hardly breathe, let alone speak. Carlos waited for her to respond. When silence ensued he said, "You are right Private, she is the best." He turned his head to see colour flood Sophie's cheeks.

She glanced towards the nurse's station, thankful that Sister Kay had her back to the ward, greeting another doctor. "Shall I help Private Skinner back into bed and get the screen?"

"No, I think we'll let the patient enjoy his freedom. It's more important that he learns to walk. I'd appreciate your help." Carlos looked into her eyes and she had a sudden urge to kiss him. Quickly, she reprimanded her silly schoolgirl thinking, unbecoming of a mature woman.

"Mr. Wainwright, my apologies," Sister Kay said as she reached the patient's bed. "All the doctors arrived for rounds at the same time this morning."

"Sister Kay, we were just telling Private Skinner how well he is doing." Carlos patted Private Skinner on the shoulder. "Keep the good work up, soldier. I'll be by tomorrow."

Carlos and Sister walked down the ward to an orthopaedic patient scheduled for surgery while Sophie found an excuse to go to the supply room. She gathered some dressings on a tray, turned, and walked into Carlos. She almost screamed, dropping the metal tray which Carlos caught by reflex.

"Carlos, what are you doing?" Sophie asked, taking the tray from his hands.

"I want to invite a friend to dinner. Are you free tonight?"

"Um…" Sophie hesitated, trying to think through her flustered mind.

Carlos frowned. "It's only dinner. We can talk about old times."

"I'd like that but I don't get off until six and curfew is nine. Archaic." Sophie rolled her eyes. "But tomorrow is my day off." *What am I thinking? I'm accepting a date from Carlos. Not a real date. He said it himself. Dinner with a friend. And I'd like to know why he's become a doctor.*

"I'll pick you up at five."

"No, there are rules about doctors and nurses too. I study in the library on my day off. Meet me at the library at five o'clock. Now go. If Sister catches us, I'll be in trouble."

Carlos left the supply room just in time as Sister entered and stared at Sophie. Had she seen him leave? She waited, expecting a reprimand.

"Nurse Romano, that tray will not walk itself to the patient."

"Yes Sister," Sophie mumbled and rushed to the ward, realizing she had only gone in the supply room as an excuse. Now she had to decide who needed the supplies.

Hillary approached her, making the decision easy. "There you are. Come with me. Mr. Watson needs his dressing changed." Sophie stood and observed. As a probationer, she was not allowed to change dressings until her third year. Hillary bent over the patient and whispered to Sophie. "Did the nice doctor ask you out?"

"How did you guess? Sister didn't see anything, did she?"

"No, she was with that other doctor." Hillary's voice changed from a whisper to almost a shout. "The wound is healing well. Before you adhere the new dressing you must…" Hillary stopped talking as Sister Kay joined them.

9

Lies That Change Lives

Concentration eluded Sophie as she sat in the library staring at the open text book. The words blurred and her thoughts jumped between the impending date with Carlos and studying fractures caused by explosions. She looked up as the big oak doors squeaked and Carlos walked into the library.

"Hello," Carlos said.

"Shush! Not so loud," Sophie whispered. "I'll pack my books and we can go."

Carlos picked up her satchel. The librarian waved with an approving glance at the couple. Sophie smiled, as they walked out to the street and, to her surprise, Carlos opened the door of a black automobile.

"You have a Model T Ford?"

"You know the makes of autos?" Carlos grinned. "You amaze me. Yes, it's American, but they made this model in England before they ordered the factory to make vehicles for the war. They call it the ordinary man's auto or something like that. Did you know that most Americans drive?"

"An automobile is a luxury for most people in Britain."

"For me it is essential to get to the hospital for emergencies. At least it's not a Bentley, which is what my father wanted me to drive. The government gives me a petrol allowance and because I'm a doctor, they can't commandeer my car for war services."

Sophie gave him a quizzical look. "But you can take ladies to dinner?"

"It's quite possible that I'm called to an emergency or injuries from an air raid. Those Germans are getting brazen with their Zeppelin attacks." He stretched his neck backwards and looked up. "It looks like a clear night. I can see a few stars."

"Does that mean Zeppelins will attack? I worry on clear nights. What will happen? Most people run to the Underground but our patients can't."

"I've wondered about that too. But for tonight let's not worry and have a nice dinner."

"Where are we going?" Sophie scanned her clothing. "I'm not dressed for dinner. I don't own a dinner gown."

"You look beautiful I…" He paused. Sophie waited for him to finish his sentence but he coughed and paused again. "I thought you'd enjoy a little Italian for old time's sake."

"That sounds nice. The last time we had dinner together was with my father in Derby."

"I remember that night. I can still see you walking downstairs in that green satin gown. You looked so beautiful." Carlos sighed, sounding sad and remorseful.

She stayed silent in the passenger seat as they drove to the restaurant.

Carlos pulled alongside a small storefront draped with fancy blue curtains. The sign above just read 'Restaurant' with a tiny

Italian flag after the word. "Antonio cooks and serves the best Italian food in London."

A round chubby man, Antonio, greeted them with Italian flamboyance; his arms reaching as though to catch every Italian word he spoke. Sophie had trouble keeping up. It had been a long time since she had used her mother tongue.

Carlos attempted to order the food but Antonio put his hand up "I have something special for you... Specialita bellissimo!" He kissed his pinched fingers and threw the kiss in the air. His arm still in mid-air, he snapped his fingers and beckoned to the waiter. "Luigi, the special wine!" Then he retreated to the kitchen.

Luigi almost ran to the table with a carafe of ruby red wine. Carlos swirled the wine in the glass, holding it by the stem. He sniffed the aroma, took a generous sip and swallowed. A broad grin spread across his face. "This is excellent. Where did..."

Luigi bowed slightly with a wry smile as he poured two glasses and whispered. "Chef's secret."

Sophie surmised the wine had not come through the usual channels.

Carlos raised his glass towards Sophie "To old friends!"

"To old friends!" she repeated, her eyes fixed on Carlos. She saw more than friends, or was that what she wanted to see? Suddenly, there was an awkwardness between them. She needed to break the silence. "When did you become a doctor?" she blurted out. "I thought you were destined to take over your father's business."

"My parent's plan. Not mine but I went along with it. I hated the Bologna office. It was nothing like working for your father." He hesitated, his eyes lingering on hers. "And you?"

Sophie ignored the inference. "Why medical school?"

"During a business trip to London, I met up with a friend who was studying at London University. I saw an opportunity; an easy way out of the business. My father approved, a degree in business would be good for his business, except I switched to medicine. He was angry but I didn't care. I'd found my passion in medicine and continued my studies in surgery. It delighted my mother, although I suspect the drawing room ladies grew tired of hearing about my accomplishments." They both laughed.

Luigi interrupted their conversation, placing two steaming plates of a colourful pasta dish on the table. "Chef's specialita; Buon appetito!"

The aroma alone teased Sophie's taste buds. She twirled the pasta on her fork and savoured the flavours. "This is wonderful. It's years since I tasted such food."

Carlos took a large gulp of wine, his lips lingering on the glass and his eyes peering above the glass, towards Sophie. "I'm sorry for what happened all those years ago. When I got to my father's office in Bologna, I regretted writing that letter." He thoughtfully played with an imaginary crumb on the white tablecloth. "Had I known about your father's death and the fire at the mill, I would never have sent it. I didn't find out until I returned to Derby at Christmas. I tried to find you. I went to your old house but no one had heard of you. Sophie, I am so sorry."

"I replied to your letter, begging you to reconsider. I told you about the fire and Papa's death. I lost everything and you abandoned me. Your letter broke my heart. I thought we were engaged to be married. I needed you so badly and marrying you would have solved all of my problems. And when you didn't reply..." Sophie had to stop, feeling the back of her eyes prickle and her throat tighten. "I explained I had to leave. I asked you to contact Mr. Fotheringham, my solicitor, as he would know of my whereabouts. Dalton, our butler was the only friend I had. He stayed with me after the staff was dismissed and looked after me while they auctioned our possessions." Sophie struggled to hold back tears. "I needed you. You were my fiancé, even though your mother seemed to think we were having a summer fling."

"My mother!" Carlos frowned. "You mentioned her the other day. I don't understand."

"I went to see her, to ask for your address. She said you didn't want to see me. She said I was too young to marry, among other hurtful things. I gave her the letter to send on to you." Sophie took a deep breath.

"I never got the letter and she never told me you had visited." Anger flooded his face, pink turning purple. "I will never forgive her for this. I can't believe what she has done."

"What do you mean?" Sophie frowned. He spoke the last sentence as though his mother had committed a terrible crime.

"She has changed the course of my life and her cruelty to you is unforgivable. How did you survive?"

"Dalton took me to his sister's house and we stayed there until he found another position as a butler in London. His sister, Doris, had a small house and children, no room for an unwanted boarder. Doris was very kind and found me a maid's position, with room and board, at The Sackville Hotel in Bexhill-on-Sea."

"I am sorry. That must have been difficult."

"No. It wasn't hard. I did well and made great friends. I stayed there until I decided to train as a nurse." She thought about Bill and the real reason she'd left Bexhill but chose not to enlighten Carlos. She wanted to be angry with Carlos but, in fact, she had always been angry but at the wrong person. His mother was to blame. If she had given him the letter, would things have been different? They fell into silence and ate their meal but Sophie's anger for the injustice bubbled inside. She wanted to lash out. Finishing her second glass of wine, she felt brave and confident.

"I'm surprised your mother hasn't found you a suitable debutante. Someone with good breeding—a father with a title and large estate or at least a wealthy merchant—someone socially acceptable, which she declared I was not." Surprised at the venom in her own words, Sophie stopped talking before she said something she might regret. Carlos was staring at her. She smiled to herself. *It looks as though I hit a nerve.*

"I loved you so very much and I missed you terribly. I wanted to marry you. I wish I could turn the clock back and I wish with all my heart I had not listened to my parents' lies. Things would have been so different." He motioned to the waiter for more wine.

Sophie shook her head. She already felt dizzy from the wine and Carlos' words. She noted Carlos was talking in the past tense. *Why should that bother me? Aren't my affections in the past too?*

"I have something to tell you. As you guessed, my mother tried to find me a debutante but I turned them down. I was too busy with studies and most of the ladies were pretty, even beautiful, but quite brainless decorations."

"That must have frustrated your mother. Were you expected to attend debutante balls?" Sophie forced a sharp sarcastic laugh. She was behaving badly but she couldn't help herself.

86

"Until war broke out. Then there were no balls to attend. I went home for a short time after I graduated. Mother began her match-making again but I was not interested until I met Rosamond." Carlos cleared his throat. "I wish I'd found you earlier." He paused and took a long breath. "We announced our engagement in the spring."

Sophie felt the colour drain from her cheeks and her mind spin with confusion. "Oh, I'm happy for you."

Carlos frowned. "Are you feeling unwell? You are very pale."

"Too much wine. I'm not used to it and it has been a few days of surprises." She needed to talk of something other than engagements. "I've been studying shell-shock and trench panic and I believe the right kind of nursing can help young soldiers." There was silence. Carlos didn't respond so Sophie kept talking. "I nursed a young man this month with shell-shock and Matron commented that I was good with these patients so I..."

"Stop chattering. We only just found each other again and you're chattering along about shell-shock. What about us?"

Sophie squinted, creasing her forehead into a deep frown. "Us?!" The word shot out of her mouth. "I don't understand. You are engaged to be married. There is nothing between us except memories of an eventful past. We have moved on to different lives. There is no us." Her thoughts were not the same as her words. She suspected the feelings were deep and mutual but the window of opportunity had passed.

Mrs. Wilderby had her hand on the doorknob when Sophie bounded up the steps of River House and slid through the door.

"Just in time. Another minute and the door would be locked," Mrs. Wilderby said. "Did you have a pleasant evening, Nurse Romano?" Her words were said to the door as she watched Carlos drive off. "Walking out in the company of a man with an automobile? He must be important."

Sophie tried her hardest to smile. "I'm not walking out with him. He's an old childhood friend I bumped into at the library. Good night, Mrs. Wilderby!"

As she climbed the stairs, Sophie noted her reference to childhood. At sixteen years old, although mature for her age, she had still been a child when she fell in love with Carlos. Puppy love was not sustainable. Had she expected it to re-kindle? She thought about Bill and how her love for him was quite different. It was a mature, sustainable love, except that Bill didn't love her. Hardly sustainable if it's one-sided she mused, opening the bedroom door.

"Is there something wrong with me?" she asked, not realizing she had spoken aloud.

"What...?" a sleepy voice answered.

"Sorry. Go back to sleep," she whispered, relieved that Trixie turned over with a contented sigh. Discussing the evening's events was the last thing she wanted to do.

Walking to Bartley Hospital the next evening, Sophie yawned but picked up her pace as though to defy the tiredness caused by switching to the night shift. As nurses in training, they rotated through different wards and tonight she was due to start on the Women's Ward. Although sad to be leaving the brave young men and staff, which included Hillary, she was looking forward to a change. Also, she'd be away from Carlos.

Most of his patients were male soldiers so she assumed she would not see him on the Women's Ward.

The night supervisor, Sister McPherson, was a cheerful, short, round woman with forty-plus years' experience. She should have retired, but because of the war she had offered to stay on. Many of the staff considered her too old to work. Sophie thought it an opportunity to learn from a seasoned nurse, even if she had a reputation for snoozing during the night shift. Sophie's main concern was working with Nurse Riding. Matron considered Mavis a victim and with Sister Singleton on permanent leave, she was back working nights. Sophie was not looking forward to working with Mavis.

10

Monsters in the Sky

The only light on the ward beamed onto the desk where Mavis sat filling in charts. Sophie walked around the ward checking on patients. The steady sound of sleep with the occasional sigh as someone turned over was different from the noisy snoring and snorting on the Men's Ward. As she returned to the desk, she thought she heard weeping.

"Did you hear that?" Sophie whispered to Mavis.

"Probably one of the chest patients wheezing. Here, take over. I'm going for some tea."

Sophie lifted her watch on her uniform. "It's not break time for another hour."

"So what! It's quiet. I'm going to the canteen. You can finish the charts."

"I'm only supposed to do them under supervision. What if Sister…" Sophie said no more. Mavis wafted her hand dismissively, calling far too loudly for a sleeping ward. "I don't care. I hate nights and I'm going for tea."

Sophie sat at the desk and listened but all she heard was creaking bed springs as patients turned over, disturbed by

Mavis's loud comment. She was reading the charts when a loud BOOM broke the silence, followed by two more. Sound rockets that warned of German attack. Her heart stopped and her blood ran cold as the boy scout's whistle sounded, confirming the danger. The shrillness sounded desperate—an air raid was imminent. She glanced at the patients. Those that could, jumped out of bed and were standing, looking to Sophie for guidance. Sophie glanced towards the door. Where was Mavis? Fire drills had instructed the nurses to escort mobile patients to the cellar. Orderlies and the remaining nurse helped patients into wheelchairs. Immobile patients stayed on the ward with a nurse. With no Sister or senior nurse, it was up to Sophie to take care of these women.

The corridor was loud with animated, fearful voices as patients left the wards guided by nurses trying to hide their own fear as they headed towards the cellars for safety. Sophie told those that could to follow the crowd and she would join them as soon as she could. She worried as there was still no sign of an orderly or Mavis. She grabbed three wheelchairs but realized she couldn't push everyone at the same time and neither could she leave the ward.

A loud crash followed by a heavy thud shook the floor under her feet. The ward vibrated from another massive explosion, causing a uniform scream from the patients. Sophie sucked in a deep breath to keep calm and figure out how to keep the four remaining patients safe. She helped three into wheelchairs and pushed them into the corner of the ward that had no windows. Mrs. Jones a large elderly lady lay in her bed staring at the ceiling, semi-conscious and unaware of the air raid. Sophie needed an orderly to help lift her into a wheelchair. Another explosion shook the building. She glanced at the window above the bed. Mrs. Jones had to be moved and that meant moving the bed. Thankful it had casters, it still took Sophie ten minutes to move the heavy bed to the corner. Satisfied she could do no more, she sat down with her patients, knowing that if a bomb landed on the hospital, there was nothing more she could do.

Seeing the pale scared faces, she smiled. "We're safe here. This won't last long. You know we rarely get attacked..." Sophie stopped, seeing the worried faces she realized they feared for their families living close by. Where had the bomb dropped? Whose house had it crushed? And nothing she said would reassure them their families were safe because they probably weren't safe. Instead she talked about the seaside, remembering her days at the Sackville. The women shared stories of charabanc trips to Brighton or Eastbourne. They talked until they realized the bombing had stopped and were filled with relief as the bugle sounded the all clear.

The corridor was noisy again with patients returning to the wards. Sophie's patients crawled into bed, complaining about the crowded conditions in the makeshift cellar. Sophie had assumed Mavis would be in the cellar but no one had seen her. Where was Mavis?

Sophie took roll call and all the patients were back in their beds, shaken and worried but safe until the next attack. At last, Mavis turned up. She gave no explanation and Sophie didn't ask.

The night shift finished at 7 a.m. There was a hue of dawn on the horizon or was it fires burning from the bombs? Sophie, beyond tired, thought of calling a cab but decided the walk would do her good. Her tummy rumbled. In the chaos, she had not eaten all night. The thought of Mrs. Wilderby's breakfast quickened her step. She shuddered as she walked past the Emergency Department lined with casualties; a line of ambulances unloading the injured from last night's attack. A fire truck blocked the road and she picked her way through rubble on the street; parts of a house no longer standing. A family, mother and three children, stood stunned on what had been the front steps of their home while a fireman attempted to comfort them with little success. All they wanted was to pick up what was left of their belongings but couldn't because it was too dangerous to go inside. A boy, around two years old, cried while his older sister, maybe ten or eleven, gathered him in her arms, comforting him the best she could. A boy, about the same age as the girl, twins perhaps, had his arm around his mother, the man of the family. Sophie assumed the father was fighting the war in France or Belgium. Tears filled her eyes at the scene of misery and devastation. What could she do? How could she help these families? She stared at the fireman as he approached her. "Miss, we need you to move on." And as though he read her thoughts or recognized her uniform, he continued. "There's nothing you can do here. We'll look after them." She gave him a weak smile as she headed to River House.

Mrs. Wilderby, usually calm and organized, was flustered, anxiety showing on her face. The bombing had cut off the gas and she improvised, attempting to boil water and cook eggs in the fireplace. She cursed that the old coal burning stove had been removed only the year before to make room for a modern gas cooker.

Sophie sat alone at the table eating boiled eggs with bread

and butter and drinking hot tea. The day shift had left ages ago. Mavis, the only other night nurse, had gone to bed without eating.

"I'm sorry, Nurse Romano. I'm sure you are hungry after a long night. This is the best we can do. Cook couldn't make bread this morning so the bread is yesterday's."

Sophie placed her hand on Mrs. Wilderby's shoulder as she bent forward to pour tea. "This is wonderful, thank you."

"I wish all the girls were as appreciative. I'm afraid there were lots of complaints this morning because we had no hot water."

"A little cold water hurt no one. After seeing the bombed-out house by the hospital, I am grateful for this lovely breakfast."

"Was it bad?" Mrs. Wilderby asked.

Sophie nodded, her mouth full of bread. She swallowed. "Yes, a nice looking family has lost their home. They looked so forlorn. I wanted to do something but the fire brigade moved me on."

"You have a good heart, Nurse Romano. Now off to bed with you and get some rest." Sophie hesitated. She wanted another cup of tea. "Here," Mrs. Wilderby handed her a cup and saucer. "Take it up with you."

Sophie smiled. Having tea in the bedrooms was frowned on unless you were in bed because of illness.

"Thank you. I am tired."

Banging on the front door woke Sophie. She turned over, glancing at the clock. Noon and she hadn't had enough sleep, but the knocking grew louder. She wondered why Mrs. Wilderby wasn't answering. Swinging her legs out of bed, she pulled on her dressing gown and tied the belt as she ran downstairs.

A man in a chauffeur's uniform stood on the step, obviously taken aback by Sophie's attire., "I'm a nurse working nights, which means I sleep during the day and you woke me up," she said, annoyed at the intrusion. The man said nothing so Sophie continued. "Perhaps you have the wrong address. This is a nurse's residence."

"I know. I'm looking for Miss Beatrix King. Sir Robert sent me to pick her up."

"Why? Is she expecting you? She didn't mention anything to me and I'm her roommate. Is there an emergency?"

A door banged shut at the back of the house and Mrs. Wilderby came into the hall, holding a wicker basket full of brown paper packages from the butcher. "Nurse Romano, what is going on?"

"This gentleman has come to pick up Nurse King."

Mrs. Wilderby raised an eyebrow, scanning Sophie's dressing gown. She was not impressed that one of her girls was standing in the front doorway, dressed in night clothes and talking to a man. "Go back to your room. I'll deal with this."

Sophie climbed the stairs, checking over her shoulder and wondering if there was a real emergency. The chauffeur didn't seem concerned. She heard Mrs. Wilderby invite him to wait in the common room.

The bed looked inviting and Sophie crawled under the covers, hoping to get an hour's sleep. When her head hit the pillow, her eyelids shot open and refused to close. Expecting to wash in cold water, it surprised her when the geyser popped a flame and produced hot water. The gas was back on and Mrs. Wilderby would be pleased. She dressed and went the library to study. Her shift didn't start until 10 p.m. She could have a rest after dinner.

The librarian nodded and smiled as Sophie pushed the big oak doors open, savouring the library aroma. She grinned, wondering what exactly was a library aroma? Musty paper and ink, dusty old print, the compilation of scents from hundreds of hands fingering pages, the faint smell of stale food and cold tea. All overlaid by the odour of human skin, masked with a hint of perfume but mostly men's pomade. Sophie's grin widened, breathing in her favourite aroma and listening to the library sounds. The silence broken only by ancient squeaky floor boards, whispers and turning pages. A contrast to last nights' bombing, she needed the essence of the library more than sleep to gather energy for that night's shift. Her studies included anatomy for the upcoming Christmas exams. Chewing the end of her pencil, she looked up and noticed the library had a decorated Christmas tree in the corner. She wondered how long it had been there. Christmas, she thought. My first Christmas away from the Sackville, always such a busy time. She was surprised at the sadness and loneliness she felt, missing Anna and Bill and even miserable old Mr. Pickles. The librarian tapped her shoulder to whisper. "Miss, the library is closing in ten minutes."

Sophie nodded her thanks and packed her satchel, wondering what Mrs. Wilderby had for dinner. She thought it might be stew as she had been to the butchers that morning.

The smell of onions greeted Sophie when she opened the front door, setting off pangs of hunger. She ran upstairs, dumped her satchel and coat on the bed, expecting to see

Trixie, but there was no sign of her and the room looked tidy. Had Trixie gone home?

Mrs. Wilderby placed a steaming casserole and a large ladle in the centre of the table and the kitchen maid handed her a dish piled high with mashed potatoes. The dining room was full, except that Trixie was missing.

"Where's Trixie?" Sophie asked.

"Her father sent the chauffeur to take her home. Her mother is not well. At least that what Matron told me," Mrs. Wilderby said.

"I saw him. He woke me up and he didn't look concerned."

"Sir Robert telephoned Matron. Nurse King changed, packed a bag and drove off in the back of a Bentley."

Mavis rolled her eyes. "Spoiled princess. I bet she just wanted to get out of night duty."

"She's not on nights," Hillary said.

"She's scheduled to start next week. The new roster went up today. I hate nights, but I don't have a father doting on me." Mavis pulled a face. Sophie wondered if she realized how witch-like it made her look.

"Time to get some sleep. I'll see you later," Sophie said, already part way up the stairs.

Her eyes skyward, Sophie watch the searchlights do their nightly dance. It was almost musical, the way the beams of light crossed each other, stopping momentarily to an invisible beat as clouds passed through the light. Mist gathered over the houses; a good sign. The Zeppelins would not attack tonight. The rubble from the morning's chaos had been cleared away but the shell of the house gaped onto the street as if in horror.

The ghostly shapes of curtains moved in the breeze where there was once a window. The family had gone and Sophie hoped they had found somewhere kind and safe.

Mavis was already on the ward, taking details from the nurse finishing her shift. She beckoned to Sophie. "Mrs. Jones needs settling for the night."

"Is she getting worse?"

The other nurse answered "She's been unsettled all day, but she is conscious. Talking to her seems to help."

"I'll go and see her." Sophie pulled a chair up beside Mrs. Jones' bed. "How are you today?"

"Better. Nurse, can I go 'ome today, I wanna go 'ome."

"Not today, but soon." Sophie took her hand. "When you are well enough, the doctor will let you go home. Does your family visit?"

She shook her head, pulled her hand from Sophie and brushed her cheeks. "I remember you from last night. You pushed my bed."

"Yes, I thought you were… sleeping."

"Sometimes I can't talk but I hear. I liked your story of the seaside. Were you a maid? I were a maid at the Red Lion. They 'ad guest rooms." She laughed. "At least that's what they called 'em. Rented by the 'our. I didn't stay long."

"I worked at a hotel in Bexhill. It was very posh, but there were shenanigans, even with the elite. Maids see it all." They laughed together.

"It's time for you to sleep." Sophie straightened the sheet. "Mrs. Jones, is something wrong?" Sophie saw her eyes fill with tears. She realized that despite her comatose state, the weeping she had heard the night before was Mrs. Jones.

"Thank you, Nurse. You are kind. There's nothing you can

do. I miss 'em, that's all." Mrs. Jones said no more and closed her eyes.

By eleven, the patients were settled. Sophie had reassured them that the London mist she'd witnessed on her way to work would prevent bomb attacks that night. Already tired from the night before, the patients rested.

Mavis worked on the charts of two women patients who had suffered serious injuries during the air raid.

Holding the new charts, Sophie whispered to Mavis. "Did the nurse say anything about their injuries?"

"Both are under observation. Bed four was struck by falling masonry. It's in the chart. She looks okay to me. A few broken bones and a bump on the head. The doctor gave her morphine for the pain. Dr. Morgan listed the other one with bad nerves and gave her a sleeping draft. She's out cold."

"Mavis, don't you care about the patients?"

She shrugged her shoulders. "I'm going to take my tea break."

"Early again! Where did you go last night?"

"None of your business. I got stuck because of the bombing. I won't be long tonight."

Working with Mavis was a challenge. Her dismissive attitude towards the patients upset Sophie and she wondered why she had even trained as a nurse. How had Mavis even passed her exams? Then, remembering Mavis's association with Sister Sin who was in charge of training, she guessed the 'how.'

11

A Visit to Selfridges

The big red bow and the red holly berries on the green wreath looked cheerful and welcoming on the front door of River House. A Christmas tree lit up the common room window, dawn light catching the shiny baubles and tinsel.

Trixie had returned the previous evening against her father's wishes. Her mother had fully recovered so there was no reason for her to stay. She ordered the chauffeur to drive her back to London with the Bentley full of cut holly and a fir tree from the estate stuffed in the boot. Mrs. Wilderby, Trixie and Hillary had spent the evening decorating and celebrating Trixie's return. Sophie helped before leaving for her last shift on nights, celebrating her final night working with Mavis.

The only time the nurses had two days off in a row was between day and night shift. After getting some rest, Sophie, just off nights and Trixie preparing to go on, planned an afternoon of Christmas shopping. Trixie grew up shopping with her mother at Harrods in Kensington where all society ladies shopped. For the first time, she planned to try Selfridges on Oxford Street. Built and owned by a blasé American, he'd designed the store to serve ordinary people. Ordinary meaning middle and upper class, with a bargain basement for the better off lower class population.

Sophie had never even set foot in a department store and her excited tummy flip-flopped with anticipation. It took her back to when she was eight or nine years old when home was a silk farm in Italy. Papa would drive her and her mother to Lucca to buy Christmas presents. The shops in Lucca were small and personal.

Giggling, they dressed in their best clothes. Trixie, the height of fashion, wore a navy serge suit and pink silk blouse with a matching broad-brimmed hat decorated with ostrich feathers. Sophie's wardrobe was limited to one smart grey wool suit with a simple, grey, utility hat; not particularly fashionable

Trixie looked her up and down. "You need a different hat." She pulled a hatbox from the wardrobe. Removing the tissue from around a black broad-brimmed hat with grey feathers and a tasteful black satin bow, she held it up. "Try this?"

Sophie stood in front of the mirror with a slight pout on her lips, offended at Trixie's disapproval of her attire. Placing the hat on her head, she broke into a smile. She looked stunning. "The hat is perfect!" She secured it with a hatpin and giggled. "Thank you."

Each picked up her handbag and gloves, linked arms and headed for the tube station. They were almost tripping with excitement as they ran down the steps for the train to Oxford Street. Once on the platform, Trixie screwed up her nose. "What is that smell?" Her eyes went to a sad and filthy family with crying children. "My shoes are sticking to the floor." Her lips down-turned in disgust and she pulled her arms in tight to her sides.

The pungent odour had hit Sophie too. Unwashed bodies mostly and the unmistakable scent of fear, difficult to describe but ever present. "They use the Underground for shelter when the Zeppelins attack," Sophie said, sensing the fear that seemed to be ground into the tiled walls. A swoosh of air and a loud rumble forewarned passengers of the approaching train. Sophie glanced at Trixie, realizing this was her first experience on public transport. She linked Trixie's arm and guided her to a seat, suddenly feeling out of place with her fashionable broad-brimmed hat. Passengers were staring at them until she spotted another well-dressed lady accompanied by a gentleman. The war had changed things; private transportation was rare. Trixie sat statue-like, staring straight ahead with her nose wrinkled in disgust. Sophie had used the tube before but agreed it was dirty and smelly that afternoon. They decided to return on the omnibus, above ground.

Relieved by fresh air and sunlight, they stood still, taking in the bustle of Oxford Street before walking towards Selfridges. People were laughing, carrying bundles of holly and mistletoe. One man passed them with a Christmas tree on his shoulder, a little boy holding his hand and skipping at his side. In a few short steps, their mood changed. The festive atmosphere brushed away the dirt and melancholy from the underground.

A crowd had gathered around Selfridge's first window and, standing on tiptoe, the girls stretched their necks to see what was going on. A man and woman worked in the window, adding the finishing touches to a magnificent display of a mannequin family around a Christmas Tree. A toy train circled the tree, the track winding through toys and Christmas presents.

The doorman doffed his cap, wishing Sophie and Trixie a good afternoon. He opened the large wood and glass doors, revealing a glittering hall of sales counters and smiling shop assistants. Perfume wafted over them from the cosmetic counters. Trixie stopped, breathing in the soft scent, while Sophie watched, knowing her reaction had more to do with expunging bad odours, than relishing the perfume.

"May I help you, mademoiselle?" Sophie shook her head and moved away.

Trixie acknowledged the sales assistant's enquiry. "I would like to purchase some perfume; a Christmas present for my mother. What can you recommend?"

Feeling awkward and somewhat out of place, Sophie stood a couple of paces back from Trixie, trying not to make eye contact. This was not the bargain basement and she didn't belong. An atomizer hissed, releasing a soft floral scent. Suddenly Sophie was a child of nine or ten, sitting on the dressing table stool next to a beautiful woman, her mother. The mirror reflected a loving smile as she squeezed the gold-fringed bulb, misting perfume on her neck and shoulders. Sophie had giggled as the tiny droplets felt cold on her skin. The memory shocked Sophie and almost brought her to tears. There was a time, when her mother was alive, that she had belonged in the same class as Trixie.

Trixie's voice broke the memory. "Sophie, this is divine! Come try it?" She frowned. "Is something wrong?"

"No, not at all. The perfume reminds me of my mother."

Trixie frowned. "I've never heard you speak of your mother."

"She died when I was twelve." Sophie took a deep breath, sensing her mother's presence. Stepping forward, she caught a glimpse of herself in the gold rimmed mirror on the counter. For a brief second, she thought her mother was staring back at her but it was her own reflection. In that moment she looked so much like her mother; the dark hair, olive skin, bright determined eyes. Her father had always told her she looked like her but that was the first day she'd seen the resemblance. It filled her with confidence.

"Sophie! Are you listening to me?"

"Oh, sorry. Please buy the perfume for your mother. She'll be delighted. I know because that was my mother's favourite perfume."

Sophie ignored Trixie's quizzical look as they waited for the sales assistant to wrap the bottle. Her mother's memory had wiped away Sophie's sense of inadequacy. She enjoyed shopping with Trixie and admiring her purchases, which were all charged to her father's account; a privilege Sophie missed. Eventually, they walked down the stairs to the bargain basement where Sophie's few spare shillings would buy her presents for Mrs. Wilderby, Trixie, Hillary and Emily.

Trixie stopped by the men's department and asked the assistant if they had any handkerchiefs with the initials C B on them. The assistant pulled a tray from the cabinet behind him, displaying a variety of fine linen handkerchiefs with every conceivable combination of initials. Trixie picked one with the initials C B embroidered in cobalt blue.

"I'll take three and could you box them, please?"

"Who are those for?" Sophie asked with a puzzled frown.

"Oh, someone I met when I was at home. A friend of my brother's."

"Did your mother finally find a beau you like? Tell me more?"

"There's nothing to tell. He's a pilot and showed no interest in me. For once, my mother was not trying to make a match. He loaned me his handkerchief and I want to return it. Now, we'd better hurry or we won't have time for tea in the Palm Court."

Sophie was pleased to be staying on the Women's Ward, working days with Hillary and Sister Kay. She'd found the night shift frightening. The Zeppelin attacks were more frequent and although the hospital had never had a direct hit, it seemed the bombs were getting closer. Mavis had disappeared two or three times a week and usually when there was an air raid, leaving Sophie to cope with the patients. Sophie had asked if she was meeting a boyfriend but Mavis told her to mind her own business. Sophie detected fear in her tone; as though she wanted to tell someone but dared not divulge her secret. When Mavis requested to stay on nights, Sophie was convinced the long tea breaks were for a beau. It made sense she'd be afraid of being caught, risking immediate dismissal.

Sophie lay in bed, worried about Trixie. She felt sorry for her. Tonight was her night off but tomorrow she would start working with Mavis. The Sister Sin incident had scared both of them. Had Mavis requested nights knowing she'd be working with Trixie?

She heard Trixie turn the doorknob and sat up in bed, waiting for it to open. "It's okay, I'm still awake. Can I talk to you about something?"

"Of course," Trixie said, throwing the covers back and sitting cross legged on her bed. "What's up? Is it that dishy Mr. Wainwright?"

"No. I told you he's engaged to some debutante. We're just

friends." It annoyed Sophie that whenever she thought about Carlos, a pain shot through her heart and she immediately changed the subject. "It's Mavis. Are you going to be okay working nights with her? I think she's up to something."

"I know you told me she goes for long tea breaks. I bet she has a boyfriend." Trixie gave a laugh. "And if I know Mavis, it's forbidden fruit; an old sugar daddy or a married man. Don't worry, I can look after myself. Now go to sleep. I'm going to write Christmas cards and try to get my body to stay awake. It is only ten days until Christmas Day. I've never worked on Christmas Day." Trixie glanced at Sophie who was already fast asleep.

Sophie woke early Christmas morning and dressed quickly, hoping to get to the dining room before Hillary. She heard Mrs. Wilderby clattering around the kitchen even as the table was set for breakfast with a tray of festive sweetmeats in the centre. Clutching three small parcels tied with a red ribbon, Sophie placed them under the tree. Mrs. Wilderby had promised the girls' a Christmas dinner and special evening. Sophie noticed there were several little parcels already under the tree. She felt a twinge of excitement.

"Good morning, Sophie, and Happy Christmas! I have a special breakfast for you. You're early. Hillary isn't down yet."

"I'm right here, Mrs. Wilderby," Hillary said from the door.

Mrs. Wilderby went back into the kitchen and returned carrying a platter of thick sliced ham in one hand and hot steaming buns in the other. "I even managed to find butter for the buns." Sophie saw the pride in her face. It was difficult getting butter and ham in wartime and she hoped the others appreciated Mrs. Wilderby's kindness.

"Thank you. This looks wonderful," Sophie said and gave Mrs. Wilderby's shoulders a squeeze.

"Stop that! You're making me blush. You know I do my best for you girls. Now don't forget dinner tonight. I arranged with Matron to have the shifts covered so both day and night shift can eat together."

Hillary and Sophie walked together, their bellies full and looking forward to Christmas dinner. The streets were quiet; there had been no bombing that night but the gaping holes and sinister shadows in the early dawn light felt ominous. Sophie shuddered, sensing the day might not be as celebrative as expected.

"Why so serious?" Hillary asked.

"I'm not sure. Something doesn't feel right."

"Working on Christmas Day doesn't feel right. But Papa always worked Christmas Day. It's the biggest day of the year, except for Easter, for the church but he always squeezed the family in between services, so as children, we never missed out."

"I know what you mean. Working at the Sackville over Christmas didn't seem like work as we celebrated with the guests and Chef always had a special dinner for the staff. But it's not that. It's more like a premonition that something bad might happen."

"You and your premonitions! One of these days you'll get out one of those Ouija boards. My grandmother had one and my father, being a clergyman, called his mother-in-law a witch. That's the only time I heard my parents argue."

"That's funny, a vicar and Ouija board. I think it's all trickery but I do get scared when I have these strange premonitions."

Hillary turned her head slightly towards Sophie, concern wrinkled the bridge of her nose. "You're serious?"

"It's probably just the excitement of Christmas."

12

Christmas Day

Sophie walked to the half empty ward, having difficulty subduing her inner feelings. Patients who were well enough were discharged to spend Christmas with their families. Despite Trixie's efforts to make the ward festive, the atmosphere felt sad. Many of the patients were holding back tears, missing their families, and some were too ill to care.

Sophie sat beside Mrs. Maggs and her baby son, Charlie, both victims of a German bomb. She held her bony hand, the veins blue against the translucent skin; the hands of an old woman, not a young mother. Fragile, undernourished, scared and alone, Mrs. Maggs' head turned, the effort almost too much as she gave an exhausted sigh. "I miss my Stanley so much. I'm afraid he'll come 'ome and I won't be there." Her eyes, rimmed red, flooded with tears again as her cheeks became mottled pink against her white skin. "Nurse, they told me he'd gone AWOL." She brushed the back of her hand across her face. "Do you know what they do to deserters? My Stan's a good man. He would never run away."

"Shush, calm yourself." Sophie wiped the tears from Mrs.

Maggs face. "The War Office tries their best but sometimes records get mixed up. When Stan makes it home, he'll know where to find you. Try not worry and get some rest. You need your strength to take care of little Charlie. And Sister has a party planned this afternoon."

"There is no 'ome, it's an 'ole in the ground."

Stuck for words, Sophie patted her hand and tried to subdue the anger she felt towards the damned war. She noted Mrs. Maggs vital signs on the chart. Her pulse was fast and her temperature slightly above normal. Nothing to be alarmed about or was it? She wondered if Private Maggs was causing her unpleasant feelings but it didn't seem that way. In fact, she had a good feeling about Stanley Maggs.

The good feeling did not last long as Emily tugged at her sleeve, whispering. "Sophie, I need to see you." Emily glanced at the bed and pulled Sophie away.

"Emily, what's wrong? I didn't think you were working this ward today."

"I'm not. I'm back on children's. I came to see you." Emily continued to drag Sophie towards the nurse's station, oblivious to her surroundings until china teacups rattled, followed by a harsh voice yelling. "'ere, watch where you're goin'."

"Oh sorry," Emily said to the tea lady, only missing a full collision with the tea-cart by inches. Emily pulled Sophie behind the screens where the Christmas treats were being stored. She felt a vice grip on her stomach. Whatever Emily was about to say had something to do with her intuition. Instinctively, she knew what it was.

The colour drained from her face and her head spun. She gripped the back of a chair. "Is there something wrong with baby Charlie?"

"Yes. His little body is shutting down. We suspect he has internal injuries. The doctor doesn't expect him to survive."

"Oh no! Mrs. Maggs is already distraught, worried about her husband. What can I do?"

"First, don't give up. I have seen babies come back from death's door with nothing more than love and encouragement. Charlie needs to be with his mother. Normally, the mother comes to the Children's Ward, but Mrs. Maggs is not well enough. I want to bring Charlie to the ward."

"But, Emily, what if he dies in her arms?"

"What better place for a baby to be? The problem is convincing the doctors that this is good for both of them. Can you explain to Mrs. Maggs that the baby needs nurturing without telling her why? I'll do the rest."

"I don't understand why the baby can't be with his mother."

"There are many reasons—allowing the mother to rest, the risk of infection and nursing a child is different to nursing an adult."

Sophie told Hillary what was happening just as Sister Kay came into the ward. A huddle of idle nurses was cause for reprimand and usually sent the nurses scurrying. A kind, understanding person, Sister quickly realized something was going on.

She pointed to Sophie and Hillary. "Why are you not with patients and, Nurse Finnegan, what are you doing here?"

Emily explained the situation and the little group waited, hardly daring to breathe until affection and understanding spread from Sister's eyes.

"We do not require the doctor's permission for baby Charlie to come for a Christmas visit with his mother. Now back to work. Nurse West, you will accompany me on rounds this morning. Nurse Romano, go and sit with Mrs. Maggs and prepare her for the visit with her son."

"What do I say to her?"

"You will know. Start by telling her the good news."

Good news, Sophie thought, *how can telling a mother her baby is dying be good news?* She opened her mouth to ask, but Sister was already halfway down the ward with Hillary running at her heels. In contrast, Sophie felt her legs grow heavy and slow as she walked towards Mrs. Maggs' bed.

"How are you feeling?" Sophie asked, still trying to find the right words in her head. "I see you haven't drunk your tea." Sophie slipped her arm around the woman's spindly frame and lifted her up, plumping the pillows at her back. "Here, drink your tea while it's hot."

"Me mam always said there's nothing like a 'ot cup of tea."

Sophie's mind jumped to family. She would need the family's support. "Has your mother been to visit?" As soon as the words were out of her mouth Sophie knew that was the wrong question.

"She worked at the munitions factory at Silvertown. She were killed just before Charlie were born. Me dad never got over it. All I have is Stan and Charlie. Stan has a sister, but she moved out of London. I don't know where she lives." The anguish in her voice and the worry on her young face ripped at Sophie's heart. Tears filled her eyes and Sophie was close to breaking down when Sister's voice flipped her back to her duties.

"Nurse Romano!" Sister's eyes pierced into Sophie, not in reprimand but empathy. Sophie nodded, acknowledging the reminder to return to work.

She took the empty tea cup from Mrs. Maggs. "I have a lovely surprise for you. Nurse Finnegan is bringing Charlie down for a visit."

"Oh, thank you!" Mrs. Maggs face glowed, her eyes bright with anticipation. "Does that mean he's getting better? When… when can I see him?"

"Very soon." Sophie took her hand. "Mrs. Maggs, Millie, I need to explain. Charlie is very poorly, but we think being with you will help him feel better…" Sophie hesitated. Should she say more? A firm but comforting hand tapped her shoulder. Sister had read her mind and the nod told her, enough said. She had done a good job.

Sister bent forward. "I hear Nurse Finnegan is bringing your son to visit. And here she is. Happy Christmas, my dear!" Sister and Hillary moved on to the next bed.

Emily walked down the ward with a bundle in her arms. Sophie was surprised at how small the bundle appeared; the child was ten months old. Even taking into account Mrs. Maggs' slim build and assuming the father was also thin, Charlie was tiny for his age. It wasn't hard to see that both were undernourished. Poverty and war were hard on families.

Mrs. Maggs sat up with her hands outstretched. As Emily placed the baby in her arms, the tears flowed once more. Charlie opened his eyes, looked at his mother and smiled. Everyone was sure he'd said 'Mama.'

Sophie took an extra blanket and laid it over mother and son. "I'll leave you to enjoy your son. Call if you need me."

"Nurse, is Charlie all right? He's so limp in my arms." Sophie's heart missed a beat as she pulled the covers back, relieved to see his arm reaching for his mother. Another smile broke on his little face.

"He's fine but weak. Talk to him. Tell him how much you love him and cuddle him. He needs to feel you."

Mrs. Maggs began to hum and then sang to Charlie. "Rock-a-bye baby on the tree top. When the wind blows the cradle will rock…" Charlie never took his eyes off his mother. Mrs. Maggs' angelic voice brought the ward to a stand-still. Sophie could hardly breathe.

An hour later, Emily returned for Baby Charlie. Anticipating Mrs. Maggs' reluctance to give up her son, Sophie sat with her and explained that Charlie needed the warm incubator on the Children's Ward.

Emily gathered baby Charlie in her arms and looked up at Sophie, smiling, "He has pink cheeks. He's had no colour for days so this is a big improvement."

As if to reply Charlie said, "Mama."

"Did you hear that, Nurse? Charlie said Mama."

"I did. I think Charlie is feeling much better. I will try to bring him down again this afternoon."

"Take good care of 'im, please!" Mrs. Maggs leaned back on her pillow, her face pasty white but her cheeks bright pink.

Placing the back of her hand on Mrs. Maggs forehead, Sophie frowned, not sure if the warmth was from a fever or just flushed from the excitement. She beckoned to Hillary. "She might have a fever."

Hillary took her temperature and noted on the chart it was up slightly from the morning. Sophie pulled the screens around her bed and lifted the covers. Mrs. Maggs had several abrasions on her lower legs. Hillary cleaned them and left them open to heal. She carefully removed the dressing on the large wound on her thigh where a piece of embedded glass had been surgically removed. Mrs. Maggs winced as Hillary dabbed the sutured area with antiseptic. She placed sterile gauze over it. "Sophie," she whispered. "I need the doctor to see this wound. I think an infection is starting. Can you tell Sister while I finish the dressing?"

Sister agreed Mrs. Maggs needed the doctor's opinion and sent a young probationary to find whoever was on duty. Her tasks completed, Sophie disappeared behind the screened area and made up plates of biscuits, Christmas cake and mince pies for the afternoon party. Matron had enlisted a doctor to dress up as Father Christmas. He'd spent the morning on the children's ward and was to visit the other wards that afternoon during visiting hours. Sophie hoped Mrs. Maggs was well enough to have Charlie visit as she had no other relatives.

A sudden shiver of pleasure rippled along Sophie's spine as a familiar voice spoke to Sister. "You have a patient in distress, Sister?"

"A possible infection, Mr. Wainwright." Sister paused and Sophie could no longer hear as they walked down the ward. Torn between revealing herself and slipping off the ward for her lunch break, Sophie realized her behaviour was childish. Taking a deep breath, she marched with a little too much determination towards the screens and Mrs. Maggs.

Sister saw her and called out. "Nurse Romano, you were with Mrs. Maggs this morning. How was she?"

Avoiding eye contact with Carlos, Sophie replied. "Mrs. Maggs was upset and anxious this morning. Her husband is missing but the visit from baby Charlie seemed to cheer her up."

Carlos directed his reply to Sister. "The small abrasions are healing well but this injury is serious. I don't like the redness around the sutures. Keep an eye on her but I think she's suffering more from nerves, worried about her husband and the baby. Keep the wound clean and dry and let me know if her temperature goes higher. I'll ask Dr. Morgan to check when he returns later today."

Although it was a relief to hear that Mrs. Maggs didn't have an infection, something niggled at Sophie about the injury. Heading to the nurses' common room for her lunch break, she felt a tap on her shoulder. Surprised, she almost tripped over her own feet. "Sorry I didn't mean to startle you," Carlos said. "I wanted to wish you a Happy Christmas."

Composing herself, Sophie replied. "Thank you, Mr. Wainwright. A Happy Christmas to you as well."

Carlos paused and frowned. "Why so formal?"

"Hospital policy and I'm not sure your fiancée would approve."

"I told Rosamond about us and the hospital has nothing against friends."

Sophie was not expecting such a smooth answer and she tried to suppress the anger she felt, on top of whatever other emotions churned at her insides. *He told his fiancée about us.* What exactly did that mean? Did he tell her about Italy and how he had once proposed?

"I have to go," Sophie said, dashing into the common room and closing the door. Glancing around the room, she was pleased to find herself alone.

13

Poverty and Privilege

The Christmas spirit and happy greetings turned up the volume of the usual low whispered conversations on the ward. Children were loudly happy to see parents or grandparents. Exchanging little parcels wrapped with ribbons promoted animated 'thank you's.' The local church choir sang carols and Santa ho-ho-hoed his way down the ward. Sister Kay poured tea while Sophie and Hillary handed out Christmas cake and mince pies.

Emily had returned with Charlie in time for visiting hours. Mrs. Maggs sat up, cooing to baby Charlie. His feet kicked under the blankets as he responded to his mother's voice. Sophie watched and smiled. *He's going to be all right*, she thought. Sensing someone staring at her, she turned to see a thin young man in uniform standing in the doorway. She didn't need an introduction—Private Stanley Maggs had found his way to the hospital. Sophie nodded to him and, standing by the bed, pointed towards the door. "Mrs. Maggs, look who's here."

Stan's army boots seemed larger than Stan as he marched

across the ward. "Oh Millie, I found you and Charlie." Sophie slid away, giving the tearful reunion privacy.

Sister lifted her watch and at precisely 4 p.m. rang the bell. Visiting hours were over. Her concern now was to settle the patients. Although the celebration lifted moods, it had exhausted some and distressed others.

Sophie caught Emily as she came to fetch Charlie. "Private Maggs arrived this afternoon. Can you leave them a little longer?"

"That is great news. Sorry, I can't leave Charlie any longer. He has to have his medicine but Private Maggs can come to the Children's Ward. He's still listed as critical, which means parents can visit anytime."

"Is he still in danger? He looks so much better," Sophie asked, alarm raising the tone in her voice. Emily's words surprised her. Had she seen what she wanted to see?

"He seems a little brighter. Being with his mother is making a difference but he's still a very sick baby."

Baby Charlie went back to his cot and Private Maggs left with the other visitors. Eager to hear how Stan managed to get leave and find his wife, Sophie went to Mrs. Maggs first. But she found her eyes already closed. Exhausted, she slept.

Sophie and Hillary did their rounds of taking temperatures, pulses and settling the patients to rest before teatime. The ward seemed quiet after the bustle of the afternoon. They finished the charts and started getting ready for their own party back at River House.

Two tired nurses plodded their way home, both wondering if they had the energy to celebrate and do justice to Mrs. Wilderby's Christmas dinner. They need not have worried. As Hillary opened the front door, a burst of energy greeted them. Laughing friends, the smell of plum pudding and the twinkling lights on the tree quickly filled them with Christmas cheer.

"Hurry, we're waiting to open our presents," Trixie yelled. All twelve residents and Mrs. Wilderby sat round the tree while Trixie passed out gifts to everyone. It amazed Sophie at the thoughtfulness in the parcels. Hand knitted gloves from Mrs. Wilderby, an embroidered handkerchief from Hillary and several Jane Austen and Brontë sister books, which the girls would share. The biggest surprise for Sophie was a bottle of perfume from Trixie with a gold bulb on the atomizer. She gave a squirt, the scent taking her back to happy childhood days and forcing a tear to trickle down her cheek. She hugged Trixie. "Thank you for the memory."

The party had gone on long after bedtime so when the alarm woke Sophie at 5 a.m. she wanted to roll over and go back to sleep. She almost envied Trixie on nights. She could come home and sleep. But duty called. Still full from dinner the night before, Sophie passed on a cooked breakfast and headed to work.

Trixie greeted her on the ward. "Mavis is missing again. She left for a tea break and didn't come back. Sister McPherson usually doesn't notice but I think she did last night. It was a quiet night and with no air raids to confuse people, Sister asked where she had gone and why the charts were incomplete."

"She did that all the time to me but it was usually during an air raid so no one noticed. But she always returned to the ward at the end of the shift. Do you think she's okay?"

"Don't worry about Mavis. I thought I'd warn you in case Sister asked questions. Oh, and Mrs. Maggs has had a bad night. Her temperature is up again. It's in the chart. I'm off to bed," a yawning Trixie added.

"Good morning, ladies!" Sophie froze as the back of her neck tingled.

Trixie gave Sophie a sideways grin and the hint of a frown to Carlos. "Good morning, Mr. Wainwright. Do you have patients to see today? I'm off duty but Nurse Romano can help you." The grin lifted her cheeks in amusement as her head gave Sophie a subtle nod of approval.

Sophie's cheeks flushed, her voice suddenly a squeak. "Mr. Wainwright."

Carlos shuffled his feet, giving Trixie an exaggerated wave. Clearing his throat, he began. "I wondered how Mrs. Maggs was doing. I discovered Dr. Morgan won't return until tomorrow."

"Oh, of course. Well, Trixie... um... Nurse King, mentioned she had a bad night and her temperature was up. I only just came on duty." Now composed, Sophie led the way to Mrs. Maggs.

Carlos studied the chart but Sophie didn't need to. Mrs. Maggs' face was flushed, beads of sweat on her forehead. "She's burning up!" She beckoned to an orderly. "Bring the screens, find Nurse West and bring me a bowl of cold water and a cloth." Carlos wheeled the screens around the bed and lifted the sheets. Yellow puss had soaked the dressing and Mrs. Maggs groaned as Carlos removed the gauze. Sophie placed the cold cloth on her forehead and held her wrist. "Her pulse is fast." Shaking the thermometer, she added, "103.2"

"What happened? The dressing hasn't been changed in hours." Carlos glanced at Hillary as she gently bathed the red angry, festering wound. Sophie knew exactly what had happened. Mavis, the duty nurse, had not changed the dressings during the night. She glanced at the chart. Carlos's instructions were clear. The wound needed cleaning with antiseptic every four hours. Trixie had noted the vital signs during the night but 5 p.m. December 25th was the last entry for a dressing change signed by Hillary—more than twelve hours ago.

Carlos ordered the wound cleaned every hour. Mrs. Maggs moaned in pain and he prescribed morphine. Sophie stayed with her, cooling her with the cold wet cloth and feeling hopeless. There was nothing more to be done except wait for the fever to break.

Mrs. Maggs became restless, the fever and morphine causing her to dream and hallucinate. "My baby. Charlie. Where is he, I can't find him."

"Shush, Millie, shush. Charlie is on the Children's Ward. Nurse Finnegan is taking care of him." The words calmed her for a while until she suddenly sat up in bed. "Stan. They're going to shoot Stan!" Sophie gently pressed her shoulders to lie back.

"Stan is fine. He came to visit yesterday, remember? I'll see if I can find him to come and sit with you." Before she had finished the sentence, Mrs. Maggs' eyes closed and she fell into a fitful sleep. Sophie slipped Mrs. Maggs' clammy arm under the covers and continued cooling her brow.

"How is she?" Hillary asked.

"She's resting but I'm worried." Fear gripped her insides. Mrs. Maggs was critical. "We need to find her husband."

"I suggested that to Sister. She said that now the wound is clean, the fever will come down."

"Hillary, we both know that won't happen. Where is Sister Kay?"

"She's off today. Sister McPherson is covering today. She could be right and the doctor isn't overly concerned. You're tired and overreacting."

"Perhaps."

"Sister wants you on rounds."

Sophie followed Sister as they went from bed to bed, talking to patients and checking charts. Returning to the nurses' station, Sister said, "Sometimes we are in danger of getting too close to patients."

"Yes, Sister."

"One reason you will make an excellent nurse, Nurse Romano, is your natural ability to empathize and care for people. But when that empathy becomes sympathy and personal, nurses fall into an emotional trap."

"Yes, Sister." She was already aware of falling into that trap.

"If you allow your emotions to take over, it will affect your judgment. You will make mistakes, ones that will cause harmful distress to both you and the patient. It is essential that a good nurse be able to remain empathetic and caring while keeping their distance. Do you understand, Nurse Romano?"

Was Sister threatening her? Sophie gulped in air as she replied. "Yes, Sister."

"In my experience, the best nurses are those that struggle with this concept. So consider my words carefully, Nurse Romano. Now, back to your duties."

The scent of flowers caught Sophie's attention as the visitors entered the ward. Where would anyone get roses in the middle of winter in London? she thought, as a posh-looking gentleman in a wool overcoat entered. Holding roses in one hand and his trilby in the other, he walked down the ward. His gait was awkward, showing his discomfort as he made his way to a young woman, sheltered by screens. Mrs. Montague had been admitted overnight for surgery on a badly broken arm after falling off a horse during a Christmas Day gallop in Hyde Park. Normally she would be in a private hospital but enemy bombs didn't discriminate between private or public hospitals. A bomb dropped close enough the Rosewood Private Clinic to close it temporarily. Of course Mr. Montague would find flowers in London. His kind did.

Her stare moved from the privileged to Mrs. Maggs, pale and undernourished. Life seemed unfair to some people but she was pleased to see Mrs. Maggs sitting up and waiting for Stan. Perhaps Hillary was right and she was overreacting. So why couldn't she shake off the feeling that a tragedy was about to happen?

Stan arrived with baby Charlie in his arms. Holding his son came naturally to him, not like a lot of men who had difficulty bonding with fragile babies. Mrs. Maggs reached out and Stan placed Charlie in her arms. Sophie couldn't help herself and went up to greet them.

"Charlie is getting better. Nurse Finnegan said he's out of danger," Stan said, holding Millie's arm that cradled the child. "Millie's not so good, Nurse. She's real 'ot."

"Stop ya worrying, Stan. I'll be better soon." Millie leaned back, her skin still shiny from the fever. A strange expression made her face taut. Did Millie have doubts about her recovery? Sophie checked the chart. Her temperature was down to 102; still high but not critical.

"Millie has a bit of infection in her wound. The doctor is treating it." Sophie couldn't bring herself to say she will get better. "I'll leave you to enjoy your visit."

Mr. Montague stood at the nurses' station, complaining to Hillary about his wife being in a public ward and demanding that a nurse spend more time with her. Sophie's anger rose like bile in her throat. Her heart remained with the Maggs family who had nothing and never complained. She was appalled by the privileged man whining about his wife with a broken arm. Why wasn't he serving his country? He was young, in his early thirties. He should be an officer in uniform but he was obviously a civilian.

Sister McPherson appeared just in time as Sophie pushed back her shoulders and stepped determinedly towards the man with a speech prepared in her head.

"Mr. Montague," Sister said. "I'm sorry we don't have more privacy for you wife. My staff have many patients to take care…" Sister didn't finish her sentence before the interruption.

"It is not my concern whether you are understaffed. I want a nurse assigned to my wife immediately."

"I'm afraid that is not possible."

"I will not tolerate such disrespect. Do you know who I am?" Mr. Montague turned and pointed to Sophie. "Go and tend to my wife."

Sophie glared at the man and bit her tongue, waiting for Sister's response.

"Mr. Montague, I do know who you are; a husband worried about his wife, like most of the men on this ward. If you haven't noticed, there is a war going on, Mr. Montague." Sister's tone unmistakably emphasized his lack of anything military. "My nurses take care of all the patients, including your wife. Have you considered hiring a private nurse?"

Mr. Montague tensed, anger creeping up from under his coat. The red flush contrasted against his white silk scarf. His cultured upbringing only just stopped him from losing his temper. Or was it Sister's imposing stance of don't-mess-with-me that kept him silent?

"A private nurse is acceptable. Make the arrangements."

Sophie held her breath, waiting for Sister's retort but none came. "Very well, I will inform Matron and arrangements will be made immediately. Good day, sir!" Sophie smiled at Sister's firm dismissal of the obnoxious man. He nodded, escaping to his wife's bedside.

"Get back to work. I will be in Matron's office." Sister's pent up anger released in loud rhythmic steps as she marched down the corridor.

Hillary rang the bell at 4 p.m. as Sister had not returned. Stan carried Charlie back to the children's ward and the visitors departed except for Mr. Montague who ignored the bell. Sophie leaned around the screen, expecting to see a loving couple but almost fell backwards. A wall of tension and angry words greeted her. She could barely believe her own ears "Don't say a word? You hear me? You fell…"

"Mr. Montague visiting hours are over."

"I'm leaving." He bent towards his wife and kissed her cheek. She pulled back into her pillow, attempting to avoid his touch. "No need to be afraid, my dear. I have ordered a private nurse and we'll soon have you home."

"Good day!" Mr. Montague gave a nod and left.

"I'm afraid your private nurse is not here yet. I need to take your pulse and temperature." Sophie touched her good arm. "Is everything alright?"

Dabbing her cheeks with a lace hanky, Mrs. Montague gave

a sniff. She tried to smile but the corners of her mouth fell in misery. "He means well." She paused, fighting back sobs. "My arm is painful."

Sophie didn't need to be a detective to know her tears had little to do with physical pain. "Your pulse is a little fast but your temperature is normal. I see in the chart that the doctor has ordered morphine for the pain. He'll be in to see you soon. Now get some rest."

"Nurse, has my husband left the hospital?"

"Yes, visiting hours are over. Sister is strict and nobody argues with Sister, not even your husband. Now rest."

14

Nothing's Fair

A loud thud woke Sophie as River House shook to its foundations. The warning rockets blasted from the fire station. A bit late, Sophie thought, wondering why there had been no earlier air raid warning. She joined the rest of the house running to the cellar. Mrs. Wilderby passed out blankets and produced a kettle for tea. They felt two more tremors but both seemed far away and then there was quiet. The all clear bugle sounded and everyone returned to their beds. It didn't seem like a Zeppelin attack. Something was different. Perhaps it wasn't a raid.

Mrs. Wilderby yawned as she placed a large pot of tea on the breakfast table. Hillary and Sophie ate in silence but a low hum came from the kitchen wireless.

"BBC News announced that last nights' bombs dropped from German aeroplanes, not Zeppelins. The searchlights didn't catch them until it was too late."

"Are there any casualties?" Hillary asked.

"They didn't say. The bombs dropped near Heath Common, so perhaps not."

"We'd better leave early, just in case," Sophie said to Hillary as she finished her breakfast, gulping the last of her tea.

Deciding that the unexpected bombs were the reason she sensed tragedy, it surprised Sophie to see only one ambulance outside the Casualty Department. The hospital looked quiet. It turned out the bombs had landed on Heath Common, a large unpopulated park area so not the reason for Sophie's intuition.

"You're early. I haven't finished the charts," Trixie said, taking a seat at the nurse's station.

Hillary sat next to her. "Where's Mavis?"

"Who knows!"

"I'll give you a hand with those charts."

Trixie rolled her eyes towards Sophie as Mavis appeared from who-knows-where.

Wandering down the ward with Sophie, Trixie whispered. "She disappeared as soon as the warning went off. I didn't have time to get the patients out of the ward before the all clear. Mavis didn't come back."

"I thought they had discovered her."

"I guess not. Or she covered it up. I'm tempted to report her and I'm worried about the patients."

"Nurse!"

"Mrs. Maggs, what can I do for you?" Sophie's heart jumped into her mouth. Mrs. Maggs sat bolt upright, her hands groping in front of her and her eyes staring at something that didn't exist. In the half-light, her translucent skin looked ghostly. "How long has she been like this?" Sophie asked, placing her hand on the woman's chest and gently laying her against the pillows.

"She's had a bad night. Her fever is up again," Trixie said.

"Take her temperature while I pull the screens around her bed."

"104.8. I'll get some cold water and sponge her down." Sophie swallowed hard. Mrs. Maggs' eyes, opened wide, full of fear, seeing things that weren't there. Mrs. Maggs would not last out the day.

"Trixie, we need to find Private Maggs. He's staying at the Seaman's Mission. Can you stop at the mission on your way home?"

"He'll be in for visiting hours this afternoon."

"That will be too late."

"How do you know that? This patient is tough. She'll pull through."

"I don't think so. Please, will you do that?"

Trixie nodded. "Of course." She spoke with Hillary as she left the ward.

Hillary dressed the wound and noted the infection had spread from her thigh to her lower leg. Dr. Morgan arrived early for rounds and took his time examining Mrs. Maggs.

"Sister," Dr. Morgan said, making his notes in the chart. "Continue nursing the fever. The infection has spread to blood poisoning. There is little more we can do. I think it advisable to contact her next of kin."

"Stay with her, Nurse Romano."

Sophie continued to bathe Millie with cool water and talk to her. "Come on, Millie, fight. Fight for your little boy."

Stan pushed by Sophie as the screens scraped the floor, wrapping them in a cocoon of peaceful seclusion.

"I'm here, Millie. It's me, Stan." He clasped her hand and raised it to his lips.

Millie opened her eyes, smiling. "Stan, you're home. Where's Charlie?"

"He's with the nurses. I came to see you first, Millie. The doctor's real worried about you. Please, Millie, you gotta get better."

"I'm tired, Stan. Where's Charlie?"

Stan looked up at Sophie. "Can I go and get him?"

"You stay with Millie. I'll get Charlie."

"She will be all right, won't she?"

"She's very, very ill." Sophie couldn't say more. Was she hoping for a miracle? "I'll fetch the baby."

Charlie cooed and kicked in her arms as she carried him to the ward. It was wonderful to see him pink and responsive. Sophie handed him to Stan.

"Millie, do you want to hold him?"

She shook her head, whispering. "I'm not strong enough." She lifted her arm to stroke his head. "He looks better."

Charlie stopped kicking, smiled and once again said, "Mama." There was no mistaking the word.

"Love him and take good care of him, Stan. Find him a new mama. I'm sorry, Stan." Millie's eyes closed as if to sleep but Sophie knew she would never wake up.

"Millie. No, Millie, wake up!"

"Stan, I'm sorry. She's gone." Sophie gently touched his arm. She watched silent tears pour down his tortured face. He cradled Charlie, quiet and still in his arms. Father and son, their eyes locking in a bond that would never be broken. A stray tear trickled from the corner of Sophie's eye and her throat was tight from holding back her own grief, angry at a God who could allow this to happen.

"Sophie," Emily said, peering round the screen. "Sister sent me to bring Charlie back to the ward."

"Not now, Emily," Sophie shook her head towards Mrs.

Maggs' body.

"Oh no!" She hesitated. "I'm sorry, but I need to talk to you."

Emily stepped back from the screen, letting Sophie come out. "The doctor is furious. He's afraid Mrs. Maggs will pass the infection to Charlie. I have to take him back."

"It's all right," Stan said, carrying Charlie. "I can't do anything more for my Millie but I can be with my son. I'll take 'im back to the ward."

Sister Kay took Sophie's arm and sat her down at the nurses' station. "Let this be a warning. Getting too close to patients has consequences. It gets difficult when it's a young mother with a baby. You need to be strong or you will never be a nurse."

The words sailed by Sophie. She hurt too much to heed Sister's advice.

"What will happen to them now, Sister? They have nowhere to live. Private Maggs is staying at the Seamen's Mission."

"We will find a relative. Private Maggs will get some extra leave and then he'll go back to the front. We live in terrible times, Nurse Romano. Take a break and compose yourself but be back in half-an-hour. We have patients to care for."

Sipping hot tea in the nurses' common room, Sophie wept for the loss of Mrs. Maggs, for Charlie without a mother and Stan's uncertain future fighting a war. She questioned her choice of profession. She wanted to heal people, not mourn their deaths. Was Sister right? If she couldn't keep her distance, would every patient who died be a personal loss? No stranger to loss, Sophie remembered the grief she'd felt when her mother died. Her father's death had crushed her. She was beginning to fear that loving someone meant they might die. Sister was right. She had crossed the line and allowed herself to love the Maggs family. Could she heed Sister's advice, find a balance between caring and loving? "I want to be a good nurse," she said aloud. "I'll just have to learn to balance on the caring side of the line."

Wiping away her tears, she headed back to the ward. She nodded at Sister who gave her a knowing smile. "You will make an admirable nurse. Now, tend to Mrs. Montague. She is going for surgery this morning and the private nurse never arrived."

It would be easy to be distant with Mrs. Montague, a spoiled and privileged young woman with nothing more than a broken arm; albeit a bad break needing surgery. "Good morning! Are you ready for your operation? The doctor will fix that arm as good as new."

"I'm rather nervous, Nurse. I've never had an operation."

"You won't feel a thing. Maybe you'll think twice about riding in Hyde Park, though. What exactly happened?"

Mrs. Montague looked puzzled. "Hyde Park? I don't understand."

"Your husband said you fell from your horse in Hyde Park."

"Oh yes, of course! Silly of me. I wasn't paying attention. I can be clumsy."

Odd, Sophie thought. How can one be clumsy riding a horse? Never having ridden a horse, she ignored the comment and wished Mrs. Montague well before moving to the next patient and bumping into Carlos. She avoided his stare. Her emotions already on the brink of exploding and she didn't need Carlos stirring things. Determined that he would not break her heart again, she hurried across the ward.

As her shift ended, Hillary said she had to see Matron and would be late for dinner. Sophie was thankful to be walking to River House alone. It had been the longest day she could remember. Her efforts of being matter-of-fact about Mrs. Maggs' death when her heart was breaking had drained her of energy.

Usually ravenous after a long shift, Sophie played with her food and said little. Trixie made up for Sophie's silence. Normally bouncy and talkative, that night she was almost hysterical. Sophie tried to ignore her until she snapped, unable to cope with the excitement. Whatever it was, she ordered Trixie to calm down. Mrs. Wilderby frowned as Sophie excused herself from the table and went to her room.

Slamming the door, she threw herself on the bed, so tied up in knots she wanted to scream. Anger exploded as she punched her fist into her pillow and wept in sorrow. The band of despair gripped so tight it made her head pound and her body hurt. A wave of nausea swept over her and she retched into the wash basin but nothing came. Flinging herself onto the bed again, she willed her feelings to go away. She yearned to see her mother's smile. Although she hardly remembered her face, she tried to recall the feelings, her mother's arm around her or her father's hand on her shoulders. She had always trusted them to make her feel better but they had left her so many years ago. Desperate for love, and to be loved, she had put her trust in Carlos and Bill—both gone out of her life. Carlos' brief return only complicated things. I can't cope, she thought as she drifted into a fitful nightmare.

A gentle knock woke her. Mrs. Wilderby peered around the door. "May I come in? I've brought some tea."

Sophie sat up, rubbing her eyes. "I must have dozed off."

"Is something troubling you? Would a chat help?"

"That is kind of you. Does it show? I had a bad day. A patient died and Sister told me I was getting too close to patients. Now I am so confused."

"Tell me all about it. I'm a good listener and maybe I can help."

Mrs. Wilderby's kindness unleashed something in Sophie and her life story tumbled out of her, bringing torrents of tears and uncontrollable sobbing. Mrs. Wilderby held her close, all caution gone. The hurt from her parents' death, the hurt from Carlos and his mother, and Bill; even Anna's friendship. She realized how much she missed her friend. And, finally, the loss of Mrs. Maggs.

The warmth and understanding felt like being in her mother's arms. It had been a long time since Sophie had felt so safe.

The Nurse's Common Room had few comforts, only a table, a dozen straight-backed chairs, a kettle, tea pot and a tin of biscuits. But it served as respite for tired nurses. The most comfort came from laughter and friendly chatter. That afternoon Sophie sat alone, her feet up on a spare chair and a cup of tea steaming in her hand while she waited for Emily.

"Sorry I'm late. Trouble in the ward," Emily said, pouring herself a cup of tea. "Private Maggs has not let Charlie out of his sight since his wife died. Matron sent him home last night but he was back at six this morning."

"Poor man." Sophie shook her head, feeling her eyes burn. "He's so young to lose his wife. What will happen to Charlie? They have no home and Private Maggs will have to go back to war."

"The authorities will put Charlie into an orphanage unless

a relative is found." Emily sighed, shaking her head. "It's a shame because he's a good and loving father, which is more than I can say for most of the men who visit their children." Emily laughed. "It is funny to see them trying to hold babies. But not Private Maggs. There is a beautiful bond between him and his son."

"Mrs. Maggs told me that Stan had a sister who moved away from London. Why don't you ask if Charlie can stay with them until the war is over?"

"Good idea. I'll speak to him and find out where she lives. There's something else, though. I haven't said anything to Sister because it might be just grief."

"Emily, what is it?"

"I think he's suffering from war nerves. He holds..." Emily paused. "No, he clings to the baby and stares into nothing, his eyes quite vacant. I don't think it's grief alone. Sophie, would you talk to him? You know what to say to soldier patients."

"I saw signs when he was visiting Millie. I'll come by after my shift tonight." Checking her watch for the time she continued. "I had better get back to the ward. See you later."

The visit to the Children's Ward to see Private Maggs had not been as successful as she'd hoped. Deep in grief and unable to face his demons, Private Maggs wouldn't talk. But he agreed to meet Sophie at the café the next day on her day off.

15

Trixie in Love

B eing preoccupied with her own troubles, Sophie had paid little attention to Trixie, except to react with annoyance when her vibrant mannerisms and constant chatter clashed with Sophie's pensive, reflective mood. Turning the knob of the front door to River House, she tried to smile. Mrs. Wilderby greeted her with a reprimand for being late for dinner and she didn't have the energy to tell her why. The laughter from the table made her want to scream. With no appetite for food or company, she made her apologies and escaped to her room. A few minutes later, Mrs. Wilderby knocked on the door. "Can I come in?"

Sophie didn't answer.

"Has something happened? Is that why you were late for dinner?"

"I'm just in a melancholy mood and Trixie's flamboyance rubs me the wrong way. What has gotten into her?"

Mrs. Wilderby smiled. "I think she's in love."

"In love! With whom?"

"She met him on her visit home. Christopher Belingham.

He's a pilot."

CB. Now I understand, Sophie thought, remembering Self-ridges. "I'm behaving badly. If you can find an extra plate, I'll come down to eat. Thanks Mrs. Wilderby, I feel much better."

"Your plate is keeping warm. Come when you're ready."

Trixie had indeed fallen for Lieutenant Christopher Belingham, a pilot and youngest son of an earl. Trixie described him as tall, handsome, clever and attentive—without being smothering. And, most important, he supported her choice of becoming a nurse. Her mother was content with bringing an earl's son into the family. Although being the youngest meant there would be no title, Lady King was happy to have found an acceptable match for her daughter. Chris, as Trixie called him, had flirted with her on her last visit home. He had not contacted her until a few days before but since his arrival in London, he had courted her in earnest. Working day and night shifts, the roommates saw little of each other. Sophie's pre-occupation with the Maggs family had clouded her awareness of almost everything around her, including Trixie's news.

Forcing herself to join in idle conversation about beaus and courting, Sophie ate some dinner and envied Trixie's happiness, although it all seemed to have happened too fast. But what did she know about love? *I haven't been exactly successful in the romance department.* Hillary sat across the table and caught her eye. Sophie gave her a quizzical look and then realized she wanted to talk. She suddenly remembered her friend's appointment with Matron. Something else I've forgotten.

Hillary got up from the table, wished everyone a good night and Sophie followed her out. "What's wrong?" Hillary asked. "I've never seen you like this. Old losses catching up with you?"

"How did you guess?"

"I saw it coming when you got so close to Mrs. Maggs. It's hard but you must learn to distance yourself from patients."

"You're right. Sister and Mrs. Wilderby said the same."

"Ah! Mother Wilderby gave you the talk. Everyone gets a Mother Wilderby talk at some time. She's a wonderful lady."

"I felt as though I was talking to my mother. Her words were so comforting and I feel so much better. I'm sorry I have been self-indulgent. I never asked you why Matron wanted to see you? Was it about medical school?"

"The directors have asked Matron for a recommendation, which means they have accepted my application for consideration. Matron said it looks promising but warned me not get too excited until they invite me for an interview." Hillary's whole face lit up in a smile. "Sophie, this could actually happen."

"Have you written to your father?"

"No. I don't want to get his hopes up. I'll tell him if I get the interview."

"This is wonderful news."

Sophie woke late the next morning. Trixie had returned and was already asleep. Questions about Lieutenant Belingham would have to wait that evening. Appreciating the extra sleep, she felt more like her old self as she walked to the café to meet Private Maggs. She wondered if she was crossing the line or just trying to help.

Private Maggs, cap in hand, was waiting in front of the cafe when Sophie arrived. She ordered a pot of tea and two scones.

Private Maggs stared into his tea. "Doctor says Charlie can

go home in a few days."

Sophie watched as he tried to lift his teacup, the tea spilling to the saucer from his shaking hand. "Stan... May I call you Stan?" He nodded. "It's good news about Charlie." Sophie coughed, covering up a gasp at the despair and fear coming from Stan.

"I dunno what to do. Me 'ouse is gone. I'm staying at the mission and I can't take Charlie there. What 'appens when..." He stared into nothing as tears spilled onto his face. "I have to go back..." Sophie placed her hand on his and remained silent until he moved his gaze towards her. "Stan, you have seen some terrible things and losing Millie has made everything worse. I'll try to get you some help."

"I don't want to give Charlie away. The doctor said they'd put 'im in an orphanage but I can't let that 'appen." He wiped his face with his sleeve. "I were raised in one of them places and it's 'orrible. I ran away. My Millie would never forgive me."

"Stan, that won't happen if we can find a relative to take care of Charlie. Millie mentioned you had a sister up north. Can she help?"

"I don't know where to find her. She were older than me and after our mam died, she took care of me until some woman took me to the orphanage. She wrote me letters until she got married and then the letters stopped. But I remember her saying she was moving to a place called Primrose Valley." A smile broke across his face, the first time she had seen it. "I remember the name because me sister's name is Primrose too. But we just called her Rose. I didn't get any more letters and then I ran away. That were years ago."

"Stan, let's see if we can find your sister. Do you know her married name?"

He shook his head. "I need to be with Charlie. I have to go, Nurse. Thanks for the tea."

Surprised at his abrupt departure, Sophie sat nibbling on her scone, not quite sure if he wanted help or not. Finding Rose might not be difficult as Primrose Valley sounded like a small place. At the very least, it would stall the authorities' plan to send Charlie to the orphanage. But Stan was a problem. His anxiety and fear, together with his abrupt departure, indicated war nerves. He needed treatment but was it bad enough to be recognized by the authorities? She didn't think so. They would, no doubt, send him back to France.

She picked up her satchel and headed to the library. She had neglected her studies and was keen to resume learning. It occurred to her that the librarian might know how to locate someone.

The library door creaked as she pushed it open and took in the delicious library smell and silence that wiped away all her troubles. Sophie set her satchel on the table and approached the librarian.

"I'm a nurse at Bartley Hospital and I'm trying to locate a relative for a patient. Do you know how I go about that?"

"We don't have much here about living people," she whispered with a giggle. "Try the County Records office." The librarian lifted her chin towards the door. "The office is just across the hall. Birth and marriage certificates will have an address. Neighbours might know if someone moved. It's difficult with the bombing and war, though. People leave and move away."

"Thank you. A marriage certificate might help. The woman I'm looking for moved away after she married."

After an afternoon of studying anatomy, Sophie was happy to do some detective work. The records office smelled of old decomposing paper and the clerk looked as though he was decomposing with it. A small man in every respect, his round wrinkled face and bald head looked something like a dried up apple.

"Birth, death or marriage?" His tiny eyes stared at Sophie.

"Marriage. Primrose Maggs. That was her maiden name."

"What year?"

"I'm not sure. Maybe 1914." Sophie sensed that without more information, this clerk would not help her. She needed to think quickly as he had already turned away. "Sir, please. I need your help. I'm a nurse at Bartley Hospital and I'm trying to locate a patient's sister. His wife just died and he has a ten-month-old baby, hurt when a bomb dropped on their house. The baby has recovered but has nowhere to go. If I don't find the sister, they'll put the baby in an orphanage." Sophie stared at the clerk with puppy-dog eyes. Expecting to see a menacing response, she saw kindness in his eyes.

"Wait here. I'll see what I can do."

The clerk returned with a large leather bound, well-worn ledger. "1914, you say?" He opened it up and placed the ledger so they could both see the listings. Nodules covered his small, permanently curled fingers. Unable to stretch his fingers, he placed a knuckle at January 2, 1914, the first marriage of the year. "Maggs you say was the bride's name? I'll leave you to go through the names."

Sophie read every listing, surprised at how many people married in 1914. It took a while as the groom's name appeared first but when it appeared, it almost jumped off the page.

Mr. Harold Butterworth, bachelor of Primrose Valley

Yorkshire and Miss Primrose Maggs spinster of the County of London Married April 10, 1914

"Sir, I found it." Sophie placed her finger against the listing, her excitement showing in a wide grin. "Thank you."

The clerk nodded. "Pleased to help."

Eager to tell Stan of her findings, Sophie went on to the Children's Ward. She was shocked to find Mrs. Montague leaning over Charlie's cot and looked around the ward for Emily. A nurse she'd never met was tending to a child at the end of the ward.

"Mrs. Montague, what are you doing here?"

"Nurse Romano, I could ask you the same question." Sophie frowned at the defensive edge to Mrs. Montague's voice.

"I'm helping Private Maggs..." She paused not wanting to say more. "And you? How is your arm?"

Mrs. Montague lifted the sling holding the heavily bandaged arm. "Mr. Wainwright has put the bones back together. It will take a few weeks to heal but, I feel quite well, thank you."

"Why are you in the Children's Ward?"

"Oh, I have a private room just across the hall. I was only a few feet away from his mother when she died. I thought I could bring him some comfort. What will happen to him?"

"His father will take care of him."

"Men are no good at looking after babies and he'll go back to war."

"Private Maggs is a loving father and quite able to take good care of his baby. We are locating a relative where Charlie can stay while Private Maggs fights for his country. Do you have children, Mrs. Montague?"

Mrs. Montague's gaze dropped to the floor. "No. Almost. I had a fall and miscarried and haven't been able to conceive since. Perry, that's my husband, is anxious for an heir and I so want a baby to hold." She took Charlie's hand and cooed into the cot.

Unpleasant vibes were creeping down Sophie's spine as she assessed Mrs. Montague's situation. Her recovery from suspicious falls, a recent mother-to-be grieving over a miscarriage and now, hovering over a soon to be orphaned Charlie. She did not like what she was seeing.

"How did you fall? It must have been a bad one."

"Oh, I was riding. I should not have been riding in my condition." She was lying. Sophie could tell, by the way she looked away and fiddled with her dressing gown belt. The broken arm had nothing to do with riding. This woman was being beaten by her husband.

"Nurse Romano, Mrs. Montague, may I ask what you are doing on the Children's Ward?"

"Emily, I came to see Private Maggs. I have some good news about his sister," Sophie said.

"Mrs. Montague, you need to go back to your room. We only allow Charlie visits from his family." Silence ensued while Mrs. Montague left the ward.

Emily whispered to her. "What is going on? That's the second time I've had to tell her to leave."

"She was here when I arrived. I found Rose Butterworth, Stan's married sister. At least I know where she is. Charlie can go to a relative."

"Charlie is no longer critical so his father has to respect visiting hours. He'll be here this afternoon. And that is good news."

"I'll be back later. And Emily, watch Mrs. Montague. I have a bad feeling about her."

"You and your bad feelings. Except this time I think there is something strange about Mrs. Montague. I'll keep her off the ward."

16

A Home for Charlie

Stan wept when Sophie told him she had found his sister. Not just because Charlie would have a home but because he'd missed her. Rose had been a mother to him before the orphanage. He eagerly wrote the letter.

Dear Rose,

How are you? It's been a long time. I'm married and have a little boy, Charlie. I'm sorry you can't meet my Millie, she w're killed in the London bombing. Charlie was hurt but is getting better. I miss my Millie terribly and I'm afraid for my son. I got no one to take care of him. I'm in the army, home on leave, but I have to go back now Charlie is better.

I don't want Charlie in an orphanage. I was treated real bad in that place. I'm asking if you and your husband can look after Charlie until the war is over? I will pay for his keep and visit when I'm on leave.

They bombed our house so I'm living at the mission but you can reply to River House Nurses Residence 45,

Common Road London. Nurse Romano was Millie's nurse at the hospital and she's been very kind to me and Charlie and helped me find you.

Your loving brother,
Stan

Emily informed the ward sister that a relative had been found. Charlie had a home to go to when the doctors deemed him well enough. There was no need to call in the authorities.

The Post Office was on Sophie's way home so she offered to walk with Stan. She watched Stan smile for the first time in days as he handed the letter to the postmistress. The relief was plain on his face, knowing someone would take care of Charlie. She waved goodbye as she climbed the steps to River House.

Trixie greeted her in the common room, as bouncy as ever. "Sophie, I can't wait to tell you about Christopher."

"And I can't wait to hear all about him. But I am surprised you like someone your mother found for you."

"Actually, it was Daddy. When I was at home before Christmas, my parents gave a reception. Did I tell you they knighted Daddy for his services to the government? I've no idea what for but it must be military as his guests are always high up military people, which includes Sir David Henderson, a Brigadier General."

"What does a Brigadier General have to do with Christopher?"

"Well, Sir David is the head of the Royal Flying Corps (RFC) and some of his pilots accompanied him to my parents' reception. Lieutenant Christopher Belingham is one of Sir David's reconnaissance pilots." Trixie twirled around the room as though she was in a ballroom. "We talked and danced and I thought he liked me but I never heard from him until two weeks ago. He'd been on some kind of exercise at Beddington Aerodrome. Beddington is near here so I've seen him almost every night before my shift—when he's not flying. Yesterday, my day off, we spent the whole day together. I'm in love. Can you believe it?"

"Trixie, slow down. You hardly know him and flying is dangerous."

"It was love at first sight for both of us. I'm not worried about his flying. He's a skilled pilot. His job is to take aerial photographs of German industrial and military stuff. His squadron doesn't fight or drop bombs."

Maybe not Sophie thought but German artillery guns would fire at RFC reconnaissance planes flying low to take pictures. Trixie did not understand how dangerous it was to fly an aeroplane, let alone take photographs of German held territory.

Mrs. Wilderby interrupted them as she placed a steaming cast-iron pot on the table. Suddenly the room was full of hungry nurses and Sophie didn't have time to finish the conversation with Trixie as Lieutenant Belingham had arrived at River House to walk her to the hospital. At first glance, Sophie had to agree that he was a handsome man and the way he looked at Trixie showed he genuinely loved her. Although Sophie really thought it might be too soon for love. *What do I know about love? I think I'm afraid of love and Trixie seems so happy.*She decided not to remind Trixie how dangerous it was to be a pilot. She deserved to be happy.

It had been four days since Stan sent the letter to Primrose Valley and there had been no reply so far. The doctor had declared Charlie fit enough to go home and they needed Charlie's bed for other injured children. The doctor said that unless Stan's sister came to fetch the child by tomorrow, he had no choice but to inform the authorities and place Charlie in the St. Vincent Orphanage.

Fortunately, she had left early with Hillary who had an appointment with Matron about medical school. Stan stood outside the hospital, waiting for Sophie. He relayed the doctor's decision about Charlie. Tears filled his eyes as he pushed a letter into Sophie's hand. Private Stanley Maggs was to report for duty in two days. He was to sail to France and join his regiment.

Stan followed her to the children's ward and they bumped into Emily just coming on duty. Sophie told her what had happened but Emily smiled. "Leave it to me. I can delay Charlie's discharge. Private Maggs, I want you to leave and come back for afternoon visiting hours." Stan nodded, confused and upset, but did as they asked.

Sophie followed Emily to Charlie's cot. "How can you delay this?"

Emily picked up Charlie's chart and made some notes, allowing Sophie to see what she had written 'Temperature 101.' Emily whispered to her. "They won't discharge him with a fever. It will get you an extra day. That's all."

"Thank you," Sophie whispered over her shoulder as she ran to the Woman's Ward.

Hillary grabbed Sophie's arm. "Sister is on the warpath. We have new patients and you're late."

Sophie hurried onto the ward, glad for the warning. Sister

was indeed angry and threatened to send her to Matron. Fortunately, they were so busy Sister couldn't spare a nurse off the floor. It was mid-afternoon visiting hours before Sophie had a break.

"I am so pleased to see you," Emily said as Sophie stepped into the nurses' common room.

"We have a problem. Mrs. Montague overheard that Charlie was going to the orphanage and wants to adopt him."

"The authorities will see this as a good thing. Prestigious family, money and means, when the mother is dead and the father has nothing. What can we do?"

"Unless you can find Private Maggs' sister, there's nothing we can do."

"Mrs. Montague is a nice lady but Mr. Montague is a bully. I'm convinced he beats his wife and that's why she has a broken arm. She never fell off a horse; this has happened before. We can't let Charlie go there. Does Stan know about this?"

"No, it's unusual, but he hasn't visited Charlie today. Charlie's temperature is still up and they have delayed the discharge. But when the night staff take his vitals, it will be normal."

Emily returned to the ward and Sophie made herself some tea. She wondered why Stan had not visited. Had his commanding officer called him early? No, he'd have sent word to Sophie if that had happened. She sensed that Mrs. Montague was grieving the loss of her baby and her supposed inability to conceive. Perhaps she thought if she had a child her husband would stop hurting her, but Sophie feared he would only bully the child as well. Her thoughts went back to Stan. Had Mrs. Montague said something to him? Did Stan think a home with the wealthy Montague family would be good for Charlie? Had he left under the assumption that Mrs.

Montague would look after Charlie? Where was Stan?!

Stan sat on the bench at St Pancras Train Station, counting his pennies to see if he had enough for a cup of tea. The train wasn't due for half an hour. He glanced up as an older lady sat beside him, the fur collar on her coat pulled up against the cold. The simple broad-brimmed hat hid most of her face but he could see a gentle smile.

"Son, would you go fetch me a cup of tea, milk no sugar and buy yourself one too? And two plain biscuits, if they have any." The women pushed a shilling into Stan's hand. Stan hesitated. He really wanted a cup of tea but he didn't know this woman. "Don't just stand there. Go!" The woman wafted a gloved hand towards the tea kiosk.

Stan felt the warm tea slither into his insides and almost sighed with pleasure. The biscuit tasted sweet and stopped his empty belly growling. The woman nudged him and handed him the second biscuit.

"Oh no, one was plenty, thank you. I needed that tea," Stan said, staring at his boots.

"That's the least I can do; buy a brave young soldier a cup of tea." She pushed the biscuit in his hand. "Here, take it. I'm not hungry and you look as though you missed breakfast."

Stan nodded and smiled at her. As she looked up from under the hat, he saw her eyes were deep blue, kind eyes same as Millie's had been. "I... didn't have enough... money."

"Where are you heading?"

"Primrose Valley to find my sister. My wife had blue eyes just like yours." Stan stopped, realizing how inappropriate his words sounded.

150

"I'm sorry," she said with generous sympathy. "War is a terrible thing," she added with no offence.

"I 'ave a little boy, Charlie. He's in hospital but he's better now. I need to find my sister to look after 'im." Stan's breath stopped and water filled his eyes. Suddenly he grabbed the arm of the bench. As it shook, he was back in the trenches. He could hear men screaming. He looked up and Millie's blue eyes stared at him. The screaming ceased as the train pulled into the station and he let his breath escape with relief. He was at St Pancras Station, not in the trenches.

"Son, are you all right?" The lady with Millie's eyes asked.

"Thank you, ma'am. I'm okay." A tear escaped down his cheek.

She took his arm. "Come with me. I'm going as far as Derby. You can keep me company on the train."

The train pulled into the station which was nothing more than a platform with a sign that read 'Primrose Valley.' No other passengers had alighted. He stood alone, looking up at the sky where a watery sun peeked through some clouds. It must be noon he thought and walked towards a pub sign hanging from a building.

"What'll it be, soldier?" A round faced barman asked.

Stan put his hand in his pocket, surprised to find several shillings amongst his pennies. His traveling companion had slipped money in his pocket while he dozed on the train. If he believed in ghosts, he would have said the lady with Millie's eyes was Millie sending him an angel. He pinched his arm, wondering if he was dreaming.

"So lad, what'll it be?" The barman repeated. "On the house."

"Thanks. Ginger beer please."

"Here, lad, no one's checking. If you're old enough to fight for our country, you're old enough to drink."

"Thank you. I am old enough, but I 'aven't eaten today and I don't hold me liquor well."

"I'll have the wife make yer a cheese sandwich. What's your name, son? Mine's Charlie."

"My baby son's name is Charlie. I'm Stan." Stan reached across the bar and shook Charlie's hand.

"So what brings you to these parts?"

"I'm looking for my sister. Primrose Maggs, but she's married now, so she'd be Primrose or Rose Butterworth. Do you know her?"

"Sure do. She's married to Harry Butterworth. She made that cheese in your sandwich. Harry owns Butterworth Farm, about three miles up the road."

The cheese sandwich tasted like nothing he'd had before. He wondered if that was because his sister had made it. He needed to pinch himself again. He couldn't believe it had been so easy to find Rose.

The farmhouse was old, but well cared for and the front door was red. So like Rose, he thought as he lifted the brass knocker. The door opened and Stan heard his sister's voice call out. "Who is it, Suzie?"

"A soldier!"

Stan looked downwards to see a little girl of about four. "Hello. Can I talk to your mother..." Stan hadn't finished when Rose appeared and stood behind her daughter.

"Oh my God. Stan!" She burst into tears and flung her arms around him. "How did you get here? How did you find me? And look at you. A soldier!" Words tumbled from her and she hugged him again. "Come in, come in." She closed the door behind him and guided him to the kitchen table. Another little girl, not much bigger than a toddler, joined them. "Girls, this is your Uncle Stan. He's my baby brother. Stan, these are my girls. Suzie is four and Dotty had a birthday yesterday and just turned three."

"Happy birthday, Dotty. I'm pleased to meet you, Suzie. I 'ave nieces. This is wonderful. Where is your husband?"

"Harry just popped up to the pub to deliver some cheese and pork."

Stan laughed "That's funny 'cause I were there and Charlie told me I was eating your cheese in a sandwich and he told me where you lived."

"He'll be back soon. Tell me all about yourself, what happened to you? I wrote to you after Harry and I got married. I wanted you to come and live with us. St Vincent sent the letters back and said you'd run away."

"The last letter I had from you was telling me you were getting married and moving to Primrose Valley. I remember Primrose and that's how Nurse Romano found you. The orphanage told me you'd married and I would never hear from me again. I was so angry I ran away and lived on the streets for a while until I got a job on the docks. Then I met Millie."

"You're married? You have children?" Rose studied Stan's face. "What's wrong?" She lifted Stan's chin with her finger and gently brushed his cheek. "Stan, what happened?" Before he could answer the back door slammed.

"I hear we have a visitor. Charlie told me your brother turned up." Harry's presence in the room overshadowed everything. The girls ran up to him and clung to his leg. He bent and kissed Rose and reached out to Stan. "I'm Harry. Pleased to meet you, Stan." Stan felt his firm grip and thought his knuckles might snap.

"How do you do?" Stan responded and realized it sounded odd.

"No need to be formal here. I'm pleased to see you. Rose talks about you all the time. She missed you when you ran off."

"He were just telling me he never got our letters." Rose said.

"I knew that place wasn't telling us the truth but, you did okay," Harry said, his voice filling the room. Stan looked at his bulk and thought of a gentle giant as his girls sat, one on each knee.

"Something terrible happened to you, Stan. I can see it in your eyes. Tell me." Rose took his hands.

"My Millie and baby Charlie, he's ten months old, were bombed. By the time I got home they were in hospital. Charlie were on death's door but he recovered. Millie were doing all right and then she got blood poisoning from where a piece of glass had cut her leg and she died." Stan could not hold back his grief and sobbed in his sister's arms. The girls leaned on their father and cried. Rose held Stan in her arms and rocked him like a baby as they wept together.

Harry took his once white handkerchief and wiped the girls faces before giving them each a kiss and telling them to go and play. "I have to start the milking. Will you be all right?" He kissed the top of Rose's head. She looked up and nodded 'yes.'

The last time Rose had held Stan and let him weep was seven years ago after their mother died. They had stayed in the tenement for almost a year. Rose cleaned houses to pay the rent but it wasn't enough and then the landlord threw them out. A well-meaning neighbour called the authorities and Stan had gone to St Vincent. Rose got a job as a live-in maid in a country house and met Harry delivering eggs and cheese.

"I'm sorry about Millie. Where is your son?"

"He's still at the hospital but he's better and the doctors want to discharge him. I don't have a home to take him to. Even if I did, I have to go back to France in two days. Rose, they want to send him to St Vincent. I can't let that happen. A nice posh lady has offered to adopt him." He burst into sobs again. "She'd give him a good life. She's rich but I'd never see him again. Rose, please, can you take him?"

"Of course we'll take him, and your home is with us. The girls can double up and Charlie can have Dottie's room. I still have the pram, cot and baby things." She giggled at the realization she only had girls' clothes. "Mostly pink, but I can find boy's clothes in the village."

Stan had the best night's sleep he'd had in months. He'd found a home for Charlie and finding his sister again was magic. The next morning, he left Butterworth Farm and caught the train back to London. Harry had insisted on writing a letter saying that he and Rose would foster Charlie as long as was necessary.

17

Fighting for Charlie

Stan watched the countryside flash by as the train took him back to London. He realized he hadn't felt this happy since he'd married Millie. As soon as the train pulled into St Pancras, he went to the ticket counter and bought a return ticket to take Charlie back to Primrose Valley. He didn't need to count his pennies for a cup of tea because Harry had given him train fare and some extra. Rose had included three small packages of cheese, one for himself and one each for Nurse Romano and Nurse Finnegan. He sipped the hot tea and ate two biscuits, thinking about Charlie growing up on a farm.

Stan's eyes looked upwards as he whispered. "He's going to be all right, Millie. Our Charlie will grow up in the country with Rose and Harry and two little girls. How about that? He has cousins and no more bombs. I wish you could have met Rose." He sensed a shadow at his shoulder and saw the lady with Millie's eyes smiling at him.

"You found your sister then? Charlie will be safe with Rose and Millie is watching over you. You'll see Charlie grow up but, be warned, it's not over yet."

Stan's eyebrows creased together, puzzled by the lady's words. Remembering his manners, he jumped up from his chair. "I'm sorry, where's me manners? Can I buy you a cup of tea?"

The lady shook her head and moved on to the café door. Stan stood up to follow. He wanted to thank her for her kindness but as his gaze searched the platform, she vanished. One minute she was at the door and the next, gone. She had disappeared into thin air without a trace and yet he could still feel her warm presence. A shadow passed over him, followed by an urge to get to the hospital.

He ran as fast as his legs would carry him, flying up the hospital steps two at a time and into the children's ward. Charlie's cot was empty.

"Nurse! Nurse! Where's Charlie!?"

"Private Maggs, you're back." Emily hesitated. "Charlie is with Mrs. Montague in her private room."

"Oh, that's a relief. I thought something had happened to him. Nurse Finnegan, I found my sister and she will take care of Charlie. I'm taking him on the afternoon train. That's where I were…" Stan stopped talking and stared at Emily's expression. "Is som'ut wrong?"

"Mr. and Mrs. Montague want to adopt Charlie and the doctors agreed it would be the best thing for him."

"No, that can't 'appen," he shouted as he ran across to Mrs. Montague's room. "I have a letter form Harry. They live on a farm. Charlie has cousins." Stan pushed open the door and yelled, "You can't have Charlie. He's my son and I found my sister." Seeing Mrs. Montague retreat into the pillows with fright, Stan lowered his voice. "I'm sorry, but it's all right Mrs.

Montague. I found my sister and she'll look after Charlie." It was then that Stan realized Charlie was in her arms and dressed in clothes that didn't belong to him.

Charlie started crying and Mrs. Montague sat him up, stroking his dark curls and rocking him. "My husband is on his way to take us home. Charlie is mine now."

"You can't have Charlie. You can't take him to your house. He has a home to go to." Stan saw the small suitcase on the chair by her bed.

"He's my son," Stan tried to shout, but the words were a whisper as tears caught in his throat.

The commotion had drawn Sister and Nurse Finnegan and Nurse Romano to the room. He stared at Nurse Romano for help. Perhaps she would speak up for him but Sister took charge.

"Private Maggs, I would like you to go with Nurse Romano. Nurse Finnegan, please take Charlie back to the nursery and then ask Matron to join us." Mrs. Montague screamed, gripping Charlie's blanket as Emily picked him up. "No need for the screaming, Mrs. Montague." Mrs. Montague gulped a breath, tears streaming down her face she stopped screaming, but began wailing. Sophie wasn't sure which was worse, the screaming or the wailing. Sister closed the door containing the noise which lessened as they walked along the corridor.

"Private Maggs, wait here please." Sophie pointed to a bench in the hallway. "I want to speak to Nurse Finnegan." Sophie touched Emily's arm. "Emily, let me go and talk to Matron. I need to tell her what kind of man she's allowing to take care of Charlie. If I'm coming with a message from Sister, I'll be able to talk to her."

"Go! Before Mr. Montague gets here. He's on his way."

"Thanks. Come, Stan, we've got some explaining to do."

Sophie told Stan to sit outside Matron's office until she called him. Beth gave her a funny look. "There's a problem on the Children's Ward and Sister sent me to fetch Matron. May I go in?"

"I'll tell her." Beth glanced at Private Maggs. "What's he doing here?"

"Part of the problem. That's why I need to talk to her before she goes to the ward."

"You'd better go in then."

A dismissive 'Enter' came in response to Sophie's knock. "Nurse Romano, we don't have an appointment."

"No, Matron. There has been an incident on the Children's Ward and Sister sent me to fetch you." Sophie hurried on before Matron could question her for being on the wrong ward. "Mrs. Montague wants to adopt Charlie Maggs."

"Yes, I know. I spoke with the Montague's yesterday and I think it is a perfect solution for the child. Private Maggs returned to the war without making arrangements for his son and other than the orphanage, there is nowhere for the child to go."

"What! No! That's not true!"

"Mrs. Montague said Private Maggs spoke to her before he left and he had agreed that she could adopt the child. Private Maggs was nowhere to be found yesterday and we know he has his papers to return to his battalion. I know Nurse Finnegan said it was unusual for him not to be with his son but grieving husbands often do strange things. And without his wife, how can he look after his child?"

"Private Maggs is right here, sitting outside your door. The reason you didn't see him yesterday was because he went to find his sister. He has a home for Charlie."

"Well, this changes things. But the Montague's would give the child a privileged life. What if Private Maggs doesn't come back from the war? What then for the child?"

"What if he comes back? He's lost his wife and now you want to give his son away."

"Nurse Romano, you are getting dangerously close to insubordination. I've reminded you before."

"I'm sorry, Matron, but this little boy needs to be with family. Have you never wondered why Mrs. Montague has so many falls? Mr. Montague beats his wife. What kind of family would you be sending him to?" Sophie stopped and held her breath. Had she gone too far?

"Your listening skills need attention, Nurse Romano. That is a slanderous statement."

"Mrs. Montague has a badly broken arm. It's not the first bone she's broken, all supposedly from riding horses. But when asked, she knew nothing about riding in Hyde Park on Christmas Day. She then lied to cover up her husband's lie. She's afraid."

"Ask Private Maggs to come in. I want to know what arrangements he's made for the boy."

Sophie called Stan to come in and he told Matron all about his sister Rose and the farm. He showed her the letter that Harry had written and the train tickets Harry had paid for. He talked about finding his sister and Charlie having cousins. Now he had a home to come back to after the war. Matron asked him if he would consider letting his son grow up in a privileged, wealthy home. Stan hesitated for a moment and his head shook with a vigorous 'no.' "My Charlie needs to be with family; raised in the country with fresh milk and cheese and far away from London bombs."

"Very well. I'll see the doctor discharges Charlie into your care in time to catch your train. Good luck to you, Private Maggs. Take care of yourself."

Sophie put her hand on the door as it burst open. A red-faced Mr. Montague entered, yelling. "What is the meaning of this? My wife tells me the nurses won't allow her to see the boy."

"Please stop yelling, Mr. Montague. The child is not up for adoption. Your wife misled me. Private Maggs did not abandon his son. His sister will take care of Charlie."

"Oh no, that will not happen. My wife has her heart set on that baby. It will do until she can provide me with an heir." He leaned over the desk and spit the words in Matron's face; his temper out of control. His hand balled into a fist and Sophie was afraid he might hit Matron. From the look on her face, so was she.

She stood up, slamming her hands on the desk. "Mr. Montague, OUT of my office now! You may return and discuss this matter with me when you have calmed down."

"You'll hear from my solicitor!" Mr. Montague stomped out of the office, knocking over a chair as he went.

Matron, without speaking, flipped her head for Sophie and Private Maggs to follow her down the corridor to the Children's Ward.

The screaming and yelling had caused a stir and Sophie heard the excited chatter as they approached the Children's Ward. The chatter stopped even before Matron arrived as the staff recognized her determined footsteps. Sobbing came from Mrs. Montague's private room but Matron ignored it and continued on to the ward. Charlie, now strong, was standing up in his cot and jumping up and down. As soon as he saw Stan his little arms stretched out to be picked up. Charlie had grown from a lifeless infant to an alert, bright, normal ten-month-old baby. "Charlie, where did ya get them clothes?" Stan looked at Charlie dressed in a pair of blue rompers and a hand knitted white matinee jacket. A blue coat and baby bonnet were laid out next to the cot.

"It may surprise you, Private Maggs, but Mrs. Montague is sorry and understands Charlie should be with his family. She would like Charlie to have them as a gift."

"I don't want charity from the Montagues. Her 'usband threatened to go to a solicitor." Stan hesitated. "But maybe Mrs. Montague were all right then. Charlie took to her and he should look smart for his Aunt Rose."

Emily handed him a bag. "You'll need these things for the journey. Nappies and milk... oh I never thought. Do you know how to change his nappies?"

Stan laughed at Emily's remark. "Course I do. It were the first thing my Millie taught me after he were born."

Stan picked up the bag and wrapped Charlie in a blanket. "I better be off. I don't want to miss me train. How can I thank all of you?"

"Just stay safe and come back to Charlie," Sophie said as they watch Private Maggs carry Charlie out of the hospital.

Matron clapped her hands, "Back to work ladies. There are patients to be nursed." Everyone including Sister scurried to their posts and Matron disappeared into Mrs. Montague's room.

Letters were rare for Sophie because she had no relatives and had never kept in touch with old friends. So when she saw her name on the envelope on the hall table, she looked at the name twice to make sure it was for her. The post mark said Primrose Valley. Her heart missed a beat. Had something happened to Charlie or Stan? Tearing the envelope, she ran to her room and unfolded the letter. She quickly checked the signature, Rose Butterworth.

Dear Nurse Romano,

Stan asked me to write to you and thank you for all you did for his wife Millie and how you rescued Charlie. Stan is back in France. I don't know where and I hope he's safe.

Charlie is settling well and my girls love him and he has three mothers. No substitute for his own mother though, may she rest in peace. Harry and I will give him a good home until Stan comes back.

If ever you want to visit Charlie, both you and Nurse Finnegan would be very welcome.

Yours truly,

Rose Butterworth.

Sophie immediately opened her writing case and penned a reply.

Dear Mrs. Butterworth,

Thank for your nice letter. I am thrilled to hear Charlie has settled in so well. I will tell Emily, Nurse

Finnegan, the good news. She nursed Charlie through his injuries and became quite attached to him as we all did.

We, Emily and I, would love to hear how Charlie is doing, if it's not too much trouble to send an occasional letter. I realize you are busy with three children and a farm to look after.

Thank you for your kind invitation and perhaps when my studies are complete, I will pay you a visit.

Please give Charlie a hug.

Yours truly,

Sophie Romano

18

Proposals

Air raids and bombs dropped from enemy aeroplanes several times a week. The hospital was now full of civilians hurt by flying debris from explosions. Sophie felt her anxiety rise. These poor people didn't know what had happened. Soldiers went to war expecting to fight and trained to defend their country and themselves, but these civilians had no defense.

Three months had passed since she'd nursed Millie Maggs and it was clear to Sophie that the war on London devastated families already in poverty. Most were not as lucky as Charlie. Despite Mrs. Maggs death, Charlie's story had ended with a family being reunited. Sophie found it difficult to cope with women in despair and asked to work on the Men's Ward. Nursing soldiers injured in the line of duty seemed easier.

Sophie could not speak of her feelings. She was afraid to admit she struggled with bad dreams of her father dying and her mother screaming for help. It wasn't unusual for Trixie to shake her out of a nightmare.

The alarm rattled Sophie out of sleep. She stretched, feeling exhausted, and remembering her nightmare. She glanced at Trixie. "I'm sorry, I woke you again last night."

Trixie yawned "You were shouting for help. It sounded like a bad nightmare. Is something worrying you?"

"Sorry, I don't remember the dream. I'm fine, just overtired. I'd better get dressed. First day back on the Men's Ward."

"Are you going to flirt with Carlos?"

"No, of course not. I told you. He's engaged to Rosamond." Sophie felt her cheeks get warm. "I have no interest in him."

"Are you sure about that?"

"Trixie, stop trying to match make. I know you love Christopher but I'm not interested in romance. I just want to be a nurse and get to an army hospital in France."

"Christopher's squadron was flying last night. I always worry until I hear from him. He's taking me to dinner tonight. It's our four-month anniversary."

"Four months. That's a long time." Sophie giggled, intending the remark to be sarcastic, but she realized that Trixie was quite serious.

Surprised to see Sister Kay sitting at the nurses' station on the Men's Ward, Sophie frowned. "Sister Kay, are you working here?"

"Matron has shuffled the staff around. We'll be working together again." It was nice to see a familiar face among the new nurses and probationers. Another batch of nurses had moved to field hospitals in France or Belgium.

"Nurse Romano, you will work with Nurse Hogan today."

Nurse Hogan was a long skinny woman with a thin, sour face. Sophie wondered if the wrinkles were from age or a bad temper. But whatever the reason, working with Sophie didn't appear to meet her approval.

The first patient, Mr. Grim, had a sense of humour and made fun of his name. "No relation to the Grim Reaper." He chuckled. "Even a German bomb couldn't get me."

Sophie laughed at his joke. "Pleased to see you have a sense of humour, Mr. Grim. How are you feeling today?"

Nurse Hogan interrupted. "Stop your chatter and take his temperature."

"Thanks for asking. You're new. I'm feeling better. Doc mended my leg." He groaned as Nurse Hogan changed his dressing. "Ouch! Nurse, that hurt."

"Quiet!" She finished the dressing and made a note in the chart.

Sophie patted his arm, smiled and rolled her eyes, getting another chuckle from Mr. Grim.

With pursed lips, Nurse Hogan hissed at her. "Watch yourself. It does not do to get familiar with patients."

Sophie felt it best not to answer. Working with the woman would be a challenge.

The ward was full to overflowing with a mixture of civilians injured in air raids and soldiers needing special treatment. The last patient on the round was Lieutenant McAllister, a Scotsman, with his leg shattered at Ypres. Sophie noticed he flinched when Nurse Hogan approached, lifting the covers to reveal a frame over a badly deformed leg.

"No need to flinch, Lieutenant. Mr. Wainwright will be in to see you. Nurse here will take your temperature."

Sophie noted his vital signs and tried to give him an encouraging smile. She knew that the chances of saving the leg were not good but she also sensed his fear. His eyes stared into the distance and he seemed not to hear.

Sophie gently tapped his arm to get his attention and he flinched again. "Lieutenant, are you in pain?"

He stared at Sophie for several seconds. "A bit. Doc gave me an injection…. I don't want to lose my leg."

"You have the very best orthopaedic surgeon. He will do all he can to save your leg. Now try to get some rest. You look tired."

"I can't sleep. Every time I close my eyes, I hear the screaming, I smell burning and I'm back in my rat hole."

"I'm sorry to hear that. Tell me, where is your favourite place?" He looked puzzled.

Sophie thought for a moment and added. "A park, a beach or a garden or a quiet place in your home, perhaps with your wife or sweetheart?"

"Kew Gardens with my wife." He managed a smile. "She's my sweetheart. We went there just before the war. I proposed to her in one of the greenhouses. A butterfly landed on her hair." He stared back in time, his look no longer vacant.

"I want you to picture that visit, smell the flowers and grass. Now, when you close your eyes, put that picture in your head."

"I see Nurse Romano is treating you well, Lieutenant."

Sophie almost dropped the thermometer as her knees gave way at the sound of Carlos' voice. What is wrong with you, Sophie Romano? Pull yourself together. Taking an extra deep breath, she stood. "Good morning, Mr. Wainwright."

"Good morning, Nurse. Nice to see you back on the Men's Ward." Sophie didn't dare look up. She thought her cheeks must be bright pink. She pulled the screens around the patient's bed before leaving Carlos and Sister Kay to their rounds. She moved to the next bed and joined Nurse Hogan, whose frosty stare quickly cooled Sophie's pink cheeks.

Exhausted from a poor night's sleep and a challenging day, Sophie retired early that night and was in a deep sleep when Trixie bounced into the room and shook her awake. "I'm sorry to wake you but I have to tell someone," Trixie's voice rose a couple of octaves. "He asked me to marry him!"

"Shush, not so loud," Sophie whispered, groggy with sleep. "Did you just say marry?" Stunned by the news, Sophie sat up, wide awake. "But you only just met him."

"It doesn't matter how long. We're in love! He's going to ask Father this weekend and we'll get married after exams. Will you be my bridesmaid?"

"Of course. But are you sure about this? Shouldn't you wait? Aren't things happening too fast? I doubt your parents will approve."

"My father is delighted because Chris is a military man, a pilot. Mother is besotted by his heritage—an earl's son. She's been trying to get me married for years."

"What about nursing? Even if you pass the exam in June, you have another year of practical training. How can you give that up?"

"I'm not giving anything up. Although Mother will expect us to buy the house with the picket fence and all that stuff. Chris says we can live on the estate. The manor house has plenty of rooms and it would only be weekends and my days off."

Sophie sighed at the flimsy arrangements. Trixie seemed to have forgotten that marriage was discouraged among young probationers. She was reluctant to dampen Trixie's excitement. "Maybe you should sleep on this. I'm happy for you but there are some practicalities you need to think about. Speaking as your friend, I think it would be wise to keep this to yourself for now."

"That's what Chris said but I want to tell everyone." Trixie's lips dropped as she pouted.

"Go to sleep." Sophie slid down her bed and pulled the covers up.

The walk to the hospital the next morning was charged with excitement. Trixie's nuptials were not the only news of the day. The admissions board had invited Hillary for an interview at the medical school. As much as it pleased Sophie, a sense of loneliness washed over her. Trixie would leave and get married and Hillary would move into circles where Sophie didn't belong. She tried to brush off the intense feelings of abandonment, but her insides churned with emotion. It scared her that she didn't understand her own feelings.

Preparing herself for a miserable day with Nurse Hogan, she walked towards the main entrance just as Carlos drove into the parking lot. She stopped, delighted to see him. Her mood lifted and she had an urgent desire to fall into his arms for the comfort she craved. He wound down the car window. "Wait, I'll walk in with you."

Sophie waited while he parked and joined her. "Why so sad?"

"Why do you ask?"

"I have known you a long time and you look upset."

"It's nothing. Just melancholy, that's all. I requested to go back on the Men's Ward but it's not as I remember."

"Nurse Hogan?" Carlos rolled his eyes. "An experienced nurse but not a nice person to work with. She has no empathy. Perhaps that's why Sister teamed you up with her. You are one of the most sensitive and intuitive nurses I've worked with. Don't let someone's negativity get you down." He slid his hand in hers and gave it a gentle squeeze. She held on tight, not wanting to release his warmth and secretly wishing it was an embrace.

"May I invite a friend to dinner?"

"Thank you. I'd like that. I'll be in the library tomorrow."

"I'll call for you at the library at five." They parted ways, Carlos to the doctors' lounge and Sophie to the Men's Ward.

Nurse Hogan stood at the nurses' station checking her watch. "You are one minute late!"

Sophie wanted to laugh. The sour face had wrinkles on the wrinkles, giving her a cartoonish look. Taking Carlos' words to heart, she decided that Nurse Hogan needed a lesson in empathy. Ignoring her comment, Sophie walked up to Mr. Grim's bed.

"How are we today, Mr. Grim? I see the Grim Reaper didn't visit overnight." Giggling, Sophie added, "I need to change your sheets and Nurse Hogan will change the dressing on the wound."

"You are funny, Nurse. I like to laugh and you used my own joke back at me." His ample belly shook as he laughed. "Can you do my dressing? That other nurse hurts me."

"I'm sorry, I can't. I'm a nurse in training and not allowed to do dressings yet. I'm sorry it hurts but the wound is open so I'm afraid whoever does it, it will sting"

"Complaining again, Mr. Grim," Nurse Hogan said.

"The wound is sore. Perhaps a gentler touch until it's healed

171

more?" Sophie held her breath.

"Perhaps it's time you learned to change dressings as you think you are so clever." Nurse Hogan pushed the instrument trolley over to Sophie.

Sophie took the forceps and removed the old dressing. Carefully dabbing the wound with disinfectant, she looked up at the patient. "I'm sorry, this will sting." She cleaned and dressed the wound.

"Good. But if you take that long with each patient we'll be here all day." Nurse Hogan moved to the next patient, leaving Sophie to finish making Mr. Grim's bed.

Lieutenant McAllister looked pale and had dark rings under his eyes. Sophie surmised he had not slept. Clearly her advice had not helped. "How much sleep did you get, Lieutenant?"

"A little. I held my wife's hand and we walked for a little while until the bad dreams came back. But it was better. It was the operation that kept me awake. The doc warned me if he can't repair my leg, he might have to amputate."

Sophie sat beside him and took his hand. "Lieutenant, you could not be in better hands than Mr. Wainwright. Has your wife been to see you?"

"I told her not to come. I don't want her seeing me like this."

"Do you know how selfish that is? Your wife will worry about you. She needs to be with you."

"I didn't think of it that way. I would like to see her."

"Does she have a telephone?" He nodded 'yes.' "I'll call her for you."

The nurses usually took their breaks around visiting time and Sophie smiled when she saw a young lady sitting at the side of the Lieutenant's bed. She wondered if Carlos could save his leg. It seemed sad to think of young men losing limbs. She had sensed his loneliness, perhaps even recognizing it because of her own feelings. Sophie found it difficult to detach emotionally from the patients. Matron and Sister kept warning her but she couldn't help it.

The following day, she and Trixie both had the day off. On the rare occasions this happened, they usually spent the time together. But that day Christopher was taking Trixie home to ask for her hand in marriage. Sophie planned a day at the library and dinner with Carlos. The urgency of being with Carlos had passed and she regretted having accepted the invitation. Did Carlos mean they were just friends or was it an excuse? Wasn't she being disloyal to Rosamond, a woman she had never met and betrothed to Carlos? If they were just friends, why did her heart race and her cheeks turn pink when she saw him or heard his voice? Did she want more? Was Carlos hanging on, hoping for more? Her thoughts drifted to Bill Blaine. Was history repeating itself? She loved Bill but he loved Anna. Even when Anna married Alex, he still couldn't love Sophie. Was she being naïve again? She remembered Italy and how she and Carlos had loved. Why was Carlos marrying another woman? His mother had been right. To Carlos it had been just a fling in Italy. He never really loved her. She wrote him a note.

Dear Carlos,
   Forgive the late notice, but I cannot join you for dinner tonight.
   Sophie

She left the library early, dropped the note off at the hospital, and returned to River House. She feared Carlos would go to the library for an explanation. The day had not been completely without merit. Her studies had revealed more symptoms of shell-shock. The vacant staring and not hearing that she'd seen in Lieutenant McAllister, together with the nightmares, confirmed her suspicions. She would talk to Sister and see if she could spend some time with him, perhaps even talk to his wife so she could understand too.

She popped into the kitchen to tell Mrs. Wilderby she would be in for dinner. Surprised to find that Trixie had returned early, Mrs. Wilderby fussed that there would not be enough dinner to go around.

Trixie sat on the bed, cross-legged and pouting when Sophie entered their room.

"You are back early. Is Christopher flying tonight?"

"My parents want us to wait for a year. Can you believe that? They have been pestering me to get married and now they want me to wait."

"Well, it is a bit soon."

"Now you are against me too!"

Sophie sat on the edge of the bed and wrapped her arms around Trixie. "No, I'm on your side. Maybe if you wait until the summer and then ask again, you could plan an autumn wedding."

"On the drive back, we talked about eloping and not telling anyone. My mother would be furious. She's planning a big wedding, which is so inappropriate while the country is at war."

"It might be better to wait. How will you finish training as a married woman? You know how they frown on married

174

nurses. And you'd never get to France."

"My father reminded me of that. I hadn't thought about it. But if we marry and keep it a secret, nobody would be wiser and I'd finish training."

"Where would you live? You couldn't move into a house or flat. You might as well stay as you are. Secrets never stay secret. If anyone found out, you'd be in a lot of trouble."

"We didn't have time to discuss everything as Chris is flying tonight. Maybe you're right."

"Why don't you plan a wedding date for April next year or after you graduate? Let your mother organize the wedding. You can choose your wedding dress and find a place to live. It could be very exciting."

"I like that idea but maybe not a whole year. I don't think I could manage that long. But planning is good. My mother would have an excuse to get to know Lady Belingham and that would keep her busy."

19

Losses

Mr. Grim sat in the chair at the side of his bed, waiting for his brother to take him home. He looked pale and old and she suspected his jovial persona covered up his true feelings. Curious, she wondered about his story. Sophie thought he must be in his fifties, too old to fight but caught in the war anyway.

"Mr. Grim, I see you are well enough to go home. I shall miss your jokes," Sophie said as she prepared the bed for the next patient.

"Thanks for your help. I'd need a long ladder to get back home." He gave a hearty laugh. "The Hun's bomb pushed my house clear through to Australia." He laughed again but Sophie sensed sadness and not humour. "My brother and his wife have offered me a home. There's just me. I never married and have no children. I served in the Boer War, you know. Ah, here he is."

An older man with the same colouring as Mr. Grim picked up the small bag and Sophie watched them leave the ward. They had the same walk and family likeness and, without saying much, they cared for each other. She wished she had spent more time talking to Mr. Grim.

"Stop daydreaming, there's work to do. The orderly is here to fetch the lieutenant." Nurse Hogan's words jarred at Sophie. How much more of her disapproval could she take? Too upset to respond, Sophie moved to Lieutenant McAllister's bed.

He sat up, twisting the edge of the sheets with his fingers, his face pale and creased with anxiety. Sophie patted his arm. "Have you taken a trip to Kew Gardens lately? That would be a good place to be at this moment."

His face relaxed and his mouth lifted into a smile. "I went last night and it helped. I slept a little." The tension returned. "They're operating this morning."

"The orderly is here to take you to theatre. You are in good hands."

Lieutenant McAllister never returned to the ward and his wife picked up his personal belonging later that afternoon. Sophie could not hold back tears and excused herself from the ward only to bump into Carlos. She'd never seen him so pale and distraught. He stared at her and blurted out, "I lost a patient on the operating table today."

Sophie guided him to a bench tucked in a corner, away from prying eyes. "I'm sorry. It's hard losing a patient."

"It's the first patient I've lost on the table. I saved his leg and the operation was almost over, but his heart couldn't take it. It was my fault. I should have been faster." Carlos slid his hand into Sophie's and they sat in silence.

Struggling to hold back her own tears, Sophie squeezed his hand. "It wasn't your fault. You did your best. We all do our best but we're living in terrible times." She had a strong desire to kiss him and stood up quickly. "I have to get back to the ward. Nurse Hogan doesn't have a sympathetic bone in her body. Death just rolls off her as if it were normal." She stopped talking. Was it becoming normal? "I thought I would get used to it but losing patients is getting harder."

Carlos shook his head, poised to speak but his eyes glistened with moisture and he tried to smile. "Thanks." Dragging his feet, he headed to the exit. She wanted to join him, comfort him, but it wasn't her place. She hoped Rosamond could assure him he was an excellent surgeon and McAllister's death was not his fault.

There would be many more deaths. Sophie wondered if she was up to the task. How could she nurse wounded soldiers in the field if she couldn't cope with death in a clean London hospital?

"There you are! Daydreaming again! Patients die all the time. Get used to it because the living patients need your attention." Nurse Hogan's words were harsh and jolted Sophie from her self-pity. She was angry at first with the unfeeling, cold woman but perhaps she needed more of what made Nurse Hogan cope. She may not have been sympathetic, but she was a good nurse and got things done.

"Why doesn't a patient's death bother you? These are young men's futures cut short, wives left as widows, children fatherless."

"I learned a long time ago that getting emotional can ruin your career."

Sophie almost jumped back as the malice in Nurse Hogan's words attacked her and then a brief flash of tenderness passed through her eyes. *Whatever happened to you, it was life changing*, Sophie thought and from that moment on, she had a new understanding of Nurse Hogan.

Mrs. Wilderby set a tureen of vegetable soup on the table with such force it spilled onto the tablecloth. "The butcher had no meat this morning, only a few bones to make soup. I don't want to hear complaints."

The soup was thin but full of flavour and Sophie wondered how Cook made something out of nothing. A few noses wrinkled but no one dared say a word.

Mavis broke the silence. "I know where to get meat."

"There is no meat to be found in London. Listen to the news. The food supply is critical; no meat, no flour or sugar. The stores are bare." Mrs. Wilderby slapped her hands against her apron. "Nothing. Rich people are buying up everything they can and hoarding it. The shopkeepers are greedy and sell to the highest bidder. The government asks us to be careful and to grow vegetables. We grow what we can in the little back garden but you can't grow meat!" Anger made Mrs. Wilderby waft her arms around in despair.

"I know someone. I can get fresh meat and flour." Mavis seemed excited to be helping but Mrs. Wilderby was skeptical.

"Where from? Tell me where the shop is."

"Well, it's not exactly a shop. Tell me what you want."

Mrs. Wilderby eyed Mavis with suspicion and hesitated for several seconds before answering. "Where does this meat come from? Is it ordinary meat? I don't want horse-meat."

"Of course its ordinary meat. My dad has a friend who's a farmer and he gives us stuff. Sometimes he gives us an old hen. I can ask if he has any."

"I want nothing to do with cheats and hoarders. If it's fresh from the farm and affordable, that sounds all right. You girls need decent food in your bellies."

Sophie detected hesitation in Mrs. Wilderby's voice as she

agreed that the offer was tempting. Mrs. Wilderby was torn between feeding her girls good food and staying within the government guidelines.

"Nurse Riding, could you ask your father if he can procure some meat for us and let me know how much it costs?" Mrs. Wilderby took a deep breath and changed the subject. "Cook made you a suet pudding with custard." The girls all sighed. Custard was indeed a treat and made up for the watery soup.

Most nurses disliked the night shift but Trixie volunteered to go back to nights on the Women's Ward. She hated working with Mavis but it meant she saw more of Chris. His squadron took to the air at night, leaving daytime to court. Trixie's parents had embraced a spring wedding. Her mother had tried to brush off her disappointment that Lady Belingham wanted no part of the wedding plans, believing her son was marrying beneath him. The Belingham's heritage went back to the 17th century. Robin King's knighthood was appointed, and although Lady King came from a society family, Sir Robin did not. Neither Trixie nor Christopher seemed to find this worrying. Sophie noticed they had little interest in their parents or the wedding. She wondered if the love birds had their own plans?

Mavis continued to do her disappearing act and, as the air raids were more frequent, Trixie was getting fed up with doing all the work. She refrained from complaining as Mavis had come through with fresh supplies for Mrs. Wilderby. The plumber's van regularly pulled up to River House, delivering supplies that had nothing to do with plumbing.

Although London seemed in crisis most of the time, and the

hospital overflowed with injured civilians, River House had, so far, escaped the bombing. Other than a round of head colds, River House was coping quite well.

Sophie had succumbed to the cold and Sister Kay had sent her home, afraid she would infect the patients. She agreed as she felt poorly. Mrs. Wilderby fussed over her like a mother hen and put her to bed with a hot drink of lemon and honey and a dash of brandy. Sophie screwed up her nose. She could have done without the brandy but relished the warm feeling it gave her tummy. Within minutes, she was fast asleep.

The bedroom door squeaked open and Trixie tried to creep in without disturbing Sophie but she was awake. "Sorry, I didn't mean to wake you. How are you feeling? Mrs. Wilderby said you had a cold."

"Better. The sleep did me good." Sophie sat up, pulling the pillows behind her, and leaned back. "I never see you these days. How are things with Mavis?"

"Bad. She leaves me to get the patients to the basement and saunters off in the middle of the air raids, re-appearing when it's over. I'm afraid to complain as she has been kind to Mrs. Wilderby, finding food. There is something strange going on."

Sophie sneezed and grabbed her handkerchief. "Why would you say that?"

"She made a comment that her disappearing act had something to do with getting the food for River House and then she added, 'among other things.' I asked her how many people the farm supplied. She gave a sarcastic laugh and said 'a few.' She's acting strange these days."

"How strange? I never see her except at dinner. She's not someone I like and I hated working with her."

"Something odd happened last night. A patient suffering

from complications from a miscarriage turned critical during the night and Sister sent for her husband. He's a policeman and arrived in uniform. Mavis ran off the ward, terrified. Sophie, I think she's into something illegal and I think it is to do with the food."

"What's illegal about food from a farmer?"

"I don't think the food is coming from a farmer. Do you think she's stealing it? Or did her father stockpile to sell for a profit?"

"Well, judging by Mavis's history of lying, it's possible, but I wouldn't have taken her for a thief. Did she come back to the ward?"

"The patient died and the poor policeman left, very upset. Sister took him to Matron's office but Mavis didn't come back. I found her shaking and scrubbing tears from her face in the Nurses' Common Room. I asked her what was wrong and she told me to mind my own business."

"Do you think we should tell Mrs. Wilderby?" Sophie asked.

A knock on the door turned their heads and Mrs. Wilderby entered, carrying a tray with chicken soup and toast. "Tell Mrs. Wilderby what?" she asked, placing the bed-tray across Sophie's lap. Trixie and Sophie stared at her, waiting for the other to say something. "Has the cat got your tongues?"

Sophie looked at Trixie. "Mrs. Wilderby needs to know."

"Ladies, I am intrigued. Please enlighten me."

Trixie relayed her concerns and waited for a response, expecting a denial and explanation about the food. Mrs. Wilderby went pale and stared at the chicken soup as though it was a feared monster about to attack. The guilt was plain to see in her gentle eyes. She closed the door and took a seat in the only chair, facing the girls.

"I had my suspicions. Some packaging was odd, as though they had re-wrapped it. Mr. Riding made me shudder. I don't like him. I sensed his dishonesty and lately the prices are more than we can afford." She stopped breathing, trying to hold back tears. "I only wanted to give you girls good meals so you'd have the energy to work, stay healthy and take care of your patients."

A loud sneeze and cough from Sophie made Mrs. Wilderby feel her forehead. "If you are no better tomorrow, I'm calling the doctor."

"Can you tell Mr. Riding you don't want any more of his products and not to come anymore?" Trixie said.

"I tried that and he threatened to go the hospital board and tell them I was buying stolen goods."

"That would implicate him more than you," Sophie said, blowing her nose. "Mrs. Wilderby, you did not know they were stolen goods. We were all witness to Mavis saying her father got the supplies from a farmer friend. You need to go to the police. Don't you agree, Trixie?"

"I'd agree except that it will get Mavis into trouble too."

"If Mavis didn't know what her father was doing, she'll be cleared. But if she is part of the thieving, she needs to be punished, not Mrs. Wilderby."

"You must not repeat this, but Nurse Riding is already in trouble with Matron for leaving the ward during air raids," Mrs. Wilderby said with a sigh.

"It was only a question of time before sister caught her leaving the ward during the night shift. I didn't know Sister had reported her absence," Trixie added, "I assumed she was meeting a beau but thieving makes it far more serious."

"We will come with you to the police station," Sophie said,

sneezing again into her handkerchief. "And we should do it as soon as possible. Before Mr. Riding has time to make excuses or hide his bounty."

"You stay right where you are, Nurse Romano. Eat the chicken soup. It is contraband but as it has medicinal qualities, we will be forgiven. Nurse King, I would be grateful if you would accompany me to the police station."

The police were non-committal, saying they would look into it, but admitted they were aware of a gang of thieves stealing supplies from warehouses. Mr. Riding's name brought a flash of recognition from the duty officer but he only said a detective would be around to see her in the morning.

The detective took statements from Mrs. Wilderby and Trixie and finally packed all the food into large boxes. Mrs. Wilderby argued that she had paid for the food and it would spoil. The detectives didn't care and took it anyway, for 'evidence' or most likely someone else's pantry.

For a second time, they removed Mavis from River House; fired from the hospital and sent home to her family. Mr. Riding was found guilty and sentenced to an extensive prison term.

20

Secrets and Little Lies

Sophie recovered from the cold. Although she felt weak and not quite herself, she decided that getting back to work would get rid of her malaise. Mrs. Wilderby even allowed her to come to the dining room for the evening meal. Expecting vegetable soup, it surprised Sophie to see a steaming roast of beef on the table. Catching Sophie's puzzled look, Mrs. Wilderby was quick to explain. "I discovered the roast at the back of the pantry. It needed cooking before it spoiled. This will do us several meals and the butcher has promised me mutton in a couple of days."

How she had hidden such a large roast was a mystery as was Mrs. Wilderby's ability to hide her guilt. Perhaps she considered being wasteful during a war as dishonest as not declaring all the Riding purchases to the authorities. In times of scarcity, it was each man for himself. Sophie suspected the authorities had seen an opportunity for a few good meals. She doubted the food would go to waste and understood Mrs. Wilderby's rationale. She nodded her approval and asked no questions. It would be the last tasty roast for a long time, so best to enjoy it.

The walk to the hospital had been a challenge for Sophie. She had to ask Hillary to slow down several times. Her chest felt tight and her limbs heavy but she brushed it off as the remnants of her cold.

Nurse Hogan greeted her with a rare smile. Perhaps their brief conversation had made a difference. "Good morning!" Sophie said in her most cheerful voice. "Who is the first patient today?" The smile disappeared and her cold response told Sophie to get on with the work. The ward was once again overflowing with injured men, including several firemen injured while pulling people from collapsed buildings. A gas pipe had exploded, causing burns. Already feeling weak, the sight of the angry painful wounds made her stomach churn and every time the patient flinched in pain, Sophie gasped. Her mind played tricks. As Nurse Hogan dressed the burns, she saw imaginary flames flare from the wounds. Her reflexes pushed her away from the bed and the vision disappeared

It had been a long morning and, relieved to have a break, Sophie sat in the common room, stirring her tea. Her head spun as she stared into her swirling drink. It had taken all her strength not to run out of the ward. She kept seeing her father's burns in each patient. Finally, she took her own advice and imagined something pleasant. Her eyes closed as she thought of walking along the beach in Bexhill, hearing the crunch of the shingle beach and whoosh of the waves.

"Daydreaming!"

Annoyed at being interrupted, Sophie glared at Nurse Hogan as she sat next to her. "Actually, yes. The beach in Bexhill where I used to work. I need a distraction."

"What happened to you? Why do burns frighten you so

much?"

"Oh, was it obvious? My father died in a fire." It tempted Sophie to ask, 'what happened to make you so cold?'

As though she'd heard her thoughts, Nurse Hogan continued. "Many years ago, after nursing four different patients back to health only to see them all die in as many days, I quit nursing. But, I loved nursing and came back. I shut off any kind of feelings to cope. People think I'm cold but I'm not. It's just my way of coping. Try it, it works."

"I don't think I can do that."

"Well, I suggest you quit nursing." Without another word, Nurse Hogan returned to the ward, her dismissal of Sophie final. The tiny window of tenderness Sophie had seen for a second time had shut tight and she doubted she would ever see it again. What a terrible way to live. But Nurse Hogan's lecture had made her realize quitting was not an option. Controlling her feelings from the past was imperative if she was to be a good nurse.

On her return to the ward, Sister Kay asked to speak to her privately.

"We have a new doctor, a psychiatrist, to help the traumatized patients. He's from the Sealey Hayne Hospital in Devon. Matron has requested that you accompany us on rounds tomorrow morning."

"Why me?"

"Your ability to help soldiers with nightmares and cheer them up has not gone unnoticed. I think Mr. Wainwright mentioned that you were a great help with the soldiers and civilians with war nerves. This doctor specializes in war neurosis."

This news should have been welcome, a way to practice

what she had learned from her studies at the library and an opportunity to learn from an expert. Instead, she felt frightened and guilty, as though secrets would be revealed. *Do I have war neurosis? But I've never been to war. What is happening in London is nothing compared to the battlefield. The burns. Why would I think of my father? That was such a long time ago. I never thought about it while I worked at the hotel. It's probably because I'm not feeling well.*

Sophie tried to push her concerns to one side. "Thank you, Sister. I have been studying shell-shock at the library and find the subject interesting."

Dr. Andrew Cuthbert was an ordinary looking man in his thirties; not particularly handsome, average height, rounded in stature, with straight brown hair and glasses that enhanced his warm brown eyes. Sophie liked him from the beginning. He acknowledged her interest in shell-shock, speaking to her and not down to her, something she found refreshing. He took the time to pull up a chair and talk to patients. His voice soothed their anxieties and his sense of humour often had patients laughing, or at least smiling.

Sophie wished she could be more engaged, but she was not feeling at all well. Her head was wobbling on her neck. She had to concentrate to keep it still and stop the spinning and she struggled to breathe, afraid the wheezing would draw attention. As much as she appreciated Dr. Cuthbert's interest in each patient, she wanted rounds to finish. Finally, they walked back to the nurses' station. Grateful she had stayed upright, she waited for an opportunity to escape to the common room. As she stepped into the hallway, and as much as she willed her body to stay upright, she fell into a deep hole. Her head hit something hard and everything went black.

First she heard whispers. Was she dreaming? She heard her mother, sweet and tender, then her father telling her she was going to be all right. Then it was Carlos calling her name and another tender male voice spoke to Carlos. Her parents disappeared but other voices were still there. She tried to get her bearings, remember something. Her head hurt and wherever she was sounded chaotic. Should she open her eyes or wait until she could remember something?

She heard Carlos. "Sophie, wake up. You've had a nasty fall." She didn't want to wake up. His voice was pleasant and soothing.

"She's stirring," a gentle voice said. It wasn't her mother's but a kind voice nonetheless. "Nurse Romano, can you hear me?"

Now I remember. Rounds with the new doctor. I must have fainted. I feel quite ill and I can't breathe. She tried to cough and a horrible sound came from her chest. Someone lifted her up and she opened her eyes and stared into the deepest, warmest, brown eyes she had ever seen.

She lay on the sofa in the Nurse's Common Room and Carlos placed cushions behind her back. The coughing stopped as she sat up but she was unsure what was happening. Matron sat on the edge of the sofa. "You fainted, probably because of a lung infection. You have a fever and are not fit to work. I'm amazed you didn't tell Mrs. Wilderby. You must have been ill for some time." Sophie detected a slight reprimand which she deserved as she had known ever since the cold that she was not herself.

"The doctors think it advisable that we admit you as a patient and I agree." Matron paused, waiting for a response, but Sophie did not have the strength to argue. "No cause for alarm. Dr. Morgan will advise on treatment for the cough and we need to make sure that the bump on your head heals." Sophie put her hand up to her head. She felt a piece of gauze instead of her nurse's cap and it hurt when she touched it.

Hillary greeted her on the ward as they wheeled her to an empty bed. Dr. Cuthbert gently lifted her onto the bed. The moving made her head spin and she was so hot she had an urge to pull off her uniform. She wanted to giggle, realizing how inappropriate her thoughts were. She must have fainted again because when she opened her eyes, she was in a hospital gown, a cool cloth on her forehead and Hillary at her side.

"Dr. Morgan is on his way to see you. How are you feeling?"

"I feel so poorly. I can't breathe and my head aches. Hillary, what's wrong with me?"

"My opinion, you came back to work too soon after your cold. You are run-down and nature said 'enough.' But the doctor will have better answers. Now, rest."

Dr. Morgan diagnosed a lung infection, resulting from the cold and a mild concussion from the bump on the head. He expressed concern about the high fever.

Sophie remembered little about the next few days. She floated in and out of sleep, or that was what she called it. Her nursing experience told her she was very ill. She didn't care. She just wanted to sleep. The fever was as stubborn as Sophie, lingering for days before it finally broke during the night. Delirious and hallucinating, she tried to get out of bed several times. Trixie sat by her side and Sister finally called Dr. Morgan as the fever reached 104 F. Trixie sponged her down with tepid water, terrified Sophie was going to die.

It had been a long night but Trixie hadn't left her bedside. As the sun was rising, Sophie took a loud gasping breath and was suddenly calm. Trixie panicked and burst into tears just as Sophie opened her eyes. The fever had broken. Dr. Morgan said she was out of danger and Trixie wrapped her arms around her friend, unable to hold back tears. "Don't you ever scare me like that again."

"You are suffocating me," a squeaky weak voice said between coughs.

"I am so glad to hear you speak." Trixie wiped the back of her hand across her wet face. "I'll change your bed. You'll feel better with clean sheets. You need rest and Dr. Morgan prescribed a new cough medicine. I hope it tastes better than it smells." Trixie was speaking to herself. Exhausted, Sophie had fallen into a restful sleep.

Carlos heard the good news in the Doctors' Lounge and came by to say hello. Still weak, Sophie wasn't very talkative and Carlos seemed troubled, as though he had something important to tell her. Sister Kay interrupted their conversation, insisting that there was no medical reason for an orthopaedic surgeon to attend Nurse Romano. Personal visits were not allowed until she was out of danger. Even in her weakened state, Sophie knew that Sister, although sympathetic, was warning Carlos his visits would be construed as inappropriate, breaking hospital rules. As days went by, Sophie hoped Carlos would come back to see her. She wanted to know what was so important. Or did she want to know? She guessed it had something to do with Rosamond. Had Carlos told her the secret about their Italian past? Perhaps he had justified meeting Sophie as a friend. Sophie knew that in Rosamond's shoes she would be suspicious. But of what? It hit her like a bolt of lightning—any future with Carlos was out of the question. He was betrothed to Rosamond and he'd made no attempt to change that. Why was she holding on to a dream that had long since passed? Her thoughts turned to Bill Blaine. Hadn't she done the same thing with him, hanging on to something that didn't belong to her? She had to speak to Carlos and end it now but Sister would not allow him to visit. It would have to wait until she was out of the hospital. She'd write a note and ask Hillary to give it to him.

Dr. Morgan agreed to discharge Sophie early as long as she convalesced at River House under the watchful eye of Mrs. Wilderby. She spent her days helping with household chores and taking short walks to build up her strength. She had not contacted Carlos but now she was well enough to walk to the café, she asked him to meet her for tea. Hillary would be the perfect messenger. Sophie slipped out of River House to meet Hillary as she returned from her shift.

Hillary greeted her with a smile. "You must be feeling better. When can you come back to work?"

"Two more days and I can't wait. I am so bored. There is something I want to do and I need your help."

"Of course. I'm always eager to help. What can I do?"

"Deliver a message to Carlos for me. I have made..." Sophie paused. "What is it?"

"Carlos was called up for service. I thought you knew."

Sophie felt as though someone had kicked her in the stomach. It had not occurred to her they would recruit him. They needed him at home. But orthopaedic surgeons were in high demand in battle zones.

"I haven't seen him. Sister made it clear his visits were inappropriate. I wanted to tell him our friendship, as he calls

192

it, had to end."

"Sometimes things just work out for the best." Hillary put her arm around Sophie's shoulder. "But judging from your face, you don't agree."

"You're right, it is for the best but I wish he'd told me." Sophie sighed. "So, your turn. Do you have any good news?"

"I do. I have a second interview with the university and if that goes well, I start medical school in September."

"Amazing! Does your father know? He must be so proud."

"I'm going home this weekend to tell him. Then I wait for the explosion when my sisters find out Papa spent their inheritance on my education."

"I thought you said your sisters were not aware of your father's money?"

"That's true and Papa assures me they will never find out. It's perhaps a blessing that drawing room talk includes fashion, domestic staff and perhaps even the hardships of war. But ladies would never consider topics such as higher education or medical school to be of interest or relevant to their lives."

"I think your father is a wise man."

21

Worried

Sophie laid her uniform out, ready to start work the next morning, as Trixie dressed, ready for her night shift. "I'm glad to be getting back to work."

"Are you sure you feel well enough? You still look pale," Trixie said.

"Fully recovered, just tired," Sophie said tentatively. Her own doubts showed in her voice and she quickly changed the subject. "Has anything happened while I was away?"

"Not really. I hear Dr. Cuthbert has been working miracles on the Men's Ward. There's a bit of talk about the sudden departure of Mr. Wainwright." Trixie glanced at Sophie. "It seems the army singled him out because of his surgical skills. Did he say anything to you?"

"No, I never heard from him. Hillary told me he'd gone." Yet another conversation she didn't want to have. Despite her resolve to let Carlos go from her life, it hurt that he hadn't tried to see or write to explain they had recruited him. History was repeating itself. She remembered the anguish she'd felt when he'd run off to Italy all those years ago and he couldn't blame his mother this time. She was too hurt to be angry and, if she was honest, she worried about his safety. The Red Cross protected hospital safe zones but was anyone safe in war? Unlike Trixie, she couldn't blindly accept he was going to be okay.

"Have you seen Christopher today?"

"No, he's on an early mission."

Sophie saw a dark shadow cross Trixie face. "What's wrong? You look worried."

"I don't think Chris is being honest with me. He assures me the missions are to take photographs, not combat. They aren't dangerous and I believed him until today when we stopped at the Rose & Crown for luncheon. There was a group of RFC pilots at the next table, not Chris's squadron but he knew the men and called them by name. When Chris went to order our drinks, I overheard them discussing a plane that came down last night."

"Did you ask Chris about it?"

Trixie nodded. "He said it was a different squadron. But why wouldn't he tell me about it?"

"I'm sure there are many squadrons at Beddington Aerodrome. It was probably one of the fighter planes."

"Perhaps. When I met Chris, I thought flying an aeroplane taking photographs was so modern, glamorous and brave…" Trixie hesitated. "I have a bad feeling about these missions."

"Chris is a skilled driver. He'll know how to steer clear of danger."

Trixie laughed at Sophie's description. "Don't let a pilot hear you say driver or steer as if they are driving a car. Pilot's maneuver. Well, I'm off. I hope there are no air raids tonight." Trixie closed the door.

Sleep was slow coming for Sophie. She worried about Trixie and understood her fear for Chris. She thought about Carlos, anger bubbling inside her because she couldn't get him out of her head.

Hillary had the day off for her interview at the university and Sophie slipped into her room to wish her luck before walking to the hospital alone.

Nurse Hogan seemed pleased to see her. "It's good to see you back."

"Thank you. I'll check the patients."

"Dr. Cuthbert is in today as he's treating Mr. Evesham. His chart says neurosis. I thought only women suffered from that complaint. And the young soldier in bed three can't talk. Shirking his duties, no doubt."

Shocked at Nurse Hogan's comments Sophie frowned and wondered if she had misheard. "What did you say?"

Nurse Hogan shrugged her shoulders. "You can read the charts. Now get on with your work."

Dr. Cuthbert arrived for rounds, accompanied by Sister Kay, who beckoned to Sophie to join them.

"Nurse Romano, I'm pleased to see you looking well." Dr. Cuthbert smiled and Sophie felt embarrassed as she caught a glimpse of the same soft, brown eyes she'd seen as she fainted in the common room.

She tried to calm her embarrassment as they walked to Mr. Evesham's bed. "Thank you, for your kindness, Doctor. I am fully recovered."

Mr. Evesham, a man in his fifties, stared at the group through pools of water, unshed tears of fear. Dr. Cuthbert spoke to him with the kindest and gentlest voice Sophie had ever heard. She watched the fear leave the patient and tears trickle down his cheeks as he described the noise of the bomb screeching to reach the street below. How he grabbed his wife's hand and ran as people scattered. But some got caught in the explosion. As he spoke the last sentence, the fear returned.

"Nurse, screens please. I'd like to speak with Mr. Evesham in private."

Ten minutes later, Dr. Cuthbert moved on to the young soldier but there was no response to his words. The soldier listened and wrote his answers on a small pad with the doctor replying verbally. Dr. Cuthbert shook his head. "Poor fellow. I can't treat him here. I am requesting they transfer him to a psychiatric hospital."

Curious about what had caused the soldier's condition, Sophie wanted to ask the doctor more about the patient. She had read about sudden speech loss after explosions on the battlefield but this was the first time she'd seen it. But she was a nurse in training and it would be inappropriate for her to speak to a doctor. Dr. Cuthbert wrote notes on the charts and left the ward.

Nurse Hogan had her righteous hat on and Sophie, not feeling her best, was tiring of orders and unkind comments towards the soldier. Sister Kay must have noticed it too because a heated conversation was taking place at the nurses' desk. Sister, normally pleasant and calm even when reprimanding, appeared agitated. Nurse Hogan was arguing, her tone close to shouting. Judging by the glances towards the soldier, the argument was to do with Private Lang. This will not end well, Sophie thought. Nurses, even senior nurses, do not argue with Sister. Sophie sensed tension but not because of the argument, she thought it might even have caused it. She suspected it had to do with the war and its consequences taking a toll on everyone. Too many patients, overworked nurses and tragic happenings, whether in London or overseas. She glanced at Mr. Evesham, a broken man and then at Private Lang, a young man's future destroyed. She had never expected to find war in London. When would it end?

Keeping her eye on the nurses' desk, it surprised Sophie to see Trixie standing in the doorway, looking frantic and waving.

"Trixie, what is it?"

"Chris didn't pick me up this morning. He always meets me as he comes off shift and drives me to River House. I tried to telephone Beddington Aerodrome but they just said Chris was not available. I'm not a relative so they won't tell me anything. I am worried. It doesn't feel right.

"We all have bad feelings these days. Perhaps his squadron is on a different mission. He has to follow orders and can't contact you. He might have left a message at River house. Go home and get some rest."

"I hadn't thought of that. Of course, he'd leave a message with Mrs. Wilderby. See you later."

Sophie hated the not knowing and fully understood how Trixie was feeling. It didn't feel good. The war had been escalating for some time and she had never thought flying over Germany taking pictures was a safe occupation. She wanted to take a break and have a cup of tea but judging by the looks-can-kill glance she received from Nurse Hogan, the argument with Sister had not ended well.

Tired, Sophie headed to River House. She was pleased to be away from the stress and tension of the hospital and

Nurse Hogan, whose temperament had turned nasty as the day progressed. She was looking forward to hearing about Hillary's interview, hoping for good news. Before she even opened the front door, more tension greeted her as she remembered her talk with Trixie.

Trixie lay on her bed, staring at the ceiling, her eyes red and face pale. Sophie closed the bedroom door. "No news about Chris?"

"Nobody will speak to me because I'm not a relative. I called his house but Lady Belingham was not available and the butler knew nothing. At least he was kind enough to suggest I call later."

"Isn't that good news. A sign he's all right?"

"So where is he? Even if he's on a mission, he would be back by now. Its twenty-four hours since he left."

Sophie could think of nothing more to say. She suspected the worst and figured it must take time to confirm if a pilot was missing or had been killed. They would notify the family first and not Trixie.

Biting her tongue, Sophie spoke with as much cheer as she could muster. "No news is good news. If something terrible had happened, you would know by now. I'm sure there is an explanation. If you haven't heard by tomorrow, I'll help you find some answers." She had no idea what she was going to do. Perhaps a white lie was called for, a telephone call on behalf of the Belingham family. She'd deal with that in the morning. At that moment, she wanted to find Hillary.

Hillary sat alone in the Common Room looking pleased. She looked up as Sophie entered. "I think I got in. The interview went well. They asked me all kinds of medical questions and I'm sure they did it on purpose, not expecting me to know the answers. I actually wanted to laugh as they talked about female sensibilities."

"What did you say?"

"I gave them a detailed description of dressing the most disgusting open wounds. One pompous fellow turned quite green." Hillary's imitation of the man's expression made them both laugh.

"What other sensibilities did you clarify?"

"Well, without blushing, I described bathing a man. Because I'm sure one sensibility was seeing a naked man. I was a bit naughty and made more of it. I thought one old bald-headed gentleman might have a heart attack."

"Can you imagine him telling his wife?" Giggles bordering on hysterics erupted.

"These gentlemen do not understand anything about nursing. I answered all their questions so they cannot say I didn't pass the interview. Then they made a big thing about the cost of medical school, implying that I couldn't afford it."

"Did you tell them to contact your father?"

"I didn't need to. Papa must have expected it because he sent me a letter and one from his banker. I still sensed their reluctance to admit a woman. Matron says they have no choice but to accept me as the university needs the money. The school is struggling with low enrolment. She said there are three women like myself so if I get in, I'll have company."

"This is exciting. I am sure you'll get in." Sophie chuckled at her inner thoughts.

"What's so funny?" Hillary said puzzled. "My father's forethought?"

"Oh goodness no, I was thinking about the interview panel. A green pompous gentleman, a shocked bald gentleman, all

trying to explain to their wives how nurses had no sensibilities." The hysterical laughter brought Mrs. Wilderby scurrying
from the kitchen.

Sophie had an early breakfast, checked the hallstand for
messages, put on her hat and coat and hurried to the hospital.
She was hoping to see Chris waiting for Trixie in the hospital
lobby but when she arrived, the lobby was empty. She
checked with the porter for any messages—nothing. Taking a
deep breath, she braced herself to meet Trixie in the Nurses'
Common Room.

She didn't have to wait long before a hopeful looking Trixie
entered. "Any messages?"

Sophie shook her head and saw rivers of tears on Trixie's
cheeks and said, "Cheer up, I've worked it out. We'll call the
aerodrome and say we are calling on behalf of the Belingham
family."

"What if they find out? It would upset Chris's mother and
she doesn't like me much."

"The call could be anonymous. We'll use a fake name. How
would they find out it was us?"

"What if they didn't believe us?"

"Do you want to know where he is? It's been two days.
Someone has to know something."

"We can't telephone from here. Someone will see us."

Before Sophie could answer yet another objection, the
porter put his head round the door. "Nurse King, there's a
gentleman to see you." He smiled at her. "You seemed anxious
so I thought I'd let you know. He said it's urgent."

"Oh, is it bad news? Has something happened to Chris?"

The porter looked puzzled, "I don't think so. It's a young fellow in uniform. I've seen him before."

Trixie flew out of the room, her feet not even touching the floor. By the time Sophie reached the lobby, Trixie was in Chris's arms.

22

Trixie and Chris

Trixie could not let him go. She clung to him, feeling the rough wool surge of his uniform scratching her wet cheeks and his words of comfort, music in her ears. She breathed in the smell of cheap army soap which she had hated and now loved. He gently pried her arms from their grip round his shoulders. "I haven't got much time. We have a debriefing later this morning, but I had to see you."

"Debriefing! What happened?" Thinking the worst, Trixie panicked. "Are you hurt?" She stepped back, looking for injuries. Seeing no sign of cuts or bruises, she suddenly felt a burst of anger and slapped his arm. "You scared me half to death. Where have you been for two days?"

He held her hand and squeezed it until it hurt, his face taught. "I had the scare of my life but I'm okay. Get in the auto and I'll tell you on the drive to River house. I might not be able to meet you for a few days. It's absolute chaos at the base and I have to get back."

Trixie wanted to be mad. Her insides hurt from worrying and her throat was sore and tight from crying. She knew something else was coming and that feeling of not knowing was going to be front and centre for a long time. All she wanted to know was what had happened to him in the last two days.

"The worst feeling was the not knowing," she said.

Chris gently pressed his fingers to her lips. "I understand, but there are things I can't tell you. The missions have changed. When we get orders, we have to go. We don't know where or for how long. We have been lucky so far, but from now on I won't be able to see you as often and we might have to wait until I get leave."

"How will I know that you are safe? Your mother won't tell me. I telephoned. She wouldn't talk to me. The butler was kind but he knew nothing either."

"My mother knows less than you do and the only news she would get would be bad news. Trixie, we are not courting in the drawing rooms. We are at war and the not knowing is all part of war. I promise you I'll stay safe. If you don't hear from me, it is because I'm following orders and fighting the war."

Trixie wished they were courting in the normal way, although she thought the drawing room analogy was a bit old-fashioned. Life was anything but normal. She loved him and wanted to be with him.

"How can I live, not knowing where you are? I hate this war."

He parked the car outside River House and placed his hand under her chin. "It's hard, but it has to be this way. I will come and see you as often as I can and if I can't come in person, I will write." Chris pulled her into his arms. "I love you so much. I hate being apart."

"Please stay safe, I love you and want to be..." Her words were muffled under a kiss she wanted to go on forever. In the middle of the kiss she realized he had not told her what had frightened him. She took a deep breath and pushed him away. "What scared you so?"

Stunned at the question, Chris stared at her, gathering his thoughts which were still attached to the intense kiss. "I beg your pardon? Who said I was scared?"

"You did! When you first picked me up. You said something frightened you on the mission."

"My last flight." Chris paused, sucking in air as though it would speak for him. "As we approached our target, I saw a blast of bright orange light." He paused again, letting air out of his lungs. "I pulled into a steep climb as high as the plane could go and headed back to Beddington. The engine sputtered and was on the verge of stalling. I've never prayed so hard in my life and I stayed airborne. I saw the white cliffs of Dover and in the light of dawn, made a bumpy landing in a farmer's field." He started laughing.

"Stop laughing. This isn't funny!" Trixie felt tears on her cheeks, angry with him for the danger and the laughter.

Chris wrapped his arms around her. "I'm safe and the reason I'm laughing is that the story isn't over. I got out of the aeroplane, thanking the Lord for saving me and suddenly there's a rifle pointed at me. I thrust my hands in the air. Had I landed in enemy territory? But knowing I had crossed the Channel, I called out Royal Flying Corps and my name, rank and number."

"Who was it?"

"A farmer had seen me flying low and thought I was a German. As soon as I convinced him I was British, he was all over me with apologies and took me to the farmhouse. His wife fed me a monster breakfast and I fell asleep on their couch."

"Why didn't you telephone?" Trixie pouted, relieved he was safe, but annoyed she had worried when he was actually eating breakfast in a farmhouse.

"They didn't have a telephone. People like you and me forget that most ordinary people don't have telephones. The nearest phone was Maidstone, ten miles away, and the only mode of transport a tractor."

"You rode on a tractor for ten miles? You could have walked it faster."

"No, the farmer didn't have petrol but I had an idea and went back to the aircraft. The field was long enough to take off and I hoped I had enough fuel. I took a chance that the stalling was because of the sudden climb. It worked and I limped back to base with about an eggcup of fuel to spare."

"That is quite a story. I wished I'd known what was happening. But I suppose no one knew until you arrived back."

"The chaps were thrilled to see me. It was exciting. Being so scared was a great feeling. Trixie, I know a way to stop you worrying about me. Will you marry me? If you are my wife, you will be my next of kin, not my mother."

"I already said yes. We're planning the wedding. You are not making sense."

"Let's run away and get married. Elope. We can keep it a secret, except for my commanding officer. But he's a good chap he'd keep quiet; I know him very well," Chris had a strange look about him as he gave a wry grin.

Trixie flipped her head to one side, "Is there something you're not telling me?"

"No, nothing I'm just lucky to have a great commanding

officer," Chris grinned again, "Our mothers can plan the big wedding for next year. I don't think there is any rule about getting married twice to the same person."

"What do we have to do?"

"Leave it to me. I have to go."

Chris waved as he drove off, blowing kisses. Trixie could hardly contain her excitement. This was a hard secret to keep but it felt special to have something that belonged only to her and Chris. Perhaps she should think it through though. Marriage was a big step but bringing the date forward in secret was romantic. She wasn't sure about hospital rules and married women but she might not qualify to serve overseas in the war. *I'll think about that if the time comes. I just want to get married.*

Having trouble keeping the smile off her face and afraid someone might guess their secret and try to stop them, Trixie declined breakfast and retired to her room.

Six days passed and there were no visits from Chris. Heeding his words, Trixie tried not to worry, but each day it got harder. The newspapers reported German aeroplanes in the skies over London but not much about British aeroplanes. Once again, she was trying to cope with the not knowing. It was the morning of her night off. Usually, after breakfast, she'd get a couple of hours' sleep and then enjoy being awake during daylight hours. But her increasing anxiety prevented her from sleeping. She stood at the parlour window watching for the postman, sensing there would be a letter. Seeing the postman walking along the street, she opened the door and grabbed the post from his hands, apologizing. The postman smiled. This was not unusual behaviour for young women waiting to hear from a sweetheart. Miss Beatrix King. The name jumped out at her as she ripped the envelope open and, reading, went to her room.

My dearest Trixie,

How are you my darling? I hope you haven't worried about me? Sorry I took so long to write. The squadron is flying every night and it is intense, not the leisurely flying and taking photographs I'm used to. I am able to use my flying skills and I'm enjoying it but, by the time we get back to base, I'm exhausted.

I have good news and not so good news. The bad news is that they do not allow us off the base unless we have leave, so I can't visit you. But the good news is that our marriage plans are in motion. Soon we will be husband and wife. I like the sound of that: Mrs. Christopher Belingham....

Trixie giggled, scanning the rest of the letter and repeating under breath, "Beatrix Belingham, Mrs. Christopher Belingham. It has a nice ring to it."

Pleased it was her day off she replied to his letter, sealed the envelope and walked to the postbox. Stopping at the café for tea, she wished Chris was sitting across from her. But soon she would be Chris's wife and that made her feel better.

Content that Chris had written and she had detected no fear of danger on his part, Trixie waited for the next letter. She didn't have to wait long. On the following Friday, the postman delivered a second one.

My dearest Trixie,

In great haste, so can't write much. I have special leave for Tuesday and Wednesday. Almost two days. I have to be back on base by six o'clock Wednesday evening. I will pick you up Tuesday morning so pack a small bag, ask for Tuesday night off and tell Mrs. Wilderby you won't be home Tuesday night. We are getting married at noon on Tuesday. I can't wait for you to be my wife. I adore you.

Love always,
Chris

A sense of guilt tempered Trixie's excitement. What excuse could she find to be away all night? Asking for Tuesday off was not a problem. She'd switch with another nurse. But telling Mrs. Wilderby she would be away overnight without a reason was a problem. She thought about asking Sophie to help. She could trust Sophie to keep her secret, but what could she do? Make a fake telephone call about a sick relative? That would not be convincing. Perhaps simple is best. I'll tell Mrs. Wilderby I want to visit home on my day off and will stay the night. I could let her assume the chauffeur is picking me up from the hospital on Tuesday morning.

The arrangements confirmed, she switched her day off and Mrs. Wilderby didn't ask questions. Trixie told her she would visit her parents on Tuesday night, returning Wednesday evening. In her letter of reply to Chris, she asked him to meet her on the side street around the corner from the hospital's main entrance. A precaution in case someone saw them driving away together.

Trixie's excitement was palpable on Monday evening as she packed a bag. Sophie sat on her bed reading and watched.

"New nightdress. That is gorgeous." Sophie felt the soft chiffon fabric. "Don't you have any clothes at home?"

"I just felt like something new."

"New dress too? Let me see? It looks fancy."

"I've folded it in tissue paper. Mother is giving a special dinner party tomorrow." Trixie quickly folded the tissue paper around the white taffeta dress. It was definitely a wedding gown with delicate pearls embroidered around the neckline.

"What's so special about the dinner? More wedding plans? Your mother is rather enthusiastic."

Trixie's heart jumped into her throat at the mention of wedding plans and she almost told her the secret. But Chris had been adamant that no one should know. She surmised he didn't want to face his mother. It was no secret that his mother did not approve of the match and hoped Chris would tire of Trixie in the year before the official wedding. If she found out they were eloping, she would definitely stop them. Trixie's mind was gathering speed, running through all the things that could either stop them or even why she shouldn't go ahead with it. Was she having second thoughts? She dispelled any doubts and imagined Chris standing at the altar saying 'I do.' It occurred to her that she didn't even know where they were getting married.

"Wish me luck!" Trixie grabbed Sophie and gave her a hug. "I'll see you Wednesday night." She closed the bedroom door

Sophie stared at the door, puzzled. What was so special about this visit home. Derogatory comments about an overbearing mother and a dismissive father usually accompanied packing to go home but Trixie had said nothing. Sophie giggled, wondering if Trixie and Chris were off to Brighton for an illicit weekend.

23

Dr. Cuthbert

Another night was spent in the cellar, listening to explosions and feeling the ground tremble. Sophie thanked the Lord the bombs had missed River House but prayed for where they had landed. The Zeppelin attacks had lessened but attacks from small aeroplanes increased. Nasty-flying-killing-machines, too small for early detection, swooped in and dropped their lethal bombs before the artillery could shoot at them. The scouts' warning whistles were useless. Even the fire brigade's rockets were often too late. Sophie wanted to cry, knowing it would be a busy and miserable day on the ward.

The all clear sounded as daylight filtered into the cellar and the smell of burning wafted on the stairs as they climbed out of the cellar. It was a natural reflex to look out of the window, afraid of what might be revealed on the street. But the houses were intact and the street looked surprisingly normal. Stifling yawns, Sophie sat at the dining room table. It was too early to get dressed and too late to go back to bed. Some had elected to grab a few winks of sleep, leaving Sophie and Mrs. Wilderby the only ones sipping hot, satisfying tea.

"You look tired, Mrs. Wilderby. Can you rest during the day?" Sophie asked, seeing deep lines of worry on the older woman's forehead. She realized she knew very little about Mrs. Wilderby or her family and the pale face and worry lines were probably for loved ones.

"No rest for me. Too much to do." As if she had read Sophie's thoughts, she added, "I have a grandson. Too young to be a soldier, for which I'm grateful, but he and his mother, my daughter, help in the air raids."

"And raids like last night worry you. I'm sure they will be all right. It never occurred to me that you had a family."

"You girls are my family. My daughter doesn't speak to me. We had a fight when Tommy was eight. That was six years ago. I was too stubborn to make up and now it's too late."

"I'm sorry to hear that." Sophie wanted to ask her more but the hurt in Mrs. Wilderby's face stopped her.

"So what about you? You are mature and confident for your age but cultured in your manners and speech. Why were you working in a hotel?"

"My parents are both dead. My mother died of a fever and my father died in a fire. My father was grooming me to take over his business—the son he never had." She smiled at the memory. "I loved him very much and miss him even now. I lost everything after my father died. The bailiff took it all except for the villa in Lucca, Italy. It's probably in ruins now. I haven't been there in years."

"Oh, Sophie. Were there no other relatives to take care of you?" Mrs. Wilderby patted her hand. Hearing her use her Christian name almost brought Sophie to tears.

"No, my aunt and uncle ran the farm in Italy but they were

murdered. Our butler took care of me and found the maid's job at the Sackville Hotel. You are the closest person I've had to a mother since I was twelve."

Mrs. Wilderby blushed slightly as her eyes caught Sophie's. "Thank you. I mother you girls because I didn't mother my own daughter. I'm trying to make amends."

"What happened?"

"I was in service. I fell in love with the master's spoiled, entitled son. We had an affair and when I was with child, the duke fired me without references. My mother, a kind soul, took me in. My father would have nothing to do with me. A disgrace to the family were his words, now permanently engraved in my head. To avoid scandal, they raised Dotty as their daughter. I found work in a manor house and my daughter always thought we were sisters. When Ma died, I told Dotty the truth and she hasn't spoken to me since."

"If it's any consolation, you are a wonderful mother. When I was ill with the cold and fever, you cared for me as my mother would have done."

Mrs. Wilderby's eyes moistened. "Enough of that, You're making me teary. Here, off to your room, young lady, and get dressed or you'll be late for your shift. I'll get on and make breakfast."

Ambulances lined up at the casualty entrance but it surprised Sophie that the route to work was clear. The bombing had been close to the other side of the hospital and some windows had shattered on the lower level. Pulsating fear filled the entrance as the porter greeted her. "It'll be a tough day today, Nurse Romano. Nurse King already left. Must have been meeting that young officer, but I didn't see him this morning. A grand couple they are."

Sophie replied, "Yes, they are." She had forgotten about Trixie. She must have had a terrible night with the patients. At least the nurse who replaced Mavis was a good worker. She thought about the porter's comment, 'a grand couple,' and once again wondered what they were up to. A wry smile spread to her cheeks as she joined Nurse Hogan.

"Looking pleased with yourself this morning," Nurse Hogan spat the words out. "We have new patients to care for and Private Lang has kept the ward up all night, according to Sister."

"Poor man. The air raid would terrify him. I imagine the air raid kept everyone up. It was close to the hospital."

Nurse Hogan shrugged. "More fuss than necessary, no doubt."

Biting her tongue, Sophie moved away to see Private Lang. "How are you today?" When he didn't reply, Sophie touched his arm and he turned to look at her. "Can you hear me, Private Lang?" He nodded and took the pad and pencil. His hands shook so badly he had trouble writing one word. 'Scared'.

"I understand. It was a nasty air raid last night. But it's over now and you are all right." He nodded and his mouth lifted slightly. He wrote 'Thanks' on his pad.

"Take it easy, soldier. I'll be back to bathe you." Sophie collected a bowl of warm water, pulled the screen around and gently washed his face and arms before letting him rest on fresh pillows. Before Sophie pulled the screens back, he was fast asleep.

Putting the screens away, she almost tripped over Dr. Cuthbert. "I'm sorry, Doctor, I wasn't paying attention.

Private Lang just went to sleep. I don't think he slept at all last night."

"No, he'd be agitated with the air raid. You have a gentle manner with shell-shocked patients Nurse..." he paused. "Sorry, I've forgotten your name. I'll leave him to sleep and come back later."

"Romano, Sophie Romano,"

"Well, Nurse Sophie Romano, I'd like you to come with me to see Mr. Evesham. A different case, but definitely war neurosis which I can treat. We assume neurosis is limited to the battlefield, but it is not. I'm experiencing more of it here in London. Ordinary people are seeing their loved ones injured before their eyes."

Nurse Hogan had joined them and literally pushed in between Sophie and the doctor. "Nurse Hogan, I'm pleased you joined us. It is extremely important to treat patients with a diagnosis of neurosis seriously." There was no mistaking the tone of his words to Nurse Hogan. No doubt Sister had apprised Dr. Cuthbert of Nurse Hogan's lack of empathy towards patients suffering war neurosis.

"Patients suffering from any form of neurosis need gentle and understanding care. Nurse Romano has studied this condition and has a natural ability to empathize with patients. You would be wise to follow her lead." Dr. Cuthbert's tone warned of consequences. Sophie shivered, anticipating unpleasant repercussions from Nurse Hogan. A skilled and experienced nurse being asked to learn from a nurse in training was a mistake on the doctor's part. Albeit, his concern for his patients and observation of Nurse Hogan's lack of empathy was valid. Her skill as a senior nurse with a matter-of-fact and precise attitude towards patients was commendable and deserved respect. However, without empathy for the mentally ill patients, Sophie doubted she would get it from Dr. Cuthbert.

Sophie felt flattered by the doctor's comments and wondered how he knew she had studied war nerves. She wanted to ask questions but she wasn't sure how to approach him. Later that day she bumped into him again, almost falling flat on her back in the hallway, his strong arms catching her a second time.

"Nurse Sophie Romano, at least one of us needs to watch where we are going."

Sophie stood upright, her cheeks flushing feverishly, but not with illness. "I should apologize. I was not watching where I was going."

"You are too kind. Let us each take blame. I must say, it is a pleasure to bump into you. I'm on my way to see Private Lang. Would you join me?"

"My shift is over so the duty nurse can help you." She paused, wanting to ask about war nerves and shell-shock treatment.

"Is there something you wanted to ask me?"

"I'm interested in talking to you about war neurosis." Sophie held her breath as it was inappropriate to speak to a doctor and could warrant a reprimand from Sister or Matron.

"I heard you study at the library. Might I suggest you read Carl Jung's books? He's a Swiss psychoanalyst and researches dreams among other things. Not specifically related to the war but his findings on how the mind works are fascinating."

"How did you know about my interest in illnesses of the mind?"

"I'm acquainted with Mr. Wainwright and he suggested I seek you out. He speaks highly of you. They whipped him off to France. I'm not surprised, he is an accomplished surgeon."

Sophie felt her body stiffen at Carlos' name and even a hint of annoyance that he would discuss her with a stranger. But it clarified that his feeling towards her were professional and she had to accept that fact.

"Carlos, Mr. Wainwright, and I have been friends for many years." Sophie was trying to sound nonchalant. "I am interested in the human mind and the effects of war. I will ask the librarian about Carl Jung. Now, if you'll excuse me, I have to leave."

Desperate to get outside and cool off in the fresh air, Sophie wondered if she was attracted to Dr. Cuthbert or was it hearing Carlos's name? "Be professional," she whispered to herself. "Neither of these men are interested in you and you don't have time for romance."

She stopped abruptly at the door, surprised at the thick fog swirling around her.

"Need company?" Hillary asked, pulling her scarf around her face.

"Yes, I hate walking in fog. It's creepy."

"I have some news. We'll be working together again."

"That is good news."

"What's going on in the Men's Ward? I'm curious as I have to report to Sister Kay tomorrow morning."

"Did they say why?"

"Nurse Hogan is being transferred to my job in the operating room."

"I am so relieved. She'll do well in theatre. She's precise with instruments but not good with patients." Sophie told Hillary about Dr. Cuthbert and rejoiced at not having to put up with 'that woman' on a daily basis. She suspected Nurse Hogan would try to seek revenge for Dr. Cuthbert's comments.

A thick fog had descended on London and Sophie was pleased to have Hillary's company as they walked to River house, barely seeing a hand in front of them. The smell of Cook's beef and barley stew greeted them with a cheerful Mrs. Wilderby setting the table.

"We'll get a good night's sleep tonight girls. The Germans won't fly in this pea-souper."

"I will never complain about fog again," Sophie said. "You are cheerful tonight."

Mrs. Wilderby glanced over her shoulder, making sure no one could hear. "I heard from a friend who lives near my daughter. They are fine and she said my grandson asked if I was alright."

"I'm happy for you. Maybe Tommy will come and see you?"

"That's what I thought. Perhaps I might be forgiven." A hopeful smile brightened her face.

"Hold on to that thought, Mrs. Wilderby." The smell of dinner had brought everyone to the table ending the conversation.

The fog persisted through the night and next day and only lifted slightly the next evening. Sophie heard Trixie arrive back later than expected due to the fog and listened to Mrs. Wilderby gave her a stern talking to her for not allowing extra time.

Trixie burst into the bedroom, giggling. She threw her bag on the bed and jumped up beside it, sitting cross-legged and glowing like a beacon.

"Am I to assume the weekend was a success? And judging by your glow, I don't think you visited your parents."

"I did, we did," Trixie opened her bag and pretended to

search for something, guilt written all over her face. She jumped off the bed turned her back on Sophie before changing into her uniform.

"Trixie, I don't believe you and you are bursting to tell me something. Did you go to Brighton and stay in a hotel?" Sophie paused as she saw the chain around Trixie's neck. "Is that new?"

"We went to Brighton. How did you guess? But we did nothing wrong." Trixie undid the top button on her uniform and held up a gold ring threaded through the chain. "We got married. Please don't tell a soul. Chris would kill me if he knew I told you. He's terrified his mother will find out."

Stunned, Sophie had trouble gathering her thoughts. "Married, wow. I didn't expect that. I had an idea you were not going to your parents. Why get married? Your parents will find out soon enough."

"Chris wanted me to be his next of kin and we just didn't want to wait. Nobody knows, and the wedding plans for next year will go ahead so our mothers can keep planning. I'll keep nursing and the secret is ours, except for you and Chris's commanding officer."

"That's quite a secret. So where did you get married? What about reading the banns?"

"Chris made the arrangements with a little church near Brighton. We're both over the age of twenty-one so no parents' consent and nobody asked questions. Chris bought me a bouquet of pink roses and I wore this dress." She spread the white taffeta dress on the bed. "Now you know why I didn't want you to see it when I was packing."

"It's beautiful. And after the wedding?"

"Chris booked a room at the Grand Hotel." Trixie blushed,

"We slept in the same bed and it was wonderful."

"Did you…?" Sophie was dying to ask for details but decided not to.

"Yes, of course we did. It was our wedding night."

"What happens if you get pregnant?"

"We took precautions." Trixie yawned. "I don't know how I'll get through my shift tonight."

"It's quiet. No air raid last night and, if the fog stays, there won't be one tonight. Married. I can't believe you're married."

24

Close to Home

The big oak doors swung open into the serene silence and the library scent filled Sophie with joy as it always did. Today she looked forward to finding out more about Carl Jung. A young woman Sophie hadn't seen in the library before stood behind the tall counter and gave her a strange look when she asked for the author by name.

"You do know who he is?" she said with an accusatory tone.

"He's a psychiatrist. Dr. Cuthbert at the hospital recommended I read his book the Psychology of the Unconscious."

The woman leaned in and lowered her whispering voice. "He's Swiss and is in charge of the British internment camp for British officers. Some say he's working for the Germans. I wanted to remove the books."

"But Switzerland is a neutral country."

"I wouldn't trust anyone in charge of one of those camps. The original book was written in German and later translated to English. You'd better be careful of that doctor friend too. There are spies everywhere and they play with your mind, especially psycho... what's-it doctors. I have just read about it.

Shocking it is. Shocking!"

"Thank you. I'll bear that in mind, but I will take the book, please." Sophie stifled a grin at this young woman's drama. Spies were everywhere, everyone knew that, but her ignorance and need for melodrama eliminated any concern Sophie might have about Carl Jung. Although it was true that any hint of German raised eyebrows.

Sophie chose a table in the corner where she could study and be alone. Despite her early confidence, she hid the reading, which was fascinating, especially an article about dreams. Carl Jung actually had a premonition about the war in a dream. Engrossed in her reading Sophie was unaware of her surroundings.

"I see you took my advice."

She jumped out of her chair, slapping her hand against her chest and gasping for breath. "Dr. Cuthbert, you scared me half to death." A couple of shushes from fellow patrons made her lower her voice. "I was immersed in Dr. Jung's theory."

Sophie sat and Dr. Cuthbert settled next to her. She felt his warm breath on her cheeks as he whispered, "My apologies. That was thoughtless of me."

Her breathing eased back to normal, although her heart throbbed from the closeness of her uninvited companion. She wondered if Carl Jung's research could explain her reaction, but she suspected it was nothing more than his kindness.

"Apology accepted, Dr. Cuthbert."

"Please call me Andrew." Another hissing sound meant to stop them talking came from the librarian. "Would you like a cup of tea? There's a café around the corner."

Sophie nodded but felt uncomfortable using his Christian name. She packed her books into her satchel. Dr. Cuthbert,

Andrew, took the satchel from her and carried it as they walked to the café. They talked at some length about soldiers and shell-shock and how the military dismissed the condition, forcing the men to return to the battlefield. An hour later, they parted ways. Dr. Cuthbert returned to the hospital and Sophie walked to River house. Quite taken with Dr. Andrew Cuthbert, she was aware that above anything it was his gentleness and kindness that appealed to her. Often skeptical of kindness, Sophie waited for people to show their mean side, but Dr. Cuthbert appeared genuine.

Glancing up at the sky, blue and clear, she felt fortified after the thick damp fog. But it also meant air raids. The Huns would be back.

Mrs. Wilderby was setting the dinner table and humming *If you Were the Only Girl in the World*, a catchy new song Sophie had heard many times. Even she remembered the words and sang. The singing got louder as nurses arrived for dinner until a harmonious chorus rang out from the dining room. Sophie wondered if the joyous singing was masking thoughts of more bombs that were to come as the sun set and darkness crept over London. She shuddered, cursing her sense of intuition, and thought about Carl Jung's premonition of war.

Trixie, usually oblivious of the dangers of war, seemed quiet and morose. She lay on her bed, staring at the ceiling while Sophie sat at the desk, reading.

"Did you know that Matron is selecting nurses to go to France and Belgium? The War Department has acknowledged the need for female nurses."

"No, I didn't know. Is she looking for volunteers? I want to go. That's why I became a nurse. I want to nurse soldiers."

"You're strange. Who wants to go to war? The conditions

are terrible."

"Who told you?"

"Emily. She said Sister told her she was on Matron's list with three other nurses and she thinks it might be us and Hillary."

"But we're only nurses in training."

"I don't want to go. I'd be away from Chris. Not that I'll see much of him. He's no longer allowed off the base without permission or leave." Trixie wound her hair in a roll and pinned it tight. "I have to go. I'll see what I can find out tonight."

The thought of getting to Belgium or France felt exciting and Sophie closed her books, unable to concentrate and ready for bed. She fell into a light sleep until she heard rockets, a warning the Germans were coming. Feet clattered on the stairs as the house woke up. Sophie got fully dressed, which was unusual as she had a thick dressing gown that shielded her from the cold and damp of the cellar. She wondered what had prompted her to dress. Was it a premonition? She pondered Carl Jung's writing and if it was having an adverse effect on her judgment. Filling her head with… what? She didn't know. Being aware of her own premonitions, she found it comforting that someone of Dr. Jung's expertise had similar experiences. Having stopped to dress, Sophie was the last on the cellar stairs. The makeshift cots were all occupied and Hillary made room for her on a large overstuffed easy chair, long abandoned by the upstairs sitting room.

A rumbling overhead made everyone look to the ceiling and then the ground trembled beneath their feet. The first bomb had landed, followed by a succession of rumblings getting closer. Listening, waiting, the fear palpable as they anticipated a direct hit and prayed it would miss. Thankfully, the rumblings grew further apart and farther away. The nervous chatter calmed into conversation, followed by yawns and eventually the rhythmic breathing of sleep.

The eerie silence had lasted for what seemed like hours. Sophie strained her ears for the sound of approaching aeroplanes while Hillary leaned against her, relaxed in sleep. She closed her eyes but opened them immediately, afraid to doze off. The silence played into her intuition. She didn't want premonitions to persist in her dreams. She frowned. If there were no bombs, why couldn't she hear the all clear?

Mrs. Wilderby glanced her way and whispered, "Would you like a cup of tea?" Sophie nodded, realizing that Mrs. Wilderby didn't sleep in the cellar. She watched and nurtured her charges. Several heads popped up from dozing, nodding for tea.

"I forgot the tea caddy." Mrs. Wilderby stood up, picking her way around sleeping bodies and before anyone could stop her, she climbed the stairs.

Sophie remembered hearing the drone of an engine and a strange whistling sound. She screamed for Mrs. Wilderby to come back when a massive explosion blackened everything. A strong smell of vinegar burnt her nostrils and she heard Hillary's voice. "Don't move the preserve cupboard fell off the wall, shattered pickle jars are everywhere." Someone lit a candle and they moved to the other side of the cellar. Sophie looked to the cellar stairs where she had last seen Mrs. Wilderby. The door to the cellar had blasted off its hinges and lay halfway down the stairs. A limp arm hung from under the door. Mrs. Wilderby was trapped.

Sophie and Hillary ran up the stairs and tried to lift the door. Sophie stroked Mrs. Wilderby's hair. "Hang on. We'll get you out of here." Tears streaming down her face, Sophie frantically tried to take the weight of the door off Mrs. Wilderby but it was hopeless. They couldn't move it.

A voice from the upper floor yelled, "is everybody okay down there?"

"We need help!" Hillary called out.

A hint of dawn shadowed the silhouette of a young volunteer in a helmet standing at the top of the stairs. "I'll get help." The man returned with two others and a crowbar. The men struggled to move the door upwards and away from Mrs. Wilderby's limp body. Hillary took her wrist, looking for a pulse and slowly shook her head. Sophie cradled Mrs. Wilderby's head, searching for life. She was twelve years old again, watching her mother die. The grief paralyzed her and she couldn't move or cry or speak. Hillary steered her to the back of the cellar as the young men lifted the body off the stairs. The silence was broken by the all clear bugle and sobbing nurses, the reality of war hitting them hard.

Dawn broke and a bright sun had the audacity to shine on such a terrible day. The young man gave Sophie a soft smile. She shook her head as she looked into Mrs. Wilderby's eyes. My mind is playing tricks, she thought. Walking along the hall, she turned suddenly and said, "Is your name Tommy?"

"Yes, ma'am."

"Your grandmother was a wonderful woman."

The young man's face brightened with recognition for a second and then twisted into grief as he quietly wept. Sophie reached out to him. "I am so sorry. She loved you and your mother very much."

"I know. My mum was ready to make amends and now it's too late."

"War does that to people. She was proud of you and the work you do."

"Thank you. I'll make arrangements to…" he paused, "claim the body. We'll give her a nice burial."

"She would like that." She watched Tommy brush the back of his hand against his face as he joined his colleagues and got back to work. A good example, Sophie thought, and with Hillary's help, she organized the house. First, they sent a message to the hospital to say they would be late and another to Matron about Mrs. Wilderby. The house was not damaged. The angle of the bomb had blown out the back door that faced the cellar, forcing the cellar door off its hinges. It was terribly bad luck that Mrs. Wilderby had gone to get the tea caddy at that precise moment.

Sophie stepped in, reviving her skills from the Sackville Hotel. She organized the cleanup of shattered china and overturned shelves in the kitchen. Unaware of the disaster, Cook arrived to prepare breakfast. A round woman who loved to eat as much as cook, she fell to her knees, distraught by the disaster. Sophie wasn't sure if it was Mrs. Wilderby's death or her kitchen in shambles that caused the wailing and animated gestures. It took four girls and smelling salts to get her into a chair. Fortunately, no one was hungry for breakfast. Grateful the gas cooker was still working, Sophie put the kettle on. As she reached for the tea caddy, she felt her fingers bend the thin metal. Her knuckles turned white around the decorative tin and she had a sudden urge to slam it, the cause of Mrs. Wilderby's death, into the wall. She was raising her arm just as Hillary took the offending tea caddy from her grip. The whistling kettle brought Sophie back into the moment. Her head gave a subtle nod to Hillary and she whispered, "thank you. I'm so angry but I'm all right." She tried a weak grin. "Really, I'm all right."

Hillary made hot sweet tea, giving the first cup to Cook who finally stopped wailing. Everyone sipped the tea, feeling the sweet liquid dissipate the shock. Sophie looked up from her cup. "Mrs. Wilderby would chastise us for wasting the sugar." A fond smile crossed everyone's face. Some wept quietly while others nodded heroically.

The handyman's van pulled up at River house and to everyone's surprise, Matron stepped out of the passenger's side, the handyman and his helper following her.

"Matron!" Sophie said. Not sure what to say, she brushed dirt and dust from her skirt.

"Are you all right? I wanted to see the damage. Is anyone hurt?"

"No Matron. It was a freak accident that Mrs. Wilderby was on the stairs…" Sophie's voice trailed off. She was finding it difficult to hide her emotion.

Matron, astute and experienced at detecting hidden emotions, stared at Sophie. "It is difficult when it comes close to home. It would be wise to prepare yourself."

"Yes, Matron," Sophie said, not knowing what else to say.

After inspecting the house and making sure it was livable, Matron called the nurses into the Common Room. "You have all suffered a terrible shock. We are used to tragedy and death in our profession, but this is different and never easy when it happens to one of our own. Mrs. Wilderby will be missed. She loved you girls and took pride in taking care of you all." As Matron paused, Sophie noticed her lips quiver. "I was a young nurse once and for a brief time was in the care of Mrs. Wilderby so I share in your grief." Hammering came from the kitchen. Matron laughed, allowing the girls to laugh with her, a welcome release from the tension. "It would seem that I have competition. Nurse West, ask the workmen to be quiet for a moment." The hammering noise stopped and Matron continued. "I came here today to offer my condolences and to make sure the house is livable." Matron hesitated. "And to ask you to return to the wards. I realize this has been a terrible shock to all of you but we need you at the hospital. Your colleagues who worked the night shift," Matron looked at her watch, "are still working at noon. If you are not feeling well or feel you can't work, I have asked Sister Kay and Dr. Cuthbert to be available to help you. Otherwise, back to work please. That is all I have to say."

Heads nodded and a muttering of 'yes' went round the room. Cook recovered but her angst was now aimed at Matron as she complained about having no pots to cook in and no dishes serve with. Her biggest question was, 'who would get her supplies from the shops?' Matron's quick reply, 'You, of course,' did not go down well with Cook.

The handyman drove Matron back to the hospital and returned with boxes of pots and pans, plates and dishes donated by the hospital.

Sophie stood alone in the dining room, listening to the normal household sounds—too normal. Cook was ranting on about Matron's expectations and the nurses chattered as they got ready for their shift. She was expecting to hear Mrs. Wilderby's quiet voice asking everyone, especially Cook, to settle down. How could anyone go back to normal? *I'm not sure I can. Was Matron giving me a warning?* Tears sprang to her eyes. Mrs. Wilderby would know what to do. She stopped her thoughts. That's it. What would Mrs. Wilderby do in this situation? Get back to work.

Sophie marched into the kitchen. "Cook, stop complaining and do your best with what you have. Matron sent enough pots and dishes for you to get started. It wouldn't hurt you to walk to the butcher's and greengrocer's. The exercise will do you good."

Cook's face turned bright red and Sophie thought she might explode. "Who are you to order me around?"

"In case you have forgotten, we are at war and everyone needs to chip in and help. Do you think any of us feel like working today? You should be grateful that Matron asked you to step into Mrs. Wilderby's shoes. I, for one, will work hard and make her proud. That is what she would have wanted."

Cook's eyes rolled towards her feet. "Very well, when you put it that way…"

Sophie was not eager to return to River House after her shift and told Hillary to go ahead without her as she had some jobs to finish; unnecessary jobs that only kept her from facing the first meal without Mrs. Wilderby. Eventually, she could find no more excuses and plodded home alone. Dinner was being served when she walked in the door. Cook had prepared a beef stew with dumplings, a house favourite. At first, the stew and the table chatter annoyed Sophie, until she realized beef and dumplings were Cook's show of respect, a tribute to Mrs. Wilderby, serving her favourite dish. The table chatter was forced and subdued as everyone tried to be cheerful. It went unsaid but nothing would ever be the same at River House.

25

Perceptions

Several days later, Sophie convinced herself the grieving and mourning had run its course and walked home with Hillary, pretending everything was normal. But another reminder waited for her as she opened the front door to River House. Sitting on the hall table and addressed to Sophie was an envelope with a black border.

Dear Nurse Romano,

I apologize for not writing sooner but we had difficulty with the authorities regarding the burial arrangements for my grandmother.

The funeral is tomorrow afternoon at 2 p.m. at St Martin's Church. My mother and I would be honoured if you could attend. Please extend the invitation to all the nurses at River House.

Yours truly,

Thomas Wilderby

The anger that welled up tight in her throat surprised her. Of course she wanted to attend the funeral but it was yet another reminder that punched her insides. She wished Carlos was there to comfort her, another surprise that she would think about him. I'm just looking for comfort, she told herself.

All the nurses, or those who were not on duty, attended the funeral. Matron joined them with several more senior nurses. Mrs. Wilderby had been well liked and Sophie surmised that most of the attendees were once probationers living at River House.

Tommy and his mother were polite and gracious, but the unusual circumstances made conversation difficult and she declined the invitation to join the family for the burial. Sophie allowed them to assume she had to return to the hospital, although it was her day off.

Desperate for privacy, Sophie walked to the omnibus only to find Cook waiting and eager to talk. The shortage of buses and drivers meant a long wait and Cook's attempt to take Mrs. Wilderby's place irritated Sophie. Cross words hesitated on Sophie's lips and went unsaid as the omnibus arrived. A cheerful female conductor chattered away, collecting their money and dispensing tickets. She wished everyone would be quiet and less cheerful.

Relieved to be home at River House, she wanted to escape to her room but Cook's way of grieving needed company and she tempted Sophie with tea and fresh apple pie. Wanting solitude even more than apple pie, Sophie excused herself to study in the library. At least she would get peace and quiet, although she doubted, she could concentrate.

The librarian gave her a smile and whispered, "Good afternoon, Nurse Romano. Can I find something for you today?"

The young woman she'd encountered when requesting the Carl Jung book stuck her nose in the air with an accusing glance. In spite of herself, Sophie wanted to smile as the young woman obviously considered her a German spy.

"No, thank you, not today."

Sophie opened her satchel and spread her papers on the table. Studying was not such a bad idea since she had exams coming up. However, her eyelids did not cooperate and Sophie dozed into a nightmare. Mrs. Wilderby was trapped behind a closed door, covered in flames. Sophie's father was banging on the door calling her mother's name, Martina, Martina! Sophie's head fell forward, jolting her awake and her pulse raced with fear from her dream. Wondering if she had called out, she surveyed the other patrons. They were not even aware of her presence, but someone was standing behind her.

"I didn't mean to startle you. You seemed distressed." Sophie swung around to see Dr. Cuthbert standing with his hands in his pockets, as though waiting to give her the comfort she craved.

"It has been a hard day," she whispered. "This is my quiet place."

"And I intruded. I apologize." But instead of moving away, he pulled up a chair. "I think you need company. I promise I'll be quiet." He glanced over to the counter and gave a nod towards the young assistant. "Have you encountered the very righteous young librarian? She suspects Carl Jung is a spy."

"I have. I asked for the Carl Jung book you recommended."

"Ah, so now she is convinced I am leading you astray. Perhaps I am, but not as a spy."

Sophie wanted to giggle and felt reassured with Dr. Cuthbert at her side. "My turn to invite you for tea. You are right, I do need company." Sophie returned the papers to her satchel, slipped her arm in his and walked to the café.

As she poured the tea, Sophie could not help herself. The words poured out of her faster than the tea from the teapot. The teacups stayed full and untouched while Dr. Cuthbert drank in her every word. He observed and waited patiently for more when she paused. His gentle touch to her hand reassured her when tears threatened and his voice soothed as her jaw clenched in anger. She finished by telling him about the funeral and the brief dream she had at the library.

Sophie had never confided so much to one person and her vulnerability made her anxious. She expected to feel relief, a burden lifted, but it was all confusion and apprehension as she waited for his comments.

"My dear Sophie, what a brave young woman you are." He paused as his head moved from side to side in empathy. "Such tragedy in someone so young. The memories must torment you. Let me help?" He reached across the small table and took her hands in his. He glanced around the café and lowered his voice to a whisper. She leaned in towards him, intoxicated by his magnetism, and at that moment, Sophie wanted to be kissed.

His voice broke the spell. "Current events, like the death of Mrs. Wilderby, have triggered events from your past. The reason I am in London is to observe civilian patients showing signs of distress after air raids. I'm fascinated by your story. Your condition is a type of neurosis. I see this in soldiers, not just shell-shocked soldiers, but men who have had trauma in their childhood. It's good that you are nursing here in London and not Belgium or France."

Sophie glared at him, her mind trying to comprehend the

change from affection to clinical. *Did I mistake his compassion for affection? Is he implying that my grief for Mrs. Wilderby will jeopardize my chances of nursing overseas? I hardly know this man and he certainly does not know me, and yet I am drawn to him as a moth to light.*

She remembered her love for Carlos and Bill. There were similarities, especially the attraction and the betrayal. Betrayal. She repeated the word in her head and it appeared larger than life. Now she knew why she didn't trust men. Whenever she opened her heart, someone betrayed her. Horror-struck, she realized she had just confided her life story to this man. She needed to get away, to run, to escape his seductive brown eyes, lock away her thoughts. Dear God, she wanted her life to have purpose—to nurse and comfort those in need.

"Sophie. What is wrong? I only want to assist you to get well again."

"My name is Nurse Romano. Dr. Cuthbert, you have misinterpreted my grief for a dear friend as an illness. I need time, not treatment." She stood up from the table, spilling the cold tea into rattling saucers. "Thank you for your time, Dr. Cuthbert. I do not require your help." Sensing his shock at her words, she dared not look into his eyes. She walked to the café entrance, relieved at the fresh air on her burning cheeks and feeling his stare on her back.

Sophie walked the streets of London, unaware of a soft drizzly rain on her wet, tearful face. She picked her way through rubble, although she noted that the cleanup crew did a marvelous job of clearing bricks and masonry from the pavement. She stared into a massive hole—a missing tooth in a row of untouched houses. Amid the shambles, a woman in a cover-all apron, scrubbed her front stoop, her head wrapped in a turban around curls secured with bobby pins. Sophie wonder why she curled her hair. No one had anywhere to go and most wives had no husbands to greet as they returned from work. The factory workers were now women in overalls carrying lunch pails, giggling and laughing. Their hair wrapped in turbans too, but for protection, not vanity. She dodged a football as it came flying across the street. Children's laughter filled the air as a young boy kicked it away. How was it that little things seemed normal and yet the world was in crisis? Or was it just Sophie's world?

Water dripped from Sophie's hat onto her face. A sudden shiver and the raw cold made her aware of her surroundings. Her coat and hat were soaked from the rain and the already grey sky darkened. She couldn't recall how long she had been walking. Panic gripped her stomach as she looked around, not recognizing the street names. She kept walking, looking for an omnibus. She found a sign and waited, relieved to see an old gentleman approaching.

"It'll be a long wait love. They moved that omnibus stop to next street. There's a hole in the road further up." The elderly man lifted a cane and pointed across the road.

"Thank you. I'm new to the area." Sophie rushed to the next street and then cursed for not asking the man where she was and how to get back to River House.

Once again, she was alone. Her bottom lip trembled and it took all her strength to stop her teeth chattering. Just as she deiced it would be warmer to walk, a young woman with a child stood behind her.

"Do you know where this omnibus goes?" Sophie asked, smiling at the little girl in the raincoat and rubber boots that looked several sizes too big.

"It goes to the common and then I don't know. Here it is. Conductor'll know."

Sophie climbed on and found a seat, grateful for the warmth. She knew her way home from the common, so she didn't ask the conductor. It seemed to be a long journey and the shivering was making her tired but she dared not fall asleep and miss her stop. They arrived at the common but it was a different common to the one near River House. She felt stupid. There were hundreds of commons around London.

"Miss, can I help you? You look lost and frozen stiff," the female conductor said, frowning.

"I am lost. I need to get to Heath Common or Bartley Hospital. I went for a walk and lost track of time." Sophie kept talking to hide the shivering.

Concern creased the conductor's face. "Are you ill, Miss? You don't look well."

"No, I'm a nurse at Bartley Hospital. I'm just cold from the rain."

"Well, you're in luck. See that omnibus over there? Its end of the line for her, so she'll be having a break. That one goes to Bartley Hospital." The conductor patted Sophie on the back. "You take care now."

"Thank you," Sophie called over her shoulder as she ran across the road and jumped on the platform as the driver started the engine. She would be home soon.

Hillary flung the door open as Sophie put her hand on the doorknob. "Where have you been? And look at you. You're soaked!"

"I went for a walk and got lost. I'm all right, wet and cold that's all."

"I'll run you a hot bath and then we'll talk. Cook said you

were acting strange when you left the funeral and went to the library."

"A bath, yes, but I don't want to talk. I want to be alone. Is Trixie home?"

"No, Chris had a 24-hour pass. I'm worried about you, Sophie."

"Don't be. Losing Mrs. Wilderby has hit me hard. Her kindness reminds, reminded, me of my mother. I need some time, that's all."

As she said the words, she questioned if time was really all she needed. Aware of her strange behaviour, she wondered if something was wrong. Dr. Cuthbert seemed to think so and getting lost in the rain was not normal.

"A hot bath, a good night's sleep and I'll be as right as rain. Not that I want any more rain." She parted her lips in an unconvincing smile. Sophie was not all right. She wanted to force the despair, pain and anger to stop and pushed it all deeper inside—a reticent volcano on the verge of explosion.

26

A Cocktail of Emotion

Sophie slept through the night, waking refreshed and ready for her hospital shift. Her persistent denial of her inner feelings seemed to work. She hadn't told Hillary about Dr. Cuthbert and, in the dawn of a new day, she questioned her reaction, recalling the shock and surprise on his face as she jumped up from the table.

After Nurse Hogan's banishment to the operating theatre, where Sophie considered she would be more adept at nursing unconscious patients than the wakeful needy ones, Sophie partnered with Hillary again. Pleasant chatter replaced the silent, austere atmosphere typical of Nurse Hogan's rounds. They chatted about Emily's news that matron was considering some nurses for overseas service. Sophie welcomed the opportunity but she knew Hillary's hopes for medical school would pre-empt her desire for battlefield nursing—that would come later.

"Nurse Romano, may I speak with you?" Sister Kay greeted them both with a serious frown and guided Sophie to the nurse's station, leaving Hillary to tend the patients.

"I warned you to be careful," Sister whispered. "Matron wants to see you in her office."

"Forgive me Sister but, am I in trouble and if so, about what?"

"You'd better go now."

Guilt gave her a twinge in the pit of her stomach with all the other protected feelings jostling to come forward. What have I done? She racked her brain for any indiscretions. Perhaps I did something yesterday on my walk in the rain? The secretary waved her into Matron's office.

"I am shocked and disappointed." There was no mistaking Matron's tone. Whatever the accusation, it was serious.

"Matron, I don't know what this is about."

"Come, Nurse Romano, you are one of my brightest nurses. I understand yesterday was a difficult day and I expect you sought comfort. But an open display of such affection with Dr. Cuthbert is unforgivable."

"Dr. Cuthbert?" Angry tears flooded Sophie's eyes. She blinked them back and her whole body tensed as she remembered his words about 'not being in Belgium or France.'

"How could he complain to you? That was a private conversation. I was upset after Mrs. Wilderby's funeral." Gasping for breath, Sophie had to stop talking.

Matron frowned. "It was Nurse Hogan that complained. She saw you at the café with Dr. Cuthbert. What she described was a disgusting display of 'whore-like behaviour'—her words, not mine. She said the doctor tried to push you away and calm you down but you grabbed his hands and embraced him, kissing him many times before he pulled away."

"What! No, that never happened. I was at the café with Dr. Cuthbert, but I didn't see Nurse Hogan"

"Nurse Hogan said you were in uniform. Concerned for

the hospital's reputation," Matron hesitated, her voice calmer, "She gave you a warning."

"I never spoke to Nurse Hogan. Matron, it was my day off. I wore a black dress for the funeral. You saw me at the funeral and I was not in uniform. Afterwards, I went to the library where I bumped into Dr. Cuthbert." Sophie heard her voice rising, the anger squeezing her head and her ears thumping in time with her heartbeat. Matron's face creased in disbelief but Sophie saw no sign of understanding. Who was the disbelief for? Nurse Hogan, a trusted, experienced nurse, or Sophie, a young probationer? Her own thoughts of Dr. Cuthbert and how she had misjudged the situation in the café filled her with guilt. She had wanted to kiss him and Nurse Hogan had seen it.

Every emotion she had felt in the last twenty-four hours threaten to erupt. She thought she might be sick and held her hand to her mouth. She swallowed hard, pushing the cocktail of bile, guilt, anger and grief deep inside. Her head spun out of control and she heard a loud thud as she hit the floor. She welcomed the blackness.

Smelling salts jolted her back into the room. Her eyes stayed closed and the smelling salts wafted under her nose again. She brushed it away. She listened to whispers around her and felt a hand on her wrist, Matron taking her pulse.

"Nurse Romano, you fainted. The stress of the last few days has caught up with you. I want you to sit up slowly." Sophie lay on the floor. Matron held her hand and she felt a strong arm on her back and opened her eyes. There was Dr. Cuthbert, lifting her into a chair. She closed her eyes, afraid to look at him and remembering the first time she fainted, being swallowed up in his gentleness. Sophie prided herself on not being the swooning type and yet she had fainted twice. Both times Dr. Cuthbert had come to her rescue. Her cheeks blushed with embarrassment.

"I am so sorry, Matron. I don't know what came over me. But I'm fine now." She attempted to stand up but her legs wobbled under her weight and she sat down again. Matron handed her a glass of water and she drank thirstily. Dr. Cuthbert stood behind her, out of her line of sight.

"Miss Filly will accompany you to the Nurses' Common Room where you can rest."

Miss Filly? Sophie thought and then realized she had never known the secretary's name. Sophie stood up and felt the doctor's hand on her back. She took a step towards the door, relieved her legs were working. Dr. Cuthbert went into Matron's office and Miss Filly took her arm.

"I'll make a cup of tea. I could do with one," Miss Filly announced as Sophie stretched out on the sofa.

"That Nurse Hogan's a piece of work."

Sophie sat bolt upright. "You heard?"

"I can't help it. It's only a wooden divider between my office and Matron's. I hear everything. Nurse Hogan is a liar. It's not the first time she's complained. She usually picks on probationers. Except the last time it was Sister Kay after she moved her to theatre. But that didn't go down well with Matron."

"Matron seemed to believe her story about me. I was with Dr. Cuthbert yesterday afternoon but I didn't see Nurse Hogan and what she said was lies."

"Matron knows that. She had to be sure. I think it surprised her when you acknowledged you were with the doctor, but she needed to hear your side of the story."

Miss Filly handed Sophie a cup and saucer and she sipped it, pulling a face. "Oh, that is sweet."

"I know, but you need the sugar for the shock. I studied first aid." Miss Filly smiled.

"Thank you. I am feeling much better," Sophie lied. The dizziness had passed but the whole affair had her on edge and she couldn't help but wonder what Dr. Cuthbert was saying to Matron.

"You look worried."

"Why was Dr. Cuthbert in Matron's office when I came around?"

"He was in my office, waiting to see Matron. We both rushed in when we heard the bang." She nodded towards Sophie's head. "Your head on the floor. Does it hurt?"

Sophie put her hand to the back of her head. "No, but there is a lump there. Do you have a first name? Mine is Sophie."

"Elizabeth Filly, but everyone calls me Beth."

The woman's name made Sophie think of a horse and strangely it suited her. It brought a smile to her quivering lips.

"I think I have ruined my chances of going overseas. Dr. Cuthbert is telling Matron right now that I'm not fit to go."

"Matron thinks very highly of you. She discusses the progress of the probationers and the nurses with the Ward Sisters at a weekly meeting. Your name and Nurse West come up often as examples of good nursing."

"Probably not so much after today. I made a fool of myself with Matron and Dr. Cuthbert."

"Did something happen at the café?" Beth asked.

"No, nothing. But I may have misunderstood Dr. Cuthbert. He has such a warm, gentle manner."

"Don't worry about that. Everyone falls for Dr. Cuthbert. Those dreamy, brown eyes and his gentle kindness. Nurse Hogan was crazy about him. I think that's why she made up those stories about you because he likes you. He looks at you quite differently."

"I don't think so, Beth. He sees me as a patient with problems and wants to make me better. I have proved him right, which might quash my dream of going overseas. Do you know anything about that? Nurse Finnegan heard a rumour about us going to Belgium."

"Oh yes, the War Department sent a letter requesting nurses. Matron asked me for the files on several nurses and your name was among them. Well, I'd better be getting back to the office. Will you be all right?"

"Thank you, I am feeling much better. I'll rest awhile and then get back to the ward. It was nice talking to you, Beth."

Sophie lay on the sofa, staring at the ceiling. The angst that had shut her body down had disappeared, leaving her with disappointment that allowed despair to take over. She wanted her life to have purpose and nursing injured, battle-weary soldiers would give her that purpose, especially frightened shell-shocked soldiers. *I have ruined my chances of ever going overseas and I might have jeopardized my career as a nurse.* An image of her father flashed before her. *Papa, you taught me to be strong, but I've let you down.* She flung her legs to the floor and sat up. In that instant, she knew her father had never doubted her abilities. And, by example, he had shown her that whatever challenges life threw at you, it was possible to adapt and move on. In spite of this revelation, Sophie felt her own fragility and the thought of facing Matron and Dr. Cuthbert sent her into another round of self-doubt. *Can I rekindle the*

ambition and strength Papa saw in me? Can I believe in myself
again as that young innocent sixteen-year-old did when she faced
a whole new world?

Upon Sophie's return to the ward, Sister Kay sent her
home under Matron's instructions to allow Sophie to rest
and recover. She hoped that Matron's reason was genuine and
not a prelude to anything else. Remembering her new resolve,
she brushed the doubts aside, but she wished Mrs. Wilderby
was there to talk to. She always had sensible answers and quite
often things were not as bad as they seemed.

In light of her thoughts and doubts, she wasn't sure if it was
positive thinking or pure stubbornness that made her pull out
her books to study for the upcoming exams, heralding the
end of the academic studies. It was hard to believe almost
two years had past and the next training phase was practical
nursing. She spread out in the Common Room so she could
hear Cook preparing dinner, needing the comfort of knowing
another human being was nearby.

The knock on the front door made her glance up from her
books. Cook came from the kitchen, chuntering under her
breath and wiping her hands on her apron.

"Good afternoon, how can I help you?" Her words were
polite but there was no mistaking the irritable tone. About to
smile, Sophie wondered what Cook would say to the unwanted
visitor, but held her breath instead as she heard the caller's
reply.

"I have called to see Nurse Romano?"

"We do not allow gentleman callers at River House. Perhaps
you could leave a message"

Sophie let out a long breath, relieved that Cook was sending
him away.

"My name is Dr. Cuthbert and my call is not social, but professional. Matron has sent me to speak with Nurse Romano." He paused. "I understand your caution. You can telephone Matron if you wish."

Frozen to her chair, Sophie glanced at the stairs across the hall, assessing whether she could escape without being seen. It was too late. Andrew Cuthbert stood in the doorway. Her intellect reminded her to be weary, but her emotions felt his soft smile wrapping her in a warm comforting blanket.

"Thank you, Cook." He turned to close the common room door.

"Doctor or not, leave the door open. It's only decent. Mrs. Wilderby would not allow it and I'm in charge now."

"I understand it is your job to protect the girls, but I can assure you Mrs. Wilderby would understand the situation. Conversations between doctor and patient are private."

Cook stuck her nose in the air, pulled the door almost shut and flounced into the hall. The sound of the telephone cradle clicking preceded Cook's voice. "Hello, this is Cook speaking from River House, connect me to Matron. It is urgent." A short pause followed and Cook finally said, "Oh, I see. Thank you, Matron." The next thing they heard was the common room door closing with a bang. In spite of herself, Sophie couldn't help but smile.

"I'm pleased to see a smile, Nurse Romano. How are you feeling?"

"I am feeling well, thank you, Dr. Cuthbert, but surprised to see you." Sophie didn't know where to look. She felt a flush on her cheeks, embarrassed and irritated.

"Matron is concerned about your health and asked me to speak with you."

Oh dear, she thought, here it comes. I'm not fit for overseas service. My career is over before it even starts. The irritation turned to anger, not at the good doctor or Matron but towards herself for behaving in such a way that Matron had lost faith in her.

"Did Matron send you to tell me my career is over because I'm crazy and not fit for service?" There, she thought, I've said it aloud.

"Sophie. May I call you Sophie?"

"I'm not sure that's a good idea, considering Nurse Hogan's lies about me. But go ahead, it's of no consequence to me."

"Sophie, I'm here as a psychiatrist and sometimes patients find it easier to talk when I use their Christian names. As far as it concerns Nurse Hogan, she is the one who has ruined her career, not you. I explained to Matron why we were in the café and exposed Nurse Hogan's lies. Matron never doubted your story." His eyebrows knitted together, puzzled, he asked, "Why would you think your career is over?"

She shrugged her shoulders. "I have a tragic past. I'm melodramatic, unstable and I can't control my feelings. Not the kind of person to be nursing soldiers in war conditions. You said it yourself, a nervous condition is better treated here rather than Belgium or France." She gave a sarcastic chuckle. "And I seem to faint a lot around doctors."

"What I said was thoughtless and not what I meant. Can we sit down?" Sophie nodded. She hadn't realized they had been standing. Dr. Cuthbert pointed to the sofa and sat in the easy chair opposite.

"Isn't this what Sigmund Freud does with his patients?"

"I believe he does. I see you've been studying. But lying on the couch is unnecessary. I just want us to talk." His smile was reassuring. "First, Matron would never let you go. You are one of her brightest nurses and she has a high regard for you as a person, and for your nursing abilities."

"So why are you here?"

"Matron is concerned about you. She tells me you have experienced several upsets in the last year and that losing Mrs. Wilderby was the final blow. I understand you help your fellow nurses with their problems and go beyond the call of duty for the patients. I heard about how you nursed a dying mother and helped her soldier husband find a home for the baby. Mr. Wainwright told me how you reassured injured soldiers afraid of losing limbs."

"You and Mr. Wainwright discussed me!" She was defensive because she had worked hard at putting Carlos out of her mind. The thought of these men talking about her gave her a strange feeling which she could not identify. She did not want to have feelings for either of these men and was grateful that she had not mentioned Carlos by name during their discussion at the café. She definitely did not want Dr. Cuthbert to know that Carlos was one of the two men who had jilted her.

"Carlos and I are acquainted. We met at medical school and have had cause to meet and discuss mutual patients."

"Oh."

"Any reference to you was about your skills as a nurse. You are exceptional but even the best of us need to talk about these things and such stress takes its toll. You have experienced many tragic losses in your life…"

Sophie interrupted. "Please tell me you didn't tell Matron about my parents."

"No, of course not. That was a private conversation between us. But from a medical viewpoint, it is significant."

Dr. Cuthbert talked to Sophie for most of the afternoon. He was an easy person to talk to and the more she talked, the better she felt. By the end of the afternoon, Dr. Cuthbert reassured her that she was not crazy but overwrought due to grief and too much work. She believed him. He didn't expect it to happen again, suggesting she come to his office to talk things through, and she agreed.

27

Called to Serve

Sophie was feeling like her old self again after several discussions with Dr. Cuthbert. She still felt sad at times, but the extreme anxiety had gone. Matron had cleared her of any wrongdoing. Nurse Hogan had had a severe reprimand but was not fired, surprising Sophie. Matron explained that soon nurses with the appropriate skills and qualifications would be leaving for overseas service and she needed to keep the pool of hospital nurses as full as possible. A diplomat, Matron did not indicate who she was considering. It was only because of the conversation she'd had with Beth that Sophie knew she was on the list of candidates. Although she had recovered from her malaise, a little doubt poked at her now and then.

Sophie worked late and started early, as did many of the nurses. She slept little, studying long into the night with Trixie, who was now working days on the Women's Ward. After Chris's last leave, they deployed him to a destination unknown. Trixie didn't say much but Sophie knew she worried about him. Few pilots made it home these days. Trixie hated studying.

Having ignored the books since she met Chris, she needed Sophie's help to catch up.

It was a warm, sunny June day for the exam. Trixie and Sophie chatted nervously, quizzing each other as they walked to the large assembly hall where the exam was to take place. Rows of desks lined the tension-charged room. Wishing each other luck, they sat at a desk and waited for the adjudicator's instructions before turning over the exam paper.

Three hours later, they met outside the hall. Trixie spoke first. "So, what did you think?"

"I'm feeling fairly confident. Most of the questions were from stuff we studied. How about you?"

"I couldn't answer the last question. I don't think I passed."

"Did you answer all the other questions?" Trixie nodded yes. "Then you passed. Those were all the important subjects we studied."

It would be the end of June before they posted the exam results and all the probationers were grateful to be busy. Air raids were hitting London frequently and more critically wounded soldiers were being shipped home for treatment, filling the Men's Ward beyond capacity. The orthopaedic surgeon who replaced Carlos was a good surgeon but had no bedside manner, making Dr. Cuthbert's job more demanding. Sophie worked alongside him daily—they worked as a team. He taught her skills that calmed the shell-shocked men and their families. On several occasions, Sophie found him watching her, staring with those wonderful eyes; his professional conversation belied his watchful glances. She brushed it away, noting she had seen it before and had misjudged its meaning.

It was July 2 and the Nurse's Common Room was buzzing with probationers jostling to see the list posted on the notice board. The exam results. Trixie stood behind Sophie as they squeezed to the front. The results were in alphabetical order. King came first. Sophie turned around and gently pulled Trixie's hands from her face. "It's all right. Congratulations, Trixie, you passed." Sophie ran her fingers down to the Rs, but her name was not there.

Trixie pushed in front of her. "Sophie, look at the top of the list. 'Honour Students' and you are top of the class." Sophie's face beamed with pride.

Cook made a special celebration meal that night. All the probationer residents at River House had passed the exams. Cook brought out a bottle of sherry and they made merry much later than normal.

Normally awake long before five, Sophie woke as the alarm rang. She swung her legs out of bed and shook Trixie awake. They skipped breakfast and joined Hillary for the walk to the hospital; a quiet group, exhausted from the late night.

Sister Kay beckoned Sophie and Hillary to the nurses' station as soon as they walked onto the ward. "Matron wants to see both of you in her office in half-an-hour." She checked her watch. "That would be 7:30."

Hillary and Sophie glanced at each other and waited to hear a reason, but Sister walked away. Sophie felt her heart miss a beat. Had she done something wrong? But that wouldn't involve Hillary. They continued their work, both watching the clock. At 7:25 they headed to Matron's office to find Emily and Trixie waiting in the corridor. The frowns and creased brows were a sign of the nurses' anxiety. Being summoned to the Matron's office was not to be taken lightly and involved being in some kind of serious trouble. Sophie tried to think of a common denominator in the group, bad behaviour, a mistake, rowdy party or boyfriend issues but there was nothing.

Beth Filly came out from her office and motioned to the four chairs lined up in the corridor. "Matron will be with you soon."

The scraping chairs echoed on the hard floor as did footsteps walking up and down the hall, a contrast to the raised but muffled voices coming from the office. No one said a word. They all stared at their feet or the green-tiled wall. The wait seemed like hours but was only five minutes. A nurse opened the door, tears flowing down her face. She walked a few paces and then ran to the end of the corridor. Sophie felt her stomach do flip-flops, afraid of what was to come.

"Matron will see you now." Beth held the door open as the four terrified nurses filed into Matron's office and stood in front of her desk.

"Good morning, ladies! Thank you for coming." Matron bent her head to one side. "Why such worried faces?" Sophie opened her mouth to answer but thought better of it. Matron added, "Ladies, I assure you, you are not in any trouble. In fact, the opposite. The four of you have shown exceptional skills and attitude towards nursing patients. I have received a request from the War Department for nurses to go to Passchendaele and work in the field hospitals. I have hand-picked you." Matron stood up from her desk and walked over to close the door. Sophie wanted to smile, knowing that Beth could hear every word whether the door was closed or open.

"Please understand you have a choice and no one will think any the worse of you if you decline. Heaven knows I need more nurses at the hospital. The conditions are poor, the work is hard and you will be faced with terrible injuries, disease and dying men. What you have seen here is nothing to what you'll see in a field hospital. I served in the Boer War so I know what I'm talking about. Serving one's country is not as glamorous as it seems. Although the field hospitals and casualty clearing stations are as safe as possible, you are close to the battlefields and it is dangerous. Please think carefully before you decide." Matron paused, looking at each individual nurse. Sophie thought she was attempting to detect any wavering doubts. Her eyes were gentle with a fondness for each nurse. She was a good leader, fair, kind and understanding. Perhaps, Sophie thought, she had concerns about sending young nurses into a battle zone. A War that had turned out to be brutal with too many casualties and lost lives. Would one of her nurses be another casualty?

"Nurse Romano, I have had excellent reports of your work with shell-shocked patients. Your maturity and level headedness will be valued in the field. Are you still eager to serve your country?"

"It is a wonderful opportunity, Matron. Thank you," Sophie said.

Matron stared at Trixie with a slight shake of her head. "Nurse King, I want you to be honest and deliberate. You will face unimaginable situations. Do you think you can cope?"

Trixie nodded her head several times. "I'm not as fragile as I appear. I want this opportunity." Trixie's answer surprised Sophie. She had expected her to refuse, wanting to stay near her husband, Chris. Her answer seemed rehearsed, as though she and Chris had discussed it. If Matron knew her marital status, she may not have included her.

"I am aware that neither of you have finished training but

you did well on your exams, especially you, Nurse Romano. As you know, the third year of training is practical. Your assignment is more practical than most, training in a war zone hospital on the Western Front. I will welcome you back to complete the last of your training after the war is over.

"Nurse West, I'm afraid you have a decision to make between medical school and going to war. As we've discussed, it is a good time to apply so think carefully."

"I don't have to, Matron. I want to be a doctor. If I get a place at medical school, I will take it."

"Nurse Finnegan, there will be no children to nurse in a field hospital but injured soldiers would welcome your skills in patience and kindness." Matron paused. "Many of the injured are barely adults and this will be a big change for you."

"I have enjoyed my work on the Men's Ward and I think I can be of service to those poor injured soldiers. My answer is yes."

"I will prepare the paperwork. Notify your families. If you need a day off, speak to Sister Kay. Be ready to leave next week. The war office will send you instructions. Now, back to your duties."

Sophie felt a strange sense of loss, even loneliness, as she sat in the library. Emily had taken the day off to visit her sister and niece and nephew and the chauffeur had collected Trixie to visit her parents. She would stay overnight. Sophie had nowhere to go and no one with whom to share the news. Her throat tightened as she pushed back tears, wishing she could share it with her father. He would have been so proud. Bill's warm smile passed through her mind. He would have cheered her on, proud that she was serving her country. And her best friend, Anna, would worry about her safety. She missed Anna but was afraid to write, fearing it might stir memories she wanted to forget. Surprised by sudden thoughts of her father, she heard a tear drop onto the open book, leaving a perfectly round wet spot. She ran her fingers over it and whispered, "I love you Papa and miss you so much." A voice replied, "I miss you too." She glanced around the room but it was as silent as a library should be. She listened and heard her father's voice again. "I'm not far away. I've always been at your side. I am proud of you and I will be with you in Passchendaele, keeping you safe."

"Thank you, Papa," she whispered and the loneliness disappeared.

A drizzly summer rain hovered in the air as Hillary helped Sophie lift her trunk down the steps. The waiting cabby grunted as he lifted yet another trunk into the taxi. Sophie gathered Hillary in her arms. "I shall miss you. Write and tell me all about university."

Sophie joined Trixie and Emily in the back seat of the taxi. The taxi drove away from River House on the first leg of the journey. It was followed by a train ride to Dover, a ferry across the English Channel and another train ride into Belgium and finally an army lorry.

Sophie gripped the hard wooden bench, trying to stay upright. A dirty canvas arched over the metal hoops that sheltered them. The lorry swerved around holes, slowed in the mud and bounced along the non-existent road. She stared through the rear opening of flapping canvas. The lush green countryside slipped in and out of grey, battle worn wildness—a stark contrast of man and nature. She felt the war and heard the cries of men rising from the ground. The lorry swerved, almost throwing her from her perch, as it turned into the camp. The gigantic bright red cross on white appeared to hover slightly above the wooden roof of the hospital. Groups of soldiers smoked and laughed and white aproned nurses hurried along boardwalks. The nurses' uniforms seemed out of place away from the sterile London hospital.

Soldiers helped them down from the lorry to a not so welcoming greeting from a stern looking sister holding a clipboard. Sophie hardly noticed smiling as she gave a long satisfying sigh. "At last, I am where I am meant to be."

You have completed Book One. Are you ready for more?
Read on ...
Book Two - Heart of Sophie's War
https://geni.us/SophiesWar2

Epilogue

Sophie, Emily and Trixie settled in the Casualty Clearing Station near the town of Ypres in Belgium, beside the village of Passchendaele, which is now a battlefield. *Heart of Sophie's War,* Book 2 of the series, takes us into the battle of saving lives and comforting the dying. Sophie makes tremendous progress with shell-shocked soldiers, but struggles with her own demons. Some favourite and not so favourite characters return.

Author's Notes

Travelling back in time to 1914 and imagining places, people and events was a somewhat daunting experience. I tried to recreate what it would be like for a nurse training, living and working in London during the Great War. My perceptions may be different to others. However, through copious amounts of research, I had a picture in my head which I tried to deliver to the page. In so doing, I may have misinterpreted or bent the rules just a little, to fit my story. I have, for the most part, made an effort to stick to historical facts, but there may be discrepancies. After I finished the book, I discovered that the term shell shock was not used until 1917. The symptoms of shell shock or PTSD as we know it today, were referred to as battle fatigue or war nerves. Forgive me, but for the purpose of the story I have used shell shock, despite not being historically accurate for the time period of 1914 -1916.

Acknowledgements

Most writers are introverts, writing alone in a cocoon of silence by choice. But there comes a time when the writer must emerge from the cocoon and face the world of readers. It is safe to say that without readers, there would be no writers. Now, coming out of the cocoon is a scary thing and, for me, I do it with the help and support of other writers. My sincere thanks go to the Historical Ladies Writing Group: Meghan Negrijn, Margaret Southall and Susan Taylor Meehan, and The Ottawa Story Spinners (TOSS): Anne Raina, Audrey Starkes, Tony Myres and Rita Myres. Your support, critique and suggestions (both positive and negative) spur me on to write. My gratitude, also goes to the beta readers, for chasing delinquent typos.

Writing the novel is only a small part of the process and, to produce a professional book, the manuscript must be polished until it shines bright amongst all the other books. Sometimes there is one person who really helps out. Meghan Negrijn has been a constant support, helping with story and structure and the editing.

Editing is not an easy job by any stretch of the imagination. Editors deal with stubborn, cranky authors and perhaps occasionally I might include myself in this category. But their expertise is second to none. A whopping big thank you to Meghan Negrijn for editing first and second editions.

Resources

Resources:

Historical fiction requires a lot of fact checking and research and the following are some of the resources I used.

Books:
The Regeneration Trilogy by Pat Barker
The Diaries of a First World War Nurse - Dorothea's War
Edited by Richard Crewdson

Websites:

- • History of Nursing
- https://www.rcn.org.uk/library/subject-guides/history-of-nursing
- • *London's World War 1 Terror*
- *https://www.history.com/news/londons-world-war-i-zeppelin-terror*
- • *Military Nurses*
- *http://www.scarletfinders.co.uk/10.html*
- • *The Air Raids That Shook Britain In The First World War |*

Imperial War Museums

- *https://www.iwm.org.uk/history/the-air-raids-that-shook-britain-in-the-first-world-war*
- *• Great War London - London and Londoners in WW1*
- *https://greatwarlondon.WordPress.com/*
- *• The Silvertown Explosion*
- *https://en.wikipedia.org/wiki/Silvertown_explosion*
- *• Shell-shock*
- *https://www.apa.org/monitor/2012/06/shell-shocked.aspx*
- *• Royal Flying Corps*
- *https://en.wikipedia.org/wiki/Royal_Flying_Corps*
- *• War Psychiatry*
- *https://encyclopedia.1914-1918-online.net/article/war_psychiatry*
- *• World War* https://www.bbc.co.uk/programmes/p01nb93y

Also by Susan A. Jennings

The Sackville Hotel Trilogy
 Book 1 - The Blue Pendant
 Book 2 - Anna's Legacy
 Book 3 - Sarah's Choice
 Box Set - All three books
 Prequel – Ruins in Silk*

Sophie's War Series
 Book 1 - Prelude to Sophie's War
 Book 2 - Heart of Sophie's War
 Book 3 - In the Wake of Sophie's War (2022)
 Prequel - Ruins in Silk *
 *Leads into The Blue Pendant and Sophie's War

The Lavender Cottage Books
 Book 1 - When Love Ends Romance Begins
 Book 2 - Christmas at Lavender Cottage
 Book 3 - Believing Her Lies
 Book 4 - Coming late 2021

Nonfiction
 Save Some for me - A Memoir
 A Book Tracking Journal for ladies who love to read.

Short Stories:
Mr. Booker's Book Shop
The Tiny Man
A Grave Secret
Gillian's Ghostly Dilemma
The Angel Card
Little Dog Lost Reiki Found

Story Collections
The Blue Heron Mysteries
Contributing author to:
The Black Lake Chronicles
Ottawa Independent Writers' Anthologies

About the Author

Susan A. Jennings was born in Britain of a Canadian mother and British father. Both her Canadian and British heritages are often featured in her stories. She lives and writes in Ottawa, Canada and is the author of The Sackville Hotel Trilogy, a combination of historical fiction, a family saga and an intriguing love story. The Sophie Series, also historical, is a collection of novels situated during the Great War. You may recognize the main character, Sophie, from the trilogy. Taking a break from the historical genre, her latest series is in contemporary women's fiction. The Lavender Cottage books feature the unusual backdrop of an English narrowboat marina.

Susan writes a weekly blog, which has been taken over by her assistant Miss Penny, Shih Tzu, with stories of living with an author.

Susan teaches the occasional workshop on writing and publishing. She is also available to speak at book clubs or other events.

She is an avid reader of mysteries and historical fiction, especially of the Victorian and Edwardian era.

You can connect with me on:

- https://susanajennings.com
- http://sajauthor
- http://facebook.com/authorsusanajennings

Subscribe to my newsletter:

- http://eepurl.com/bgY6kb

Made in United States
Troutdale, OR
02/10/2024

17565706R00170